In Search of SOLACE

A Rebel Wayfarers MC &
Freed Riders MC Crossover Story

MariaLisa deMora

Edited by Hot Tree Editing

Proofreading by Whiskey Jack Editing

Photography & model: Stuart Reardon

First Published 2020

ISBN 13: 978-1-946738-64-6

DEDICATION

For the fighters among us who keep climbing to their feet, head hung low, and still find the strength to carry on.

CONTENTS

ACKNOWLEDGMENTS

No, Gunny does not always get his way.

I know it might seem like it, because when that man talks you know I listen. But he doesn't get everything his little heart desires. For instance, you'll note this story is not titled: Fraudy Fraudy Froggy Frog. Take that, Lane.

In all seriousness, there are a few characters that I know to listen to. Know to tease out that little murmur, give them space to allow it to build, and then—once they're truly ready to talk—seize the moment like there's no tomorrow. Gunny's one of those. Every story he's brought to the table made me laugh and cry, and in the case of this book, gag a little. Swear, it's all his fault. I might complain about the guy, but when he starts talking in my head I pay attention.

And look, now he's brought us Myrt and Bane, a couple I've enjoyed a great deal. Oh, also, you're going to see a lot of old favorites within these pages, and yes, the whole story is basically a teaser for a potential new series, but in my heart Blackie has always deserved his own book. So future stories to watch for, yeah?

As ever, it takes a tribe to bring a story from tiny whispers along the edges of my consciousness to what you hold in your hands—whether in paperback or electronic. From the alpha readers of Megan and Kori, to the editorial team at Hot Tree Editing, where Becky and her crew always do my stories justice. And to Mel with Whiskey Jack Editing, a proofreader who doesn't fear to push me in all the ways that will make the story better. Thanks to all of them. From the bottom of. Thanks also to Stuart Reardon, photographer and model, for giving Bane the perfect cover.

Much gratitude to the readers. Those one-click addicts, the loyal followers, my fans-to-friends on social media, ravenous consumers of the written word who prove to me with each book that the stories are worthy.

Alla y'all make me happies.

Woofully yours,
~ML

In Search of Solace

Pain and anguish dominated Myrtle's life. Forced to take things into her own hands, she disappeared into the Kentucky mountains, shrouded in darkness with only the little she could squeeze inside a bag. Days—and hundreds of miles—later, in a different kind of tough spot, Myrt finds herself rescued by a woman who seems too good to be true. Ignoring Myrt's bruising and desperation, Vanna offers both a place to stay and a hand up.

Slowly settling into her new, charmed life, Myrt is rocked when a van rolls to a stop in the front drive and out steps a stranger. Dark and rough on the outside, he still makes Myrt feel safer than she's been in years. Could she offer her trust to such a man? Her heart?

Bane, taking on increased responsibilities with the Freed Riders MC out of Northeast Texas, rides to the rescue for the family of an officer with a friendly club. Delivering them safely to Baker, Florida—a dead-ass town in a no man's land strip of the Gulf coast—is no trouble at all. Until his relaxing ride runs smack into the most perfect woman he's ever seen. Now he hungers to wrap Myrt up safe in his arms.

Myrt, a woman under the protection of that same friendly club that was the reason he was in the area in the first place.

Well, this is gonna be fun.

Prologue

Myrtle

Stepping out of the stranger's car, Myrt Sallabrook stared around the empty parking lot and campground. The sighing of the waves sounded through the scraggly trees, and the desire to see their incessant lapping against the shore ran wild in her veins. She waved goodbye to the elderly man, who drove off still shaking his head. As she'd shut the door, he'd claimed once again it didn't sit right with him, leaving such a young girl here alone.

If he'd only known how her life had been for so long, he'd understand being alone wasn't the worst thing that could happen to a body.

Hitching her unwieldy bag higher on her shoulder, she strode to the welcoming sunshine, ready to experience something new. Later, she'd find somewhere to lay her head, somewhere underneath the trees. Once set up like she imagined, the shelter would be hidden, and it would take someone looking intently to spot her.

Exactly what she wanted.

Chapter One

Vanna

"Honey, I'm home."

Truck's greeting never failed to bring a smile to Vanna's face, and tonight was no different. He'd been away for a few days, visiting mutual friends in Texas. While they'd spoken on the phone frequently, hearing him through the crackling ether was no replacement for having his rich tone and reverberating sense of love wrap itself around her skin.

"In the kitchen," she called back, raising her voice. She reached across the table to place her hand over the trembling one of the girl who sat opposite her. Speaking softly, she told the girl, "That's my Truck, my husband, and exactly like I promised you, you're safe with us, honey." Lifting her voice again, Vanna gave him a couple seconds' warning. "We've a visitor."

He rounded the corner and came through the archway leading to the kitchen, glanced at the girl, then arrowed straight towards where Vanna sat. A moment later, she was off the chair and in his arms, his mouth on hers in a slow exploration that had her breaths coming choppy and quick, fingers tingling as she ran her hands through his hair and cupped the back of his neck, holding him to her.

"My God, woman. I missed you." The soft scratch of his beard across her cheek was familiar, as was the strength in the arms that held her close. He brushed a kiss along her jaw, the tender gesture followed by a gentle nip at her earlobe. "Glad to be home." Truck settled her in alongside him, one arm curved around her back as they turned to face the table where the girl sat. "Hey," he said gruffly, and Vanna felt his tension zing through her, transferring as if by magic from where his hand gripped her hip. "The fuck?" The breathed expletive told her he'd taken in the girl, every bruised inch of her.

Earlier this morning, Vanna had been headed towards a loop trail she enjoyed hiking, singing along to the oldies on the radio as she drove. Pulling into the trailhead parking lot, she'd noted a crude shelter built just beyond the edge of the surrounding woods. More a tarp than a tent, it was secured in an amateurish fashion, with what looked like strips of cloth tying it to low-hanging tree limbs. It would do nothing to block wind or rain; a stiff breeze would likely loft it and tear the tarp loose from its moorings.

On the bare ground underneath had been a figure, and with the lack of a cook or fire ring nearby, Vanna wondered if it was a city homeless person, thinking to escape the rat race for a time. The only problem with that idea was homeless were typically dependent on the kindness of others for assistance, needing folks around to survive. Out here, they were alone. With Vanna's the only car in the lot, she'd known from experience—barring a surprise visit from an out-of-towner—it would stay that way.

So she'd approached carefully, because she was a woman alone, but with kindness in her tone, hoping to keep from frightening whoever was bundled up in the pile of fabric visible under the tarp.

"Hello? Hey, there. I'm only here to hike, but I thought I'd check on you and make sure you're doing okay. You got everything you need?" Vanna stopped about ten yards from the makeshift tent. Her car was unlocked only a few strides behind her. Between that proximity, the fact the figure was on the ground, and the small cannister of mace on the keyring still in her hand, she thought she'd be able to argue with Truck she was being safe. Not that he'd need to know about this little encounter. *She grinned, knowing the thought was a lie. She reveled in sharing her adventures with her husband, and if she was honest with herself, it was always kind of fun to wallow in the knowledge he loved her so much he'd promise to do over-the-top things to keep her safe.* That man. *"Are you awake?"*

The figure stirred, and Vanna quieted, waiting. Pale, delicate fingers appeared and curled around the articles of clothing covering their face, tugged them down, and Vanna found herself staring into the elfin features of a girl who couldn't be more than seventeen or eighteen. Deep purple bruising circled both eyes, the raccoon effect typically the product of a terrible blow to the head. Green and yellow dotted her throat, mapping where a hand had brutally gripped. She blinked, and Vanna noted the red streaks in the sclera of her eyes, more evidence of trauma.

"I'm not gonna cause any trouble." The girl's bottom lip was split and swollen, but her words were understandable. Her voice trembled as she restated, "I don't want to cause trouble."

"You're not, honey. It's okay. Needed a safe place to catch a nap. I get it." Vanna hunkered down where she stood on the gravel of the parking lot, putting one knee to the ground. Making herself smaller would lessen the girl's fear, something she knew from having a hand in far too many rescues. Ones that felt just like this one—desperately needed. "Are you hungry? Have you eaten recently?"

"Uh, a couple of days ago." The girl angled into an awkward sitting position, one hip cocked up as if it hurt to touch the ground. She was close to the tree but not leaning against it, supporting her weight on an arm propped behind her. Both of those things spoke volumes to Vanna. "I'm okay, ma'am. Thank you."

"A couple of days ago isn't okay, honey. I've got some provisions in the car. Would you be all right with it if I got you a few things?" She took in more of the girl's condition. Her lips were dry, the skin on her fingers pinched and wrinkled. Dehydrated, too. "I've got a couple of bottles of water you might be interested in, too."

"I'm..." The girl bowed her head, breaking eye contact as she focused on the ground between them. "I'm awful thirsty."

"I'll get you fixed right up." Vanna stepped backwards as she stood, creating distance as she rose to what could be interpreted as a more threatening posture. She dropped her daypack to the ground, making a marker for how close she'd originally approached. "Give me half a minute. You here alone, honey?"

"Yes, ma'am. It's just me."

Vanna's gaze swept the lot as she made her way to the back of the little SUV she drove. Her tire tracks were the only ones in the dirt of the entryway. It had rained about a week ago. That meant either the girl had been dropped off before then or she'd walked in. This particular trailhead adjoining a tiny sliver of national parkland wasn't adjacent to any main roads. It was a long trek from anywhere with a population, one of the draws of the location for Vanna.

She spoke loudly enough for the girl to hear, aiming at reassuring her. "And it's only me. So now it's just the two of us." Hatch lifted, she rummaged around in the two crates of food items she kept in the car. She ignored the hiker-food goods for now and focused on what could be termed comfort food. Toaster pastries and water bottles, beef and turkey jerky, and a package of gum. Shoving the haul of goodies into a small bag, she grabbed another bottle of water and a protein bar for herself, picked up a folded blanket from the other pile of supplies, and walked back towards the girl, clicking the car fob to close the hatch. A couple of strides from where she'd left the daypack, she asked, "Is it okay if I sit with you for a while? The sun sure is hot." It wasn't, but she wanted to give the girl the right of refusal. Vanna bent slightly and grabbed one strap of her pack. "I bet it's cooler up under those trees."

"Yes, ma'am. Feel free to sit anywhere you want."

The girl had attempted to straighten her sleeping pile while Vanna was by the car, sweatshirts and pants folded and set aside. It had exposed her legs, which were mottled with faint bruising, evidence of an earlier beating. Whoever had put their hands on this girl had done it repeatedly, systematically, and with a definite intent to inflict harm.

Pulling a sampling of the selections from the bag, she held them out in offering. The girl eyed the items in Vanna's hands. "Thank you for everything." She accepted each of the foodstuffs tentatively, as if Vanna might snatch them back at any moment, resting them carefully in her lap as she reached for the next. "You're too kind. This is too much."

"Oh, honey, I've got more where that came from. I always carry extra with me. Never know when I might get hungry or meet someone in need." Vanna retreated a few feet away, placed her blanket and the pack at the base of a tree, settled on the cushioning surface, and then leaned back against the trunk. She opened her water and took a long drink, finishing with a satisfied "Ahhhh."

The girl followed suit, sipping more cautiously, wincing as the plastic opening pressed against her swollen lip. "This is real good. Thank you." She plucked at the seam on the foil packet of the toaster pastries, opened it, and reached inside to break off a piece. The first bite was quickly followed by another and another, until the pouch was empty. "I—" The girl laughed. "My lands. I didn't realize I was that hungry."

"Going without'll do that to ya." Vanna opened her protein bar and nibbled off one corner. "That jerky is good. The turkey is my favorite. Not too spicy." She leaned her head back and stared up through the pine needles of the limbs overhead, seeing swatches of blue sky mixed with high, white clouds. "Lemme know if you need help opening it." One of the girl's fingers had swollen into a barely bendable lump, either with a dislocated knuckle or broken. "Weatherman is calling for rain tonight. You set up for that?"

"Rain?" The tension in the girl's voice had Vanna looking back towards her. She was peering at the sky over the

parking lot, the storm approaching from the west not yet visible. "With lightning?"

"What they said." Vanna took another bite. "Want me to open the jerky for you?" The girl nodded, and Vanna stood, ducking as she walked out from under the tree. She got closer, and the girl handed the package back. "I'm Vanna." She gave a nod as she unzipped the top of the plastic and then wrestled the seam of the package open. "Here you go. I've got more water, too." She handed another bottle of water to the girl, along with the seasoned meat. "You worried about the storm?"

Making her way back to the folded blanket, she resumed her position against the trunk of the tree. The girl finished the bite of jerky she'd stuffed into her mouth before responding, swallowing hard around the dried turkey.

"Maybe? I sure don't like 'em." She lifted another bite to her mouth, then let her hand fall away. "You think it'll get bad? It's not tropical, is it?"

"No, just a storm front. Probably wind, lightning, thunder, and rain. It's the wrong time of year for tornados." Reaching into the pocket of her khakis, Vanna pulled out her phone and unlocked it, smiling at the text waiting for her.

Headed home to my baby.

Vanna fired off a quick response to Truck, letting him know she'd received his message, then opened the weather app she used.

"Looks like it's strengthened. It's hours away yet, though, so plenty of time to get you somewhere safe." She glanced at the girl, who was chewing slowly, staring off into the distance. "You got people around? I can give you a lift pretty much anywhere, honey."

"No, ma'am. I got nobody here." She restlessly reached out and touched the piles of fabric she'd folded and stacked to the side, as if in reassurance they were still where she'd left them.

A tiny thing she could control. *This wasn't Vanna's first rodeo in the human rescue department, and experience gave her insight into the girl's behaviors. Persistently calling Vanna ma'am, the sincere gratitude for the smallest of things, fear of accusation of misbehavior—everything screamed controlling and abusive relationship. Now to find out if it had been the girl's family, or a boyfriend, or if she'd escaped something else.*

"Like I said, my name is Vanna." The girl cut her eyes to the side but was clearly listening. "Vanna Reicht. I live a few miles from here, and I happen to have an empty bedroom now since my son's moved off on his own." And protective as all get out of his independence, too. The last time she'd shown up at Kitt's apartment unannounced he'd spent the hour texting responses to her questions, illustrating how unnecessary the visit was. In his mind at least. Hugged her hard when she'd left though. Boys. She smiled at the memory. "He's in the city up in Georgia, so the room sits empty. It would be a safe haven for you tonight, if you

wanted." The girl was already shaking her head in negation of the offer, and Vanna held up her palms to stave off the verbal response. "My husband is headed home now, and if I know that man, he'll roll in midnight or later. It'd be a blessing to me if I wasn't tottering around the house alone until then. You'd be doing me a favor, if we look at it like that. I'm not a fan of storms."

"I—I don't like storms much either."

Vanna pulled in a relieved breath. That's not a no.

"We've time. I'm going to go ahead and trot my happy hiking ass up the trail a couple of miles. I promised a friend to send photos of this tiny wet weather waterfall that's not far. It's dry right now, at least until that rain comes, and the rock formations are amazing. When I get back, we can pack you up and go grab a real lunch." She shoved the rest of the protein bar into her mouth and grinned as she chewed. The girl smiled back, and the expression provided a glimpse of the kind of beauty that lay behind the bruising. Vanna swallowed, took a drink of water, and tipped her head towards the girl. "You're welcome to walk with me if you want. It's not a hard hike."

"I'll stay here if it's all the same to you." The girl's fingers danced over the tops of the clothing stacks again. She glanced up at the awkwardly tied tarp. "I can be ready whenever you're back."

"Sounds like a plan, Stan." Vanna stood and shoved her trash into the side pouch of her daypack. She slung it into

place on her shoulders and grinned, tipping her chin up so a splash of sunlight struck her face, basking in the warmth for a moment. "I'll be back in a bit. Shouldn't be long." Two strides towards the trailhead, she paused and partially turned back, looking at the girl over her shoulder. "Happy to call you Stan, but give some thought to trusting me with your name, honey?"

"I'm Myrt." The girl's smile faltered and faded, chin dipping towards her chest. "Rhymes with dirt."

That had led them here, where a child-bride named Myrtle Sallabrook sat at her table. And now Vanna had to explain to Truck. *Shoulda texted him.* "Hey, there, you." She snuggled into his side, hoping to pull his attention back to her, but his gaze stayed fixed on Myrt. *Nothing for it, might as well dive in.* "Myrt, this is my husband, Truck. Love of my life, this is Myrtle. She's gonna stay with us for a few days." Vanna had needed to argue hard with the girl to get her to agree to even that much. Convinced she'd be a burden, Myrt had persistently demurred, refusing to consider more than one night until Vanna had asked straight out for her to stay. No half-baked qualifiers about being company, or helping Vanna get through the storm—simply a plain offer to stay with no strings or expectations, and the girl had accepted with an almost regal nod. *Someone prefers honesty over white lies.* "I found her like a sprite in the forest this morning, and she agreed to grace our home."

"Who did that to you, kid?" Truck's arm behind Vanna's back was rigid, and Vanna had no illusions about the anger he was holding at bay. The man's heart was big as Texas, and his caring way was one of the things she loved about him. He had an innate way with children and animals, too, as if they could see through to the gooey center of him at a glance.

"My husband, sir." His deft touch proved true once again, as Myrt answered his direct question, where she'd easily dodged Vanna's sideways advances on the same information for the entire afternoon and evening. "And it's good to meet you. You have a lovely wife." Myrt lifted a hand in an awkward wave.

"The hell he did?" Truck's voice was low, growled from deep in his chest. "Motherfucker got a name?"

"Ian Sallabrook. We're not from around here. I'm just…passing through, Mr. Truck, sir." Her shoulders rounded as she worked to make herself small. Truck caught the reaction as quickly as Vanna did, but he evidently didn't notice her cautioning squeeze of his waist.

"Myrt, look at me." He'd changed his approach in an instant, voice now smooth as satin. The patience and grace that rose from his soul covered his words, and Myrt's chin lifted until she was staring at Truck. "The things people do to us don't define us, darlin'. We are carved from the whole of our experiences, and it's only by those we learn how to change our future. Was your relationship with your husband one you chose, including his treatment of you?"

A tear broke free from the corner of one eye as Myrt slowly swung her head side to side.

Truck continued, "Did you learn from it and decide to change the direction of your life?"

Her nod, a jerky dip of her chin, was quicker to come in response.

"And are you determined to create what's right for *you* from the opportunities you're given?"

Myrt stared at him for the space of two deep breaths, then slowly and purposefully inclined her head.

"Then you aren't passing through, child. You're home."

Vanna was overwhelmed with emotion at his oh-so tactful handling of the girl, how he'd settled her when she'd been ready to bolt. *God, how I love this man.*

Chapter Two

Myrtle

Soft light filled the room as Myrtle blinked awake. It took her only a moment to remember where she was and how she'd come to be living in a fairy tale, a made-for-TV movie of rescue and redemption.

Born in the type of deep backwoods in Eastern Kentucky that the rest of the world had forgotten, the seventh of fourteen children and female, she'd always known she was disposable. Her mother had been her father's fourth wife, and when she'd passed on, Myrt had understood her time within the family was limited. When Mr. Sallabrook's wife had died from cancer, it had taken him a single day after shoveling dirt on top of her casket to come to Myrt's daddy and ask for a helpmeet. Clearly defined duties marked the boundaries of expectation. Cleaning, cooking, working the garden and barn animals, and—unspoken—holding tight to the rails of the footboard as he took her from behind.

In the years she'd lived with him, they'd never shared a bed. Sallabrook was shepherd for a holler flock of fundamental holdouts, their beliefs a far cry from the gentle Jesus teachings of the white-steepled church Myrt had attended as a child. Cohabitation was against his God's laws, and without much room in the small cabin perched high in the slope of a mountainside, her sleeping pallet was most often constructed on the porch or in a barn stall. Myrt found herself happier the farther away she was from the old man, and his peculiar way of interpreting the Bible had made that easy.

It hadn't been bad for the first couple of years. She and Mr. Sallabrook had settled into a routine easily enough, and as long as she followed his rules, everything had seemed fine. It was just sometimes the rules changed, and she'd fall afoul of them before knowing the ground had shifted underfoot.

The final year had been different. People had been moving away from their family hollers in greater numbers than ever before, and there'd been less money tithed to Sallabrook as their spiritual leader. The current bruises decorating her body all stemmed from an innocent question about an unexpected blank space in his home where a sewing machine had always stood. His first wife had been a skilled seamstress, turning out all of her mister's suits by hand.

He'd drunk a quantity of 'shine from a parishioner one night and talked for hours about the myriad ways his first missus had cared for him. How her quilts and handmade clothing had sold for hundreds of dollars up in Louisville, her skills turned towards supporting him and his causes. Then he'd looked at Myrt, the edges of his lips curling up, the expression he wore telling her without words how lacking he found her.

That's why she'd known better than to ask about the sewing machine. It had held a continued place of reverence in the cabin, and she'd carefully dusted the casing dozens of times, ensuring the wooden panels shone with polish from her efforts. The empty space where it had stood seemed larger than it should have, divots in the floorboards pressed deep from the steady pressure of the machine's weight. The words had tripped off her tongue, as if she hadn't a care in the world.

And Sallabrook had lashed out. And lashed out. And then lashed out again with feet and fists, fingers tangled in her hair as he dragged her from one side of the room to the other and back, Myrt's feet trying and failing to find purchase against the floor. He'd shoved her legs out wide, and for the first time since her father had passed her into his care, rose above her as he thrust hard, tearing his way into her while face-to-face, his reflexively contorted expression terrifying, all teeth and eyes and hard hands holding her down.

Before that day, she'd toyed with the dream of freedom. Keeping nickels and dimes in a sock she'd wedged into a cubbyhole in the barn stall she'd considered hers,

Myrt had slowly built a cache of money that had felt unimaginably huge. Riches galore.

She smoothed the fabric of her nightshirt, trying not to roll her eyes at the ignorance under which she'd labored. Sallabrook had kept her isolated on the mountain as much as possible. He'd allowed regular if infrequent visits with her family and siblings, but what little interaction with outsiders was permitted had always been limited to others in their close-knit community. She'd been a child the last time she remembered going into town with her mother and hadn't realized the true changed state of the world.

That beating had been so severe, Myrt had been crippled by pain for weeks. There'd been no self-recrimination from Sallabrook, no expression of regret or concern. He'd scooped her off the floor and stalked to the barn, throwing her to the dirt floor just inside the door and turning on his heel without a word. She'd dragged herself to the stall and curled into a ball on her flannel-covered pallet of hay. Four days later, Sallabrook had come out to harangue her for not properly preparing his suit for Sunday services. His only glancing reference to the things he'd done had been a cutting comment about her bruised ugliness making it easier for him to resist Satan.

All of it had set the tone for her life for the next year.

For twelve months, Myrt had wobbled from beating to beating, none as out of control and severe as the first had been, but all tied in some way to that sewing machine. The uncertainty ate at her, and she'd hated how she had come to flinch at any quick movement. She'd quickly learned to study every setting for weapons that could be used against her. And she'd become acquainted with the holler's witch, an old woman who'd handed down a recipe for an effective herbal tea. Sallabrook might not have cared about leaving his seed inside her, but Myrt was determined it would never take root.

Throughout the year, Myrt's resolve to leave had strengthened, and she'd gotten even better at finding opportunities to add to her stash of cash. Quarters and paper bills replaced the pennies and other small change. It turned out Sallabrook carried enough money on him on any given day that he didn't miss a dollar here and there. Or he didn't think her smart or bold enough to steal from him directly. That year had seen a change in him, too, with his visits to the 'shine man coming more frequently. His drunken snores would fill the cabin as she crept in from the barn to rifle through his wallet, plucked from his back hip as he lay sprawled across the bed.

She cleared her throat gently, quietly, scooting up on the mattress so her back was against the headboard. The window was open, and a light evening breeze had set the sheer curtains into a slight sway. Looking around the room she found herself astonished once again that she was *here.* Such a far cry from her previous life, where even the luxury of the headboard was strange. The bed was tall, mattresses unbelievably soft, so different from the hard, cotton-ticking one Sallabrook had. The stripes of welts across her back ached, but it was the kind of pain that helped center her, so instead of avoiding it, she leaned into it, pressing harder, stirring up more pain to go with the memories plaguing her. At least she didn't have to worry about her littlest sisters getting sold to Sallabrook or a man like him—one of her older sisters had taken them into her household years ago when she'd married.

That last day hadn't started out as anything memorable. She'd been up at dawn to milk the cow and gather eggs from the chickens, prepare a hot breakfast for Sallabrook, then swing into the normal flow of chores and tasks. He hadn't spoken to her as she moved around where he sat at the kitchen table, hadn't looked at her as she served his food. He hadn't given any indication of anything other than he'd been in the grip of his now-normal hangover state. Eyes bloodshot, jowls loose underneath his unshaven chin, Sallabrook had gripped his knife and fork in trembling hands to eat his meal.

He'd been nearly to the end when it happened. He'd reached out for the last biscuit at the same moment she'd gone to refill his mug with hot coffee. His hand had scarcely brushed the metal, but the explosion had been immediate, giving her no time to react. Pot ripped from her hand and hurled against the wall, he'd secured his hold on her with fingers twisted in her hair. With her physical reactions controlled in that way, he slammed her head against the wooden table, stunning her. From there, things began to blur, the memories choppy as they skipped and stuttered through her head. The blood-covered tabletop coming towards her face, again and again, strands of hair stuck in the rich red liquid. Sallabrook hadn't screamed or shouted, hadn't reminded her of her place, hadn't sermonized at her—the only sounds were the blows against her skin and his grunts of effort. His hands had fumbled at his belt. Then came the blistering pain of the leather coming down on her bare bottom and back, her flour sack dress flipped up, panties ripped away.

At the end of things, he'd left her where she fell. Crumpled in a heap on the floor of the kitchen, she'd been only vaguely aware of the door opening and closing, his exit conducted as silently as his attack on her had been, booted footfalls angling across the porch, the echoing cough of his truck's engine as it caught and ran, then the humming decrescendo as he drove away.

She'd stolen boots from his closet and a pair of dungarees he'd complained were too small and had ransacked his small library, filching the larger bills she'd previously shied away from between the pages where he'd hidden them. Riches expanded in unexpected quantity, she'd stuffed the toes of the boots with newspaper, added smoked meat and cheese to her stash, and shoved everything into an old oat bag. Then she'd cared for the barn animals, detoured through the garden to pluck some ripe produce to add to her bag, and taken a deep breath. Standing at the edge of the clearing opposite where the driveway entered, she'd looked around the place she'd spent so many years, isolated from family and the few friends she'd had, her life nothing like the fairy tales her mother once read to the children on long winter nights.

Myrt had fixed each thing in her head, turned on her heel, and strode into the woods, headed downhill.

Myrt took a slow look around for what felt like the hundredth time since Vanna had brought her upstairs and showed her to the guest room. It was huge, about half as large as the entire cabin had been. A sturdy dresser stood against one wall, a mirror attached to the top. It angled so if Myrt wanted, she could look at herself, even though the piece of furniture was nearly as tall as she was. One glance into the glass had her changing the position with a gasp. In the days since she'd walked away from the cabin, she'd only captured tiny glimpses of her countenance in reflective surfaces. The full scope of the damage Sallabrook had done hadn't been clear to her until that single look. *Satan sure wouldn't tempt him now.* The reactions of the people she'd met along the way, wavering between shock and sorrow, made more sense now, and Myrt hated thinking they'd felt sorry for her. *Not Vanna, though.* Vanna hadn't given off the vibe she'd taken Myrt in out of pity. Everything about the woman spoke towards her caregiver personality, and even in the way she'd introduced Myrt to her Mr. Truck, had looked beyond the awkwardness of the moment and into the future where she expected Myrt to be well and whole. *I bet she picks up all kinds of strays.*

Myrt's lids sagged briefly but jerked wide when her brain painted an image of a fist headed straight towards her face. She'd been suffering through the same kind of flashbacks since she'd walked off the mountain.

She'd stumbled into a highway directly in front of a sedan arrowed straight at her, the inevitability of impact seemingly the same as Sallabrook's knuckles. The elderly man navigating the highway that day was a courier and hadn't hesitated to give her a ride. That driver had taken her more than ten hours straight south. There'd been no destination in mind when she'd climbed into the car, just...away. The bruises hadn't all surfaced by then, not when she'd gotten into the car. The ripening of the colors had bloomed under her skin slowly, drawing sidelong glances, then more direct stares, from the male driver.

The farther they'd driven, the more signs she'd seen for Gulf Coast beaches, and an idea had been born.

After growing up in the slow-moving backwoods, she'd quaked with frantic anxiety watching the flow of traffic in the cities. A pretty lake, with it's lapping wavelets, would be just the thing to ease her mind. She'd imagined the Gulf of Mexico as something like a big lake, an expanse of water that drew the eye out to the horizon, and the calming sounds of waves. The driver had been doubtful about her description, trying in a kind way to explain how the water was different, and then he'd been beyond doubtful about leaving her at the beach, her only request of him not to tell any authorities, but on a deadline, and with his route already disrupted, a few reassurances from her had settled his nerves. He'd been the source of the tarp and warmer articles of clothing, a kind stranger drifting through her life.

Vanna was another one.

Myrt had been on the beach for only a few hours when an incoming storm had driven her back inland, the rising fury of the waves startling and unsettling. By the time she'd slogged through the sand and back to a road, the rain had begun in earnest, and she'd found getting a ride in bedraggled and soaked clothing was more difficult. Finally, a woman had stopped and lectured her about the evils of men—as if Myrt couldn't have told her a few things—and taken her to a women's shelter. They'd been full, and Myrt had watched as the other women turned away at the door had melted back into the darkness, somehow able to merge with the environment like an owl in a tree. She'd attempted the same, searching for a safe place to lay her head, and walked all night. Morning sun rising had shown her the road she'd been following had taken a curve into the wilderness. At the next intersection, when she'd been unsure which way to go, she'd decided that like the poems her mother had once read to her, she'd take the path less traveled.

That had led her to an empty parking lot and eventually into Vanna's sights.

Myrt scanned the room again and shook her head. *How did I go from that to this?* She tried to grasp the edge of the covers and winced when her hand gave a shout of pain. Vanna had helped with that injury, too. The second day at what she now knew was a hiking trailhead, Myrt had fainted as she'd walked towards the only water source she'd found and had woken with a sore and swollen finger. Vanna had offered to take her to a hospital, but Myrt had declined and asked for whatever treatment Vanna was comfortable giving. The memory of those moments were better left in the past, and Myrt stared down at the miraculously straight finger taped to its neighbor.

All in all, I'd say I'm pretty lucky.

She slipped her legs over the side of the mattress, wiggling her toes against the braided rug on the floor alongside the bed. A glance in the angled mirror showed her more green and yellow than the day before, the dark purples holding tight to the flesh around her eyes. Truck had called her a raccoon last night, and she hadn't quite understood what he'd meant. She saw it now and grinned, pleased when the lifting of her cheeks scarcely made her wince. Raccoons were mischievous animals, innovative in how they looked at the world around them, and able to suss out some of the hardest puzzles.

Yeap. Pretty lucky.

Faint sounds crept under the edge of the door, and she tipped her head to the side. Voices, one low and rumbling while the other had a lilting brightness, their conversation muffled by distance until it was only a murmur. The noises that came through alongside the soft murmur were different. She knew those sounds, but Myrt also understood that here in Vanna and Truck's home the noises carried a far different meaning than inside Sallabrook's cabin. The squeak of mattress springs bounded to a rhythm augmented by the pleased cries Vanna offered, her tone pleading, but not for respite or assistance. Myrt imagined the tender care with which Truck had held Vanna in his arms last night would translate to a love-filled embrace in their marriage bed.

Wanting to give them a privacy they'd never know about, Myrt stood and quickly dressed, then made her way downstairs. It took a few minutes to understand the coffee machine, which stood on the counter. Fortunately, there were clearly written instructions taped inside the cabinet door where Myrt found the canister of grounds, which meant soon enough the room filled with the delicious scent of brewing coffee. Finding all the foodstuffs needed for a hearty breakfast inside the refrigerator, she began preparations. The sounds upstairs had stopped, and rushing water filled in the silence. She mentally mapped the noise to her use of the bathroom yesterday to relieve herself and then wash up. They were bathing and would likely be downstairs soon, so Myrt laid the slices of bread she'd readied on a cookie sheet and popped it into the oven, this device also coming with easy-to-understand instructions in a plastic-covered sheet attached to the handle.

By the time Vanna and Truck entered the kitchen, Myrt had places set at the table and was blowing on her fingers in between moving the oven-baked french toast to a serving plate. With a smile, Vanna came to her and wrapped her arms around Myrt gently, her voice soft as she greeted her. "Hope we didn't wake you, honey. This all looks delicious. Soon as Truck smelled the coffee, he said you were a genius for knowing what his brain needed to wake up." Vanna stepped back and reached around Myrt to open a drawer. "Spatula will keep your fingers from burning." Instead of trying to take over and finish things, Vanna simply handed her the implement and turned away, her wordless movements telling Myrt she was trusted and her efforts were welcomed.

Truck stood next to the coffee machine and lifted a filled mug to his mouth. He blew air across the top of the liquid and then sipped, smacking his lips with a grin. "Damn good cup of joe, Myrt. Thanks, honey."

She dipped her head nervously before turning back to the pan on top of the stove. Once all the pieces of toast were on the serving plate, she carried it and a pan of fried potatoes to the table, somehow not surprised to see Vanna perched on Truck's thigh as he sat in a kitchen chair, her head resting against his shoulder. "It ain't much."

"It's food I didn't have to make, so trust me when I say it's perfect." Vanna flashed her a quick grin as she reached out with a fork to transfer a piece of toast to her plate. "I've got some syrup in the pantry." She stood, and Truck grabbed for her hip, laughing when he came up empty-handed. "Gotta be faster than that, old man."

"I'm *your* old man," he shot back, retrieving his own stack of toast. "Grab the butter from the fridge." Using the edge of his fork, he cut into the toast. "Smells real good, honey."

Myrt watched their interaction with interest, noting again how happy they were around each other. Vanna had been pleasant yesterday, truly kind and caring, but the moment Truck's footsteps were heard inside the house, she'd brightened somehow, as if she were more herself in his presence.

Syrup and butter deposited on the table, Vanna slid her plate around in front of a chair, leaving Truck to his own devices. *Probably a good idea, given the syrup.* Pleased with contributing to these two people who'd taken her in overnight, Myrt watched as they ate. Until Truck noticed she hadn't begun her own meal. Then he gently urged her to eat. Vanna's gaze on him shared her sense of pride that he would care so for someone else.

After a second stack of toast had made its way to his plate and been eaten, Truck pushed back from the table, hands folded across his stomach. He stared so pointedly at Vanna that Myrt knew it was some kind of silent signal. Sure enough, as soon as Vanna finished the bite in her mouth and swallowed, she leaned forwards, elbow to the table as she looked steadily at Myrt.

"Myrtle, I know we talked yesterday about you staying a couple of days."

A sickening feeling curdled the food in her stomach, and she dropped her chin to her throat, eyes closed. Her heart pumped loudly in her ears, drowning out everything else in the room. Here she'd been thinking they didn't mind her being around and her wanting to pay them back for their kindness, and then they'd been forced to share a meal with her while waiting on the right time to tell her to leave. Myrt's throat clicked as she swallowed, and she shoved her chair back, standing and turning to leave the room.

"Myrtle, stop right there."

Truck's loud voice froze her in her tracks, but she didn't turn, keeping her back towards the couple as she waited for the final blow from whatever proclamation he was about to make.

"She didn't hear a thing you said, babe. Look at her; she thinks we're kickin' her to the curb, when that's the farthest thing from the truth." Wooden chair legs scraped across the floor as the seating was quickly rearranged. "Make it right, Vanna, or we're gonna lose her."

His words didn't make sense. They didn't line up with what Vanna had said, what Myrt had heard, so she waited, wondering.

"Oh, honey, please. Please, come back to the table." Heat from Vanna's palm settled on Myrt's arm, and she was pulled in a half circle. Eyes averted, she couldn't bring herself to look into the woman's face, not wanting to see the rejection that must've taken up residence there. "Come on." Myrt went with the tug, passively following Vanna back to the table. She sat in her chair where it had come to rest from her quick departure, angled towards the door and well away from the edge of the table. A chair appeared directly in front of her, and she glanced up as Vanna settled herself, knees touching Myrt's.

"You thought we wanted you to leave?"

Truck's question was as gentle as the man could make his voice, probably, the sound more a soothing rumble than the growl it had been moments ago. Myrt nodded, compelled to answer him.

"Oh, honey. Furthest thing in the world from what we want." He positioned himself behind Vanna, both of them now between Myrt and the doorway. Not that she felt trapped or penned in, but the idea they wanted to put the brakes on her leaving gave her a sliver of hope. "Tell her, babe."

"Myrtle, stay. Days, weeks, months, years even. We want you here because we want you safe and healthy. You're a sweet girl, with one of the kindest souls, and we want to be part of your family if you'll let us."

The pain that had set up residence behind her breastbone eased, unclamping slightly and giving her room to take in a shuddering breath. "I thought you were already tired of me."

"Farthest thing from the truth." Vanna reused Truck's words, her firm tone filled with reassurance Myrt needed. "With our son out of the house, it's too quiet around here. I'd love to have a companion as you heal, and it'll give me a chance to make sure you take care of yourself. It's a mom thing, honey. Hurts my heart to think of you out in the world like this, or anytime. Life's hard, and I—we—want to make it easier for you."

"You don't even know me." That was a concerning truth, because she hadn't told them much about Sallabrook, a glancing slide across the top of the truth. Her husband had beaten her and she'd run away. No reason to go into the gory details simply because things were difficult. "I could be a thief."

"You're not." Myrt glanced up at Truck, surprised to see a fierce expression on his face so at odds with the tender tone his words had taken. "Trust me when I tell you I know thieves and liars and bad people of all types. So when I say I believe my gut, it's because I've had exposure and am a damn good judge of people." He lifted his chin. "You're no more bad than my Vanna is. You're sweet and kind and young. So fuckin' young, honey. I expect you'd cut off your hand before you did anything to hurt her or me. I'm seldom wrong about something like this, so don't even think you can feed me a line of bullshit."

"I don't understand." This was the best way to approach it, the way her mother had told her the schools used. A give and take of ideas, where admitting to ignorance was seen as the highest merit of honesty. Myrt's mother had been educated, having gone to college a whole semester before her disastrous marriage. *If she hadn't died...*

"We have a room. You need a room. Vanna's alone in the house a lot now, and my..." He sighed softly. "My job means I have to be gone sometimes." His slight hesitation was more pronounced because the rest of his words were so definite. His jaw firmed, and he stroked a hand down his beard. "I don't like when she's out here all alone. Kitt, our boy, had a dog, and havin' an early warning system always made me sleep better. But the pup moved out with him, which leaves Vanna here by herself. If you could see your way clear to staying with us for a time, that'll soothe my mind, honey."

"Myrt, I hate I hurt you like I did." Myrt's cold fingers were covered by Vanna's warm palm and gripped gently. "I started off wrong. What I was trying to say was, you and I had talked about a couple of days, but I wanted to extend our invitation indefinitely." Vanna gave their joined hands a shake that Myrt felt to the soles of her feet. An emphasis to her words, a physical reassurance that this was a real offer. "We want you here, and not only because you make a mean breakfast." Myrt looked up in time to see Vanna share a watery smile with Truck. "We want you here because we need you, maybe more than you can believe right now. But it's the truth."

Each breath was more difficult, her throat tight. Vanna's kindness stirred something inside Myrt, eventually eliciting the kind of gratitude her mother had modeled. Myrt stared down at her lap, her gaze slowly coming into focus on the clothing she wore. Everything on her body was from the generosity of this woman who had crowded close to try to right an imaginary wrong. Myrt turned her hand inside Vanna's grip, folding her fingers around the other woman's and holding tightly.

"It's been a long time since someone made me feel worth saving." Her lips were dry, a condition hardly changed when she ran the tip of her tongue across the surface. "Since someone talked to me like I mean something. Just that right there's worth nearly anything. Makin' me feel like somebody. It's hard to hold on to yourself when everything comin' at you is ugly. You're offering me a slice of sweetness right here, and I'm not stupid. I'm going to hold to it until you take it back."

"We won't." Vanna's fingers spasmed in hers, an expression of pain crossing her face. "Not takin' anything back. Not ever. You're part of the family now, honey."

Chapter Three

Vanna

Unsnapping the clothespin, Vanna removed the towel from the line. Dropping the fastener into the bag hanging nearby for that purpose, she snapped the fabric away from the breeze, ensuring any creepy crawlies that might have taken up residence were forcefully evicted. Matching edges, she folded the towel into a square, then into a column, and then into thirds, dropping the finished product into the basket at her feet. Two steps along the line and she repeated the process, interrupting her movements only to bring the fabric to her face and sniff, the smell of detergent mixing with the rich pine of the surrounding trees.

The back door of the house creaked behind her, and Vanna glanced over her shoulder, smiling at Myrt, who was making her way outside with another basketful of wet things.

In the weeks since Myrt had come to live with Vanna and Truck, they'd settled into an easy routine that was comfortable and good. The girl was up way too early of a morning, but Truck had come to appreciate having coffee ready and hot when he rolled out of bed. If Myrt had her way, she'd feed them a banquet breakfast every day, and it was only when Vanna had shared her worries about Truck's diet that Myrt had slacked off on her over-the-top efforts. Now cut fruit was as likely to make an appearance as a ham and cheese omelet, which Vanna appreciated far more than Truck did.

Days like today, when the two women worked together for a common goal, were some of the best. Vanna hadn't enjoyed a companion like this in a long time.

As if on cue, her phone buzzed in the pocket of her jeans, and she slung the towel she was working on over her shoulder, digging the device out. She tapped the icon to accept the call, and a woman's image lit up the screen, a broad smile on her face as she cradled her youngest child against her shoulder.

Sharon had come into her life much as Myrtle had—caught up in desperate need, filled with terror at having experienced the worst of humankind. As with Myrt, Sharon had lived with Vanna, sharing the house with Kitt, Vanna's son. That had been before Truck, and the profound changes he'd wrought in Vanna's life. It had also been before Gunny had found Sharon, latching on like she was the most precious thing he'd ever known. *They saved each other.*

"Vanna Mom!" Girlish shrieks came from the background, and Vanna could see the tops of Sharon's two daughters bumping up and down. From the corner of her eye, she saw Myrt's head lift quickly as the girl stopped in place, a wave of surprise rushing across her face.

"Cade and Kitten, I can scarcely see you girls. Where are you?"

Sharon rolled her eyes, and the video jittered before she stopped trying to push the girls away. "Stop it now, kiddos. Josh, get down, buddy. Time to go play in the backyard. There are bugs there, remember?" The little boy whose cheek rested on her shoulder shook his head back and forth, snuggling in tighter against her neck. "Vanna, I wanted to talk, but this is just...ugh." Sharon blew bangs off her forehead with a stream of air. "I'll call you back?"

"No, just hand the phone to Cade. Let me talk to the girls for a minute, then I'll get her to bring it back. That'll give you a minute to see why Josh boy doesn't wanna go hunt for bugs. Tell him Vanna Mom's worried about her boy. Bugs are a big deal."

"Okay, give me half a sec—" Sharon turned away from the phone, her brows drawn together. "Cade, can you take—no, Kitten, Cade's going to hold the phone. Stop. Cade, can you please—?" The view changed from Sharon's profile to a close-up of a girl no more than ten years old.

This was Cadence, Sharon and Gunny's oldest. Katherine was two years younger, followed by Joshua a year later. Cade, Kitten, and Josh were the light of Vanna's life, and she loved the kids as if she were their blood grandmother, instead of an adopted one.

"Girls, oh my goodness. I swear you grow inches between every time I get to see you. And look at that pretty tattoo. Does Daddy know you've got a cartoon on your cheek? It's gorgeous. Both of you are my little sweethearts." She kept up the quick and engaging patter, tag-teaming the girls effectively while in the background she could hear Sharon talking to Josh. After catching up on the outcome of an earthworm experiment (turned out the children had found out captured earthworms could escape a bowl if left unguarded overnight), listening to them sing her an off-tune rendition of a popular country song, and soaking up the excitement of seeing her girls again, Vanna gently guided the interactions back around to the girls' mother, and a few minutes later the phone was returned to Sharon's hands. Sans Josh, who now seemed to be off chasing his sisters through the backyard, accompanied by the bright barks and low woofs of Sharon and Gunny's pack of dogs.

"Whew." Sharon puffed her bangs up as she walked into the shade next to the house and sat where she could watch out over the backyard. The home and terrain were familiar to Vanna, her many visits over the years giving her a good sense of things. "That was chaotic to the extreme."

"What was up with Josh?" Vanna studied Sharon's face, noting the fatigue etched in the tiny lines at the corners of her eyes. "He's getting too big for you to cart around like that, kiddo. Gonna wreck your back."

Sharon's gaze flicked past the camera and into the distance, the smile stretching her lips loving and kind. "My boy will never be too big for Momma's lap."

"Might want to check that wish before tossing it out into the universe. Have you seen the size of the boy's daddy?" Vanna tossed the towel over the line and left it there for now, walking slowly towards the house. "I'll be back in a minute, Myrt. Leave me some work to do, okay?"

"Yes, ma'am." The girl's unwavering politeness was lost in the quiet tension held in her words, and Vanna glanced to see Myrt's shoulders had pulled in, her head dipped down and to the side as if avoiding a blow.

"God bless," she murmured and sighed as she stepped into the kitchen. "What's shakin', Shar?" On the phone, Sharon's brows drew together. "I'll tell you all about my visitor as soon as you dish on why you called me today." Something she'd intended to do over the past couple of weeks, but each call had been cut short by one child or another needing something. "So, the faster you give me whatever it is you've got to tell me, the sooner you hear all about my adventures."

"You're something else, Vanna." The phone traveled away from Sharon's face, and Vanna saw the edge of a table as the device was wedged into place. *This'll be a longer conversation, then.* "Josh didn't want to look for bugs because Kitten put worms in his bed, and he didn't see them before climbing under the covers. They squished, and you know how he feels about hurting anything."

"Kitten did that?" Vanna didn't try to contain her laughter. "Does she know that's not nice?"

"Oh, yeah, she knows now. Doesn't help Josh's guilt over smushing a half a dozen earthworms. You should have seen his face when Gunny was talking about taking him fishing soon and demonstrated how to bait his hook. It was only a gummy worm, but my poor Joshie was traumatized." Sharon's eye roll revealed exactly how she felt about her husband's efforts with their son. "Gunny sometimes doesn't know what to do with our sensitive child."

"Hey, now, Cade's plenty sensitive." The oldest girl was the caretaker of the trio, had been since Kitten had been born, persistently bringing her baby sister all her favorite toys and blankets until Gunny had explained Kitten had her own things. "Kitten's the one who's misnamed, for sure."

"More like a roaring lion than a purring kitten," Sharon agreed. "I thought middle kids were supposed to be the peacemakers. Why isn't she more about making sure everyone's okay?"

"Because she takes after her mother." Sharon's expression of fake shock had Vanna laughing again. "No, she's Gunny all over again. I bet if we could talk to his grandmother, we'd find a lot in common."

"Yeah. I'm glad the kids have my folks as well as Jase and his family, but I feel like we're all missing out because they don't have the same connections on Daddy's side of the family." Sharon shook her head, strands of hair escaping her messy bun to trail along her cheeks. "It's good they've got Vanna Mom, too. You help keep us all balanced."

"Think you can peel him loose anytime soon and come for a visit?" Vanna hoped but didn't expect she'd be successful. It was worth a little wheedling, though, just in case. "Vanna Mom misses her kids. I miss you and Gunny, too, but man, I miss those kids."

"Unlikely. He's in Milwaukee this week and will be in Kansas City the next. They've got him roaming all over to help keep things smooth with all the change that's happening."

Gunny was an officer in the Rebel Wayfarers motorcycle club. He was based out of Fort Wayne, Indiana, where Sharon was calling from today, but traveled wherever the club needed him. Vanna understood, probably more than most, because Truck was also a member, based out of the Little Rock clubhouse but given special dispensation to stay close to home most of the time.

Most of the time. Vanna glanced up at the clock, mentally counting down the hours until Truck's bike would roll into the driveway. "Truck's over in Adken again. That new chapter is taking a lot of his time these days. He was in Texas a couple of weeks ago, and when he got back, I'd hoped he'd be home for a while, but Sparks asked for him by name." Sparks was the president of a club that had been absorbed by the Rebel Wayfarers MC only a few months ago, a transition that had gone smoothly, all things considered. The same day the club had patched in, a prominent member of another club had patched over, all of which raised the tension level considerably.

"It's always something." Sharon's smile was tinged with sadness and didn't linger long on her lips. "So what if I could bring me and the kids, but no Gunny?"

"I'll take it. When can you be here?"

"Depends. What kind of company do you have and how long will they be there?"

Tit for tat. Vanna wouldn't have expected any less. As possessive as she was over Sharon and her family, it was returned tenfold. "Myrtle is a young lady who found herself in a situation. One I was in a position to help her escape. She's been with me for a few weeks—" Sharon's brows rose at the revelation, probably because Vanna hadn't mentioned the girl before. "Don't do that. Every time we get on the phone lately, there's an emergency. This might be the longest conversation we've had since I don't know when."

Sharon smoothed out her features and nodded. "Carry on, please." Her regal tone had Vanna chuckling.

A shadow crossed the porch, and Vanna sighed, then pitched her voice to carry. "So Myrt's been with me for a while, and I hope she'll stay a long, long time. I enjoy the company, and she's a huge help around the house." Myrt's head appeared around the corner of the open door, chin still angled down to hide her expression. The basket in her hands was filled with folded towels, which meant she had not only hung up all the wet ones but also finished taking down the dry ones. "Wanna meet her? Come here, Myrt. Let me introduce you to my daughter, Sharon." Vanna stood and turned her back towards the girl, holding up the phone as if she were taking a selfie, trying to capture both of them in the frame. "Sharon, this is Myrtle, my new house companion. Myrt, this is Sharon. You've heard me talk about her and the kids, and her mess of a husband, Gunny."

"Pleased." Myrt's head bobbed, and she weaved to the side, around Vanna, and into the house before Sharon got a chance to respond.

"You sure you want the tribe to come and stay for a few days? I won't take offense if you say you've got your hands full, Vanna."

"Not a chance, girlie. Bring on the chaos." Vanna smiled out the window, her imagination bringing the scene to life with children playing hide-and-seek among the laundry drying in the bright sunshine. She returned her gaze to the phone's screen to see a fondly amused expression on Sharon's face. "When do you think you can make it here?"

"I'll call Gunny when I hang up and make sure he can't come, then I'll text you. Probably Saturday if that suits?" Sharon's head tipped to the side, and she bit her bottom lip. "I miss you like crazy, Vanna Mom."

"Sooner if you can make it, but Saturday will work." Vanna felt her shoulders drop as she relaxed and confided, "I can't wait."

***

Vanna

"Hello?" Vanna blinked up at her ceiling, the surface lost in the darkness of night invading her bedroom. Fear trilled its uncomfortable electric feeling up and down her back, causing her toes to curl. She hadn't looked at the phone's screen before answering, but it wouldn't have mattered. Early morning calls were always picked up.

"Vanna, darlin'?"

She took a breath to steady her nerves. "Truck? Is everything okay?" *Thank God it's him.* If anyone else had spoken in her ear, she would have assumed the worst. Her mind wandered. "Is Kitt okay? Did someone call you?"

"No, darlin'. Nothing's wrong. It's all good, all good, baby." Truck's voice was pitched to soothe and comfort. She knew he'd never lie to her, so it couldn't be anything with her son.

"Then what's going on that'd have you calling me—" She shifted the phone to see the screen, then put the speaker to her mouth again. "—at three in the morning. Something's wrong, even if it's not you or Kitt."

"Sharon's on her way down—"

"Oh, God. She's got all the kids with her. Is she okay? Are the kids okay?" Imagined scenes of wrecked and mangled vehicles filled her mind, tiny bodies flung hither and yon inside the van. "Please tell me they're okay."

"Vanna, darlin', if you'd let me get more than a couple of words out, you'd already know they broke down."

"Oh, no. She's got the babies. Truck, where is she?" Vanna levered herself off the mattress, scurrying towards the closet. "I can be dressed in half a minute and on my way in a minute more. Where am I going?"

"Truck, you need to let Momma know they're safe and have roadside comin'." The voice in the background was well known and loved. *And surprisingly calm if Sharon and the kids are in trouble.* Gunny wasn't known for keeping his shit together when his family was involved.

"Is that Lane? Can he tell me what's going on, since you obviously don't have the right information?" Balancing on one foot, she managed to tug a sock into place, only hopping once or twice. "Gunny! What's going on?"

"Jesus, Truck." Gunny's laughter settled her in ways nothing else would have. No way would he be laughing if his family were in peril. "Just tell her."

"I'm fuckin' tryin', you jackass. Now back the fuck off before I slap you silly." Truck's growled words settled Vanna even more. "Momma, you still there?"

"Yeah, Truck. I'm here. Take your time." She sat on the edge of the bed, holding the other sock in her hands. Now that the urgency of the situation seemed to have fled, she found her situation amusing. "I've got one sock on and the other off, a shirt but no bra. I got nowhere to be but here, so you tell me what you need."

"No bra?" Truck's tease was clear and made her grin.

"Jesus, Truck, don't do a sex call right now." That was an unexpected voice, and unlike Gunny's, it wasn't in the background but on the call.

"Blackie? Oh, honey, it's good to hear from you." Blackie was one of Vanna's oldest friends, someone she'd turned to for advice time and again over the years. He lived with his wife over in Northeast Texas. "What're you doing up this time of day?"

"Waiting on Truck to let you know you're going to have an unexpected visitor." He chuckled, the sound dark and rumbling through the phone's speakers. "And listening to you losin' your shit. Not something I've been exposed to frequent-like, so it's interesting to hear."

"Don't you start, too, Blackie." Truck sounded even more annoyed now, which was surprising because she knew the two men were friends.

"Hey, you're the one called me for a favor, man. I'm owed a little bit of repayment for makin' me drag my ass outta bed this time of the morning. I'm on Central, remember, so it's early as fuck here."

"Can someone please tell me what's going on with Sharon?" A shadow at her doorway had her heart beating fast again until she recognized the silhouette as her houseguest. "Myrt, come on in, honey. Might as well make a party of it." Vanna patted the corner of the mattress, and when the girl settled in, wrapped an arm around her and pulled her tight. "Truck's just about to give me some good news."

"You're going to have an unexpected visitor." Blackie dove right in, as Truck sputtered in the background. "Dispatched one of my men to help Sharon, and he'll be riding the rest of the way with her, to make sure they don't run into any additional issues."

"Who?" Vanna knew most of Blackie's club by name and had a good relationship with all the men.

"Bane's comin'. He was close when we got the request for assistance, so easiest for Blackie to ship him over to help." Truck was apparently trying to regain control over the call. "He's a good guy."

"I know. I've met him. Sweet boy." Myrt stirred at her side and stood before walking to the doorway and miming drinking from a mug. Vanna nodded her support of what she imagined was making a pot of coffee, watching the girl disappear into the shadows near the top of the stairs. "I'll get a room ready for him. You're sure Sharon and the kids are okay?"

"Yeah, darlin'. I promise. You think Gunny'd be willing to hang out here otherwise?"

A deep tone said something with a grumble in the background, and Vanna smiled, shaking her head.

"No, I don't suppose he would." She lay back on the bed, curling onto her side, wrapping herself around the phone. "So tell me about your day? I feel like it's forever since we got to talk."

"I'd rather talk about you not wearing a bra." Truck lowered his voice an octave, adding a teasing tone.

"And that's my cue to hang up." Blackie laughed. "Later, Peepers."

"Later, my friend." There was a click and a hum; then the call returned to normal. "So, what do you want to know about my current braless state?"

Chapter Four

Myrtle

Tires crunching on gravel caught Myrt's attention, and she stood from the side of the bed to angle towards the window, looking down at the driveway in front of the house. Fear trilled through her for an instant at the sight of the unfamiliar vehicle. The side door opened before the van had even come to a complete stop, and three children poured from the inside, followed immediately by three dogs of varying sizes. The fear was swallowed by amazement as Vanna appeared, kneeling in the front yard as she swept all three kids into her embrace.

A tiny woman who had to be Sharon exited the van's passenger door, more slowly than the kids had, but still with some speed as she trotted to the heap of kids now piled on a reclining Vanna, the tangle of arms and legs spread out on the grass. Laughter seeped in around the closed window, and Myrt grinned as Sharon scolded the kids before realizing Vanna had instigated the dogpile. Then the actual dogs angled in from the side, adding to the confusion as they barked excitedly and pressed close.

More movement at the van caught Myrt's attention, and she froze in place as a man climbed out of the driver seat, closing the door with a firm press of his hand. He didn't look anything like she'd expected. She'd known it wouldn't be Gunny, the man in so many photos Vanna had on her walls, pictures of this family she claimed as her own. Having heard a multitude of tales about the love story that was Sharon and Gunny, Myrt couldn't imagine what it would have been like to be a stranger traveling so far with Sharon and her kids.

She stepped closer to the window, and his head jerked up, aimed right at her. Steely blue eyes pinned her in place, and she stared into the most handsome face she'd ever seen on a man. Grizzled scruff softened the edges of his jaw, and his inky hair was scarcely long enough to curl behind his ears, the symmetry of his features adding to his perfection.

A voice called, and he looked away. Myrt felt a profound relief, breaths whooshing in and out of her lungs as if she'd been held underwater for long minutes, only allowed to surface just before she drowned.

Edging to the side, she used one finger to pull the curtain out an inch, giving her a narrow view of the front yard. The man, who looked younger than Sharon as he stood next to her, stretched out a hand to Vanna and helped her recover her feet with three kids still holding tightly to her. He looked pointedly up at the window Myrt had vacated and said something that had Sharon and Vanna looking up, too. Myrt felt like the worst of frauds as she kept hiding, but nothing she could say to herself was enough encouragement to reveal herself again. Something about the man had her panicked, and she hated the way her heart trip-trapped in her chest, tattooing out a beat of retreat.

Vanna spoke to them, the kids' arms wrapped around her legs and waist, their affection clear. Then the women, kids, and dogs all turned as a unit and headed for the front door. The man looked back up at the window, gave a slow nod as if he knew Myrt still watched, and returned to the van. He opened up the back at the same time a cacophony of sounds made their way up the stairs, indicating Vanna and the Robinson crew had entered the house.

"So stupid." Myrt rested her forehead against the back of her hand, keeping one eye locked on the man as he retrieved suitcases and backpacks from the cargo area of the van. "Vanna said Sharon would understand."

"I do." Myrt's argument with herself was interrupted by the unfamiliar voice at her door, and she swung around to stare slack-jawed at Sharon. Shoulder to the doorframe, the slight woman looked harmless enough. "You don't have anything to fear from me, Myrtle." Myrt glanced away, back towards the window, then pointedly returned her gaze to Sharon's face. "You don't have anything to fear from anyone here. Vanna's house is the safest place I know. It's always been my sanctuary when things get hard. I wouldn't bring anyone here who would threaten this place, or what it means to me."

Myrt chewed her bottom lip and nodded, dropping her gaze to the floor.

Sharon continued talking as if Myrt trying to blend into the background wasn't unusual. "Willy's a real good guy. When I told Gunny I was driving down, he didn't want me and the kids on the road by ourselves. I took off on my own anyway and then had trouble a few hundred miles back. Willy dropped everything and came to help. Made it so I could come see Vanna. So my kids could see their Vanna Mom." Sharon shifted, and Myrt flicked her gaze up to see she'd pushed away from the doorframe, standing straight. In her expression, Myrt saw the fierceness Vanna had spoken of with such love, explaining the source of it was Sharon's story to tell but that her girl had come a long way from when Vanna had first met her. "And if he makes you uncomfortable in any way, you tell me. He'll answer for anything he does. I swear to you on the oath of the sisterhood."

That was odd enough Myrt had to ask, "Oath of the sisterhood?"

"Uh-huh." Sharon nodded, the fierce expression never wavering. "It's the 'sisters before misters' oath. Us girls have to stand together, and that means I'll have your back, Myrtle."

"You can call me Myrt." She forced the corners of her mouth up for an instant before releasing the uncomfortable smile. "Rhymes with dirt."

Instead of the grin she'd expected, an expression of deep sorrow passed over Sharon's features, leaving behind an echo of pain Myrt didn't understand.

"Myrt, derived from Myrtle, who shares a classic beauty with a gorgeous flowering shrub." Sharon acknowledged her preferred name with a gentle correction, which drew a line under what had bothered her. She nodded as if her statement had the authority to change Myrt's first words. "Myrt." Leaning back, she shouted down the stairs. "Willy, can you bring up the bags? Kids are sharing the room at the end of the hall. I'll be with Vanna Mom in the main bedroom, and you'll have the one next to Myrt."

"Sharon, can you please stop calling me that?"

The man's voice was gruff but rolled through with amusement like honey in a rich, dark coffee. His tone was sweetly affectionate, proving his annoyed words a lie.

"If he's not Willy, then who is he?" Myrt whispered her question, surprised when it traveled enough so Sharon could hear.

"His club name is Bane." Sharon shrugged, as if renaming the man wasn't a big deal. Myrt had heard and understood enough from Truck to know he owned his club name in a proud way, even more than his given name. "I like to pick on him a little."

"More like a lot, little sister." The voice only preceded him by an instant, and then all Myrt could do was stare at the man who loomed over Sharon's shoulder. "You must be Myrtle." He nodded, his chin going down and up as his gaze never left Myrt's face. "Pleased to meetcha." He took another step, now looking at Myrt from over Sharon's other shoulder, another pace farther along the hallway. "I'm gonna get things sorted for the hordes." His biceps bulged, visible in the sleeveless leather vest he wore, as he lifted the suitcases and bags out to the sides in further explanation. "I'll be right back."

Bane disappeared, and again Myrt found herself short of breath, as if every ounce of oxygen had been sucked out of the room for the length of time he'd been visible.

"Oh, sister." Sharon took a step into the room Myrt had come to think of as hers, a pleased expression on her face. "I'm glad to see that whatever happened to you…and before you ask, no, I don't know. Vanna's good at keeping secrets. But I'm awfully glad to see no matter what it was, it didn't kill that curiosity. Bane's a good guy. I've known him for a couple of years, met him on a trip to Texas. He's never had a steady girlfriend in all that time."

Myrt swallowed hard and dropped her gaze, taking a step backwards so her shoulders bumped the wall. "I don't know why that should matter to anything."

"Just sayin', sister." From the corner of her eye, Myrt saw Sharon retreat a step. "I'm going to head down to check on my kiddos, make sure they haven't talked their

Vanna Mom into anything they shouldn't have." From the hallway, she yelled in the direction Bane had disappeared. "I'm going downstairs. Totally just headed down to check on my kids. No other reason. But I'm going now. Floor's yours." She aimed a smile at Myrt and winked, then disappeared.

Myrt's feet were stuck to the floor, legs stiff as boards. Butterflies had her stomach turning over and over, and she couldn't catch her breath. It seemed like hours passed, weeks even, before the assertive tread of what had to be Bane's boots came striding up the hallway towards her open door. Saliva pooled in her mouth, and she closed her eyes to block out the view of the doorway. The footfalls slowed and came to a stop, then began again, but instead of aiming towards the stairs, preparatory to going down to the main floor, they grew louder, angling towards where she stood.

"Myrtle? You okay, honey?"

She swallowed and choked, hands flying up to cover her mouth as she bent at the waist, coughing.

"Hey, hey, you okay?" A hand gripped her arm while a second settled in the center of her back, patting gently. "Slow down, honey. Take a breath."

Face flaming, she coughed again, finally pulling in an unimpeded lungful of air.

"There you go." The palm between her shoulder blades rubbed in soothing circles. "Take a minute, catch your breath."

"I'm fine." She choked yet again, trying without success to reassure him as she folded over. The hand around her upper arm pulled her back upright, then tugged her tight against his side, his arm strong as it braced across her back. The fingers that had been caressing her disappeared, then reappeared cupping her chin as he angled her head up and back.

"Take a breath, honey. You're gonna be fine."

Seen from this close, his eyes looked more robin's egg blue than steely, the dark brows drawn together, framing them beautifully. He was so handsome.

"Myrtle, you got a voice?"

His gaze held her fixed, and her voice trembled as she answered him. "I'm okay." Her lips refused to lift, even in a semblance of a smile. "Sorry for the bother."

"No bother, honey." One corner of his mouth quirked, curling into a cheeky grin. "Long as you're okay now. That's all I care about."

His arm around her back gave her a squeeze, the backs of his knuckles pressing into the side of her breast. She tingled all over, nerves up and down her spine firing while heat pooled low in her belly. The butterflies were back in earnest, fluttering madly as Bane looked at her. Looked *into* her, stirring something deep inside.

Myrt jerked free from his hold, stumbling sideways until her shoulder jarred against the wall. A picture not far away swayed and teetered, settling back into place against the wall after a couple of terrifying moments. She turned away, cheek to the wall, and whispered, "I'm fine. Please...please go."

It was silent in the room for long enough that she'd taken a half a dozen breaths before the leather of his boot soles scuffed against the floor. "All right. Okay, I will."

The shuffling came closer instead of retreating, and she squeezed her eyes closed, flattening herself against the wall in avoidance. *If I can't see him...* She knew it was an idiot's thought, a fool's idea, but she couldn't stop the refrain from running through her head. *I can't see you.*

"Myrtle." Her name was spoken so close she felt the touch of his breath against her cheek. "I didn't mean to scare you." She slid down the wall away from him, heedless of the way the rough plaster scraped her cheek. "I'm goin'. Don't hurt yourself, honey. I'm...I'm goin'."

She tracked his footsteps through the door, then left towards the top of the stairs and down each groaning tread to the main floor and out the front door, slamming shut in his wake.

And still her arm tingled, the nerves on her skin where it had touched his sparked, and her breasts ached. It was as if she'd grabbed tight to a live electrical wire, energized by the current as it flowed through her, unable to shake it loose.

All because a man named Bane was nice to me.

The rolling of her stomach was for a completely different reason.

***

Bane

He rocked to a stop next to the van and heaved out a frustrated breath. *No fuckin' ride.* Hands on his hips, he stared back up the road they'd followed from the highway, overwhelmed by the silence surrounding this house in the middle of no-fuckin-where. *Son of a bitch.*

When Horse had taken a call that the ole lady of a national officer in a friendly club had run into mechanical problems in eastern Arkansas, with no brothers of that officer within easy range, he'd tagged Bane to be Sharon's rescuer for her trip home. Horse was the enforcer for the Freed Riders MC, the club Bane had patched into a couple of years back. That officer with the ole lady in trouble had been Gunny, with the Rebel Wayfarers MC. Presented the problem, without question, Bane had hitched a ride with a brother and gotten on the road, treating the ask as an honor. Keeping the ole lady of an RWMC lifer like Gunny safe, then being trusted by his own president as escort for the duration of her trip, was a privilege.

He knew the honor was only because the RWMC wasn't aware of his history, which felt like all kinds of a lie.

When Bane had first landed in east Texas and found the Freed Riders, he'd latched tight to the idea of patching into the club. That had been years after he'd left his hometown of Philadelphia in the dust. With the back of his vest bare of any patches, he'd approached an officer named Horse and laid out all the reasons and benefits that had seemed most likely to get him through the door. Unfortunately, that attempt had run up against a big ole nope. Horse had listened to him, but still shaken his head and said the efforts Bane was willing to put in wouldn't ever be enough, could never be enough, because of his former affiliations.

To say the disappointment had been crushing would be an understatement. From where he'd stood—and everything he'd witnessed between the members—the brotherhood within the FRMC represented everything he'd ever needed. *Third time's a charm, and all that.*

Still, Bane hadn't blamed them. FRMC would have been the third patch to ride between his shoulders. Even divorced by geography as diverse as Michigan to Wyoming, and then Texas, that was a fuckton of history to be dragging in his wake.

Of course, then there was the *real* reason.

William Douglas Crow, known to his FRMC brothers as Bane, had been born into an interesting life.

The youngest grandson of an old-blood mob member, he'd broken from tradition and set aside the blind loyalty bred into him. Bane had shunned the kind of violence in which his family seemed to revel, staying well clear of the pack of sycophant jackals. The final straw that had sent him running was the clear and present threat of being forced into his brother's motorcycle club. Called the Monster Devils, they'd been known for their lack of self preservation, unafraid of upsetting the status quo with war after war. Bane had longed for a sense of belonging, but knew he'd never find it in that bloodthirsty bunch.

That isn't how it's supposed to be.

He shook his head. Bane had deftly managed to stay well clear of both family organizations, not wanting to be associated with a way of life he no longer recognized. But blood was blood, the bonds strong—so he'd known if put in the same position but on the other side of the table, he'd have said the same thing Horse had done. *Protect the club.*

Stubbornness seemed to run in his family, though, because Bane hadn't given up. As he'd told Horse the next night—showing up with a black eye and bruised jaw as evidence Horse's prospect had done per request and delivered a thoroughly discouraging message—except Bane wasn't listening. He'd decided he wouldn't stop working to show the FRMC the kind of member and brother he could be.

It had taken ten days. Ten beatings where he refused to lift a hand to defend himself. Ten mornings when he'd prayed he wouldn't piss blood. And ten times Horse had patiently listened to the whole of his spiel and then slowly shaken his head.

Eleven had been his magic number, it seemed.

This trip would be a brief foray out of his club's Texas territory but could be a huge step forwards in the depth of trust Horse and other FRMC officers had for him. As well as increasing his standing with the RWMC men—something he'd been working hard to gain since meeting several of them a handful of years ago.

Following a multi-club party, Blackie, the FRMC president, had tasked him with inter-club relations, hoping to leverage the already-friendly level of trust between their Freed Riders MC, based in Longview, Texas, and the Rebel Wayfarers MC, based out of all-the-fuck-over.

Tipping his head back, he gave up staring at the road and shifted his gaze to the slowly swaying tops of the trees surrounding the house. *Blackie, via Horse, asked me personally. I can't fuck this up.* The gig was supposed to be watching out for Sharon and the kids, with a side quest of making sure Vanna was safe with this most recent rescue in her home. The women in the house had more than one connection to the clubs, Sharon being sister of Captain, an RWMC officer, as well as Gunny's ole lady. Factor in Vanna being Gunny's adopted mother as well as Truck's ole lady.

Truck was a sergeant-at-arms for the RWMC, posted out of their Little Rock chapter, even if he now resided in the

Florida panhandle. He was married to Vanna, and both were well known to Bane. Cross-club meetings, rallies, and chance encounters had given Bane a good idea of what kind of man Truck was. *A fuckin' good one I'm damned lucky to call friend.*

Then there was Vanna's association with Blackie and the Freed Riders MC, and how before Truck stormed into her life, she had long worn a *Property of* patch for them without even being an ole lady. Protected by the club itself for her service, friendship, and loyalty. *Layers and layers.*

Breathing deeply, Bane lifted a hand to ruffle through his hair. He dragged his fingers through, trying to dampen the nerves plaguing him since he'd first seen the woman through the window. He'd known Vanna had a guest. That had been the topic of several discussions between Gunny and Sharon, conversations conducted over speakerphone, caring only that the kids were asleep. It had given Bane a good idea of what he'd be walking into. The two of them had drawn correlations between this woman and Sharon, and as he'd driven through the night, Sharon had talked in painful transparency of the challenges in her life prior to Gunny's entrance. The cover of darkness had given her courage, and she'd shared a lot of what had happened to bring her to Vanna's house so long ago.

Myrtle's story sounded much the same, from what evesdropping could tell. Vanna had rescued the poor thing and asked her to stay awhile, and the girl had agreed. Hell if he'd be the one to spook her into going before she was ready.

Seeing her up close hadn't given him any concerns about the authenticity of her need. She was painfully thin, the angles of the bones underneath her skin close to the surface and casting shadows across concavities more exaggerated than normal. Her collarbones jutted from the edges of her shirt's neckline, and her wrists were birdlike in their fragility.

The way she'd looked at him, though, had driven all ideas of her physical condition out of his mind. Her gaze had devoured him, head to toe, and the most alluring blush had risen from her chest to her cheeks, the blood singing underneath the covering of her skin, just enough to show off her interest. Even Sharon had seen, based on the encouraging look she'd given him as she exited the room. Then Myrtle—and what a unique name, old-fashioned in a way that seemed to fit her well—had choked suddenly. He hadn't known what to do other than patting against her back like burping a baby. The episode had eased, and she'd leaned against him, relaxing into his hold for the briefest of moments.

In an instant, though, she'd been feet away, hiding her face. He'd never seen someone try to melt into a wall before, but she'd pressed tight to it as if she could obtain invisibility through will alone. Alarm, not something as simple as fear but a more extreme terror, had been reflected in every line of her body. His attempts at understanding had been shut down. She'd asked him to go, and he'd done the only thing he could. He'd exited the room.

In body.

In his mind, he was still right there, listening to Myrtle's every breath, absorbing the rightness of her in his arms, her slight weight as she leaned against him, and the expression on her face as she'd looked at him.

A look that had said a lot.

Myrtle was a damsel in distress who wouldn't be against being saved by a knight.

White knight, right. He snorted at the thought. *I'm about as far from good guy as I can get.*

Which meant he wasn't the right one to try and save her.

Oh, but he'd like to.

***

Myrtle

Peering around the corner of the house, she looked out across the nearby field and sighed.

He was there. Standing next to the gate with Vanna, Josh on his back, arm wrapped around supporting the boy's bottom.

Bane.

Even in her thoughts his name sounded mysterious.

He glanced up, and she stopped in place when their gazes connected. He stared, studying her so intently Vanna started to turn. Bane saved Myrt the embarrassment of being caught peeping by talking louder, shifting so Vanna turned with him, putting her back to the house.

He was a good man, a kind man, all the things Sharon had promised he was.

Why then was Myrt so afraid of finding herself alone with him?

***

Bane

Letting Josh slide to the ground, Bane stepped behind the gate and stood as casually as possible with a raging boner.

All it took was a look from Myrt and he was a goner.

Later, he promised his dick, as he had every day of the week they'd been at Vanna's.

He suspected Vanna knew his frustration, since a bottle of lotion had mysteriously appeared on the nightstand in his room.

So later he'd jerk one out, imagining the sweet lips and soft words of the woman currently hiding around the corner of the house from him.

So fucked.

Bane laughed, caught Vanna's look of confusion, and shook his head.

Or not fucked, as it may be.

Chapter Five

Myrtle

Perched on the edge of the bathtub, Myrt scrubbed across her forehead with the palm of one hand. The other rested against her stomach, fisted and pressing deep, as if her actions could force the nausea away. In the week Sharon and her kids had been here—*and Bane*, her mind needlessly reminded her—*as if I could forget him*—the sickness had settled into a terribly regular routine, there all day but far worse in the early morning.

She concentrated as she counted the days and then counted them again. The words of the holler's witch echoed in her mind.

"Day one to day one hundred twelve of delayed courses, here are your tools." Old Tabitha gently placed stalks of dried plants on the table in front of Myrtle, spreading them in a fan with her at the center. *"Equal measures, just a scooch more than a pinch with hot water, steeped for*

twenty minutes. Three cups a day for three days, no more. Otherwise your water will sicken."

"My water?" Myrt glanced at the younger woman seated to the side of the table.

"The herbs can be hard on the kidneys." Young Tabitha went back to studying her nails, fingers curved over her palms as she ignored her grandmother's narrowed look.

"Oh." Myrt recognized the plants and herbs, naming them in her mind to help cement the memory. "And after a hundred and twelve days?" Not that she'd give anything a chance beyond the earliest indications, but it was always good to know the options. "Are there things to help bring on my period if it's greatly delayed?"

"Nothin' that won't leave you sickened near to dyin'." Old Tabitha sat back in her chair, creating space between her and Myrtle. "And nothin' certain to any of this. You may not start your womanly cycles again for a space of months. Sometimes it's better to let nature take its course."

Those plants had been readily available in Kentucky. Sometimes reaped from the woods, the folds of land on the sides of the mountain offering up secret hoards. At times taken from cultivated flower gardens in town, Myrt creeping around the edges of yards in the dark, hands gathering up her dress as a sling to hold the treasures securely.

She had no idea what she might find in Florida.

A loud thumping echoed through the house, and Myrt stiffened, a sense of unease washing over her. Someone banged at the front door, demanding a response, the cadence setting up an echoing racket in her chest as her heart thundered fast.

The pounding continued, even with Vanna's called greeting of "Just a minute" to tide over whoever it was. If anything, the knocking increased in speed and force, the fist attacking the surface of the door.

"Can I help—*oh!*"

Vanna's pained cry had Myrt out the door and at the top of the stairs in a flash, in time to see Ian Sallabrook rock to a stop in the middle of the dining room. He'd left Vanna cast to the side, one hand cradling her other wrist.

"Where is she?" His bellowed demand woke the children sleeping up the hallway from where Myrt stood, and as the first tiny cry lifted to the heavens, his gaze turned upwards and landed on her. "Girl, get down here, now."

Her feet had grown roots, tangling with the carpet on the floor, holding her in place. Everything else faded away except him and his reddened face, cheeks mottled purple with rage. His top lip lifted in a sneer, exposing his long, yellowed teeth. His lips moved, and she read the words, not able to hear anything over the fast beat of her heart echoing in her head. "I said get down here now. You're gonna regret this, girl."

He jerked backwards, whirling around, and time sped up again, sounds rushing to her ears in a wave.

Bane had a hand wrapped tightly around Sallabrook's arm and was dragging him towards the door. Sallabrook futilely tried to fight him, but the younger, stronger man never flinched at the weak blows aimed his direction. Then they were outside, the screen door tapping gently into place.

"Vanna, are you okay?" Sharon called, as she firmly moved Myrt to the side and descended the stairs, Josh in her arms and Kitten trailing behind. A hand slipped into Myrt's, and she looked down to see Cade at her side, staring up at her. The little girl rubbed Myrt's knuckles against her own cheek, then tugged her hand, leading her down the stairs one tread at a time.

Vanna was seated in the kitchen by the time they made it downstairs, a bag of frozen vegetables wrapped in a towel and placed on her wrist. She had Josh in her lap, Kitten standing at her side. Myrt saw the top of Sharon's head dart past the window outside and understood she'd gone out the back door and was headed around to the front where Sallabrook continued to shout.

"I'm so sorry." Myrt let Cade's unwavering grip lead her to a chair near Vanna and maneuver her around to sit.

Vanna looked up, her gaze filled with compassion as she cradled Josh to her body, his cheek nestled against her bosom. "Oh, honey. His problem isn't yours. Not as long as

I'm around." She shook her wrist free of the makeshift ice bag and flexed her fingers, pulling them into a tight fist with a fierce smile stretching her lips. "You're my family and this is your house. He's got no call to come barging in like that."

The front screen door opened and closed, and the inside door latched into place with a force that was just this side of a slam. Myrt twisted in sudden fear that somehow Sallabrook had overwhelmed Bane and Sharon and was now in the house to complete whatever mission he'd imagined for himself. Instead, she saw Sharon's head thrown back in laughter and Bane grinning widely, a pleased expression on his face. His gaze settled on Myrt and he sobered, coming straight to her while Sharon made her way to Vanna.

"You okay?" His hand replaced Cade's, the little girl giving Myrt's arm a soft pat as she moved away. Bane crouched in front of her, chin lifted slightly as he looked up into her face. "He didn't scare you, did he?"

"Why is he here?" She hadn't known the tears were close until she tried to talk, her throat closing unexpectedly around the words so she had to force them out hoarsely. "Why would he come here? How did he find me?"

"He wouldn't say. It's a long way from Kentucky to here, though, so him showing up on Vanna's doorstep was not random." Bane leaned closer, the nearest he'd been to Myrt since the first day he'd been in the house.

She'd successfully avoided him since then, rising early to fix breakfast, then heading into the garden before the day's heat gained teeth. After her self-assigned chores were complete, she'd found other ways to stay clear of the man, taking Cade on nature walks in the surrounding woods, spreading a blanket under the trees to hang out with Kitten or Josh, watching all three kids and the dogs play in the nearby creek—there were a thousand opportunities to avoid someone living under the same roof if a body was determined. Now, the scent she'd decided was simply Bane curled around her, bringing her heart rate down a notch. His thumb swept side to side on the back of her hand, across and back, across and back. An innocent touch, but one that threatened to unsettle her, the rough glide a promise of how it would feel if he touched her elsewhere.

Stop your dreamin' about wants and wishes, woman. She needed to focus, because the next few minutes would set the course for the rest of her life. Sallabrook had found her, which meant she couldn't stay here. Not if he might be back. *What if one of the children had answered the door instead of Vanna, or if it had been tiny Sharon? What if he'd hurt Vanna more than a sprained wrist?* Myrt would never forgive herself if that man harmed the slightest hair on the heads of any of these people she'd come to love like family. *More than family.* She didn't try to shy away from the knowledge that Vanna and Sharon, and even Bane, treated her better than her own father had. *I can't let anything happen to them.*

"Vanna." Suddenly aware this might be her last chance to touch him, Myrt clutched at Bane's hand as she turned to the woman who meant so much to her, a mother figure she hadn't known she needed, a friend and confidante. "I'm gonna have to go." Hotness trickled down her cheek, splashing to the back of her hand, swept away by Bane's persistent touch. "I never meant to bring you harm."

Her stomach rolled and then rebelled. Frantic yanking freed her hand, and she covered her mouth, barely making it to the garbage can in time. She retched again and again, coming up for air finally to find the kitchen empty of everyone except her—and Bane. He stood close by, wet washrag in hand, a glass of water on the counter nearby.

"She's not going to let you leave." He gripped Myrt's elbow gently and steered her back towards the chair, helping her sit. His bottom lip bowed up in a sorrowful expression. "Vanna Mom's hurt you'd even suggest such." The first touch of the washrag against her chin was gentle, tentative, but he gained confidence the longer she didn't fight him. He folded the fabric, then used the clean side to wipe up her temples and across her forehead, drawing it down along her hairline and the back of her neck. "I told her it was shock talking, and she agreed. She and Sharon are upstairs getting the kiddos back into nap mode. And maybe trying to give you a little privacy." Half turned away, he ran water over the washrag, then wrung it out and turned off the tap. Bane captured her hand and carefully cleaned her forearm, then between her fingers before moving to her other arm. "I promised her I'd watch over you."

"Why did he come lookin' for me?" She knew the venomous look on Sallabrook's face hadn't been her imagination. He hated her more today than he ever had, probably because she'd inconvenienced him.

"Man claimed a lot of things." Bane repeated the process with the washrag, this time leaving the wrung-out fabric draped over the faucet. He claimed a chair at the table, angling it so he faced Myrt. "Most of which I know for a fact wasn't true."

"Like what?" Myrt hated the way her voice wavered like an old lady's, touching on different octaves for each sound.

"Said you were his wife."

She lifted a hand and scrubbed across her forehead, pinching the bridge of her nose between two fingers. The refreshing feel that had come with Bane's tender ministrations fled, and her stomach clenched in a dire threat. "I am."

"He have a judge or a clergyman officiate?" Bane's tone was hard, but when she chanced a glance at him, the expression on his face was soft, tender.

"Well, no. But I'd been with him for a long time when I finally got the nerve to leave."

"Did you live with him in a state other than Kentucky for any time?" She shook her head side to side. "Myrt, if there weren't any papers, then you're not his wife. He's not anything to you. Kentucky doesn't recognize common-law marriages. Hasn't for more than a hundred years." Bane ducked his chin, bringing his face closer to hers. Enunciating deliberately, he told her, "He is nothing to you."

"He told me a bunch of times." She forced herself to hold his gaze. "He's got rights."

Bane's head was swinging back and forth before she finished. "I looked it up. Looked all of it up. He doesn't have any rights." His gaze hardened. "Not with anything to do with you. You're your own person, Myrt, and he can't come in here demanding anything."

"What did you tell him outside?"

"Told him to get back in his goddamned truck and haul his ass back to whatever hole in the hill he'd crawled out of. Informed him that he'd injured someone near and dear to a man he likely had heard of, gave him that name, and then watched as he turned as green as you were a few minutes ago." Bane's steady gaze gave her an anchor, and she locked hers with his. That bottom lip bowed up again, and she had an instant to notice the cleft that appeared in his chin. "I told him he was barkin' after the wrong woman, because from what I could see, you had a future waitin' for you out here that didn't involve him."

And just that fast, any swell of emotion fled, leaving her hollowed out and frightened. She'd been struggling to figure out a way to pay Vanna back but kept running up against the fistful of deficits she held in her hands. A wealth of cannots not even balanced by a single can. *Focus on the present issue.* "And he left? Without arguing? That doesn't seem like him."

"No, it took a couple more words to get him to vacate, but once I had his attention the right way, well, he trotted his happy ass off fast enough. Sure seems like a man who's used to gettin' whatever he wants, regardless of the cost to anyone else."

"Fair enough description of him."

"What is he to you?"

"Daddy gave me to him years ago." Bane's cheeks lost all color, going from ruddy and high with emotion to pale and shocked in a single breath. She hadn't been so careless with her words even with Vanna. *Gotta keep my head.* "I was his helpmeet."

Angling his chin away, Bane stared over her shoulder. His mouth opened and closed, then he roughly cleared his throat. He blinked twice, each taking a long time for his lashes to sweep down and up, then looked at her again, eyes burning hot. "Your daddy *gave* you to him?"

"Don't tell Vanna." Her whisper scarcely stirred the air. "Please."

"I need to understand." He ignored her request and scooted his chair closer. "Help me understand, Myrtle."

"My momma died. She married Daddy after his other wives had passed on. Her daddy, he told her it was the best offer she'd get. She'd been up in Lexington, goin' to school. She was smart and…and knew stuff. All kinds of stuff. I was her first, then she had seven more. Enough kids to put her dreams of going back to school to sleep. When she got sick, towards the end of things she made me promise I wouldn't stay. The older kids were all flyin' the coop, marryin' or takin' jobs in other towns. I had one older sister left at home, Marian. Momma said my daddy'd never part with her." Myrt realized her words were tripping over themselves to get out of her mouth, coming so fast they slurred into each other. She focused on the sweep of Bane's thumb, the glide as steady and dependable as time itself. "Mr. Sallabrook's wife had died. Daddy sold me to him for the price of a tractor. He wanted someone—a woman someone—to cook and clean, do chores. That kind of stuff."

"And other stuff, too, right? He wouldn't be so angry if he'd only lost his slave labor." Bane's fingers tightened around hers, not painfully, but as if telling her she was safe talking to him. "It was more than just that."

"He's the preacher. It wasn't proper for us to live together. But yeah…other stuff, too."

"Preacher my ass," Bane muttered under his breath, then sighed heavily as she ducked her chin. "Sorry, Myrt. I'll put a leash on my mouth for ya."

"It's okay, Bane. I'm not offended." Her shying away hadn't been criticism but embarrassment. She met his gaze, holding it for a moment before angling her eyes down, breaking the shaky connection between them. *I can't look at him and tell him even the smallest of things.* "It wasn't bad at first. He was patient with me learnin' everything he liked. Dealing with all the things his wife had let go, seein' as she was sick for so long. Took me probably two years to figure out how to get the house and barn like he wanted them. Once it was right, it was easier to keep it like that."

"Two years? How many years were you with him?"

She angled her head to the side, not wanting to see pity in Bane's expression when she admitted how long she'd been captive to Sallabrook. "A few."

He gripped her chin between a finger and thumb, bringing her head around to face him. "Don't hide from me, Myrt. You don't have anything to be ashamed of."

"That's what Mr. Truck told me, too. He said what people do to us is their responsibility, not ours. Not mine." She shrugged and tugged her chin free of his hold. "Easy to say, harder to do."

Bane snorted, and she chanced a glance at him in time to see amusement on his face. It was so at odds with their conversation that she couldn't look away. He grinned, then muttered, "Mister Truck, like it's a title. Gonna razz him about that, for sure." The smile fell away, and he stared at her. "Regardless, he's right. Like I said, you got nothin' to be ashamed of, Myrt."

"It only got bad the last couple of years." Tired of trying to hold his gaze, she dropped her chin, wrapping one arm around her waist. Her other hand was still held and controlled by Bane, and she didn't want to examine her reasoning for leaving it where it was. "Seemed like once he got mad at me, he couldn't find his way back from the brink." She blinked back tears. "He's right to be mad, though. I stole a bunch of money from him."

His fingers made that reassuring squeeze again, and Myrt's heart skipped a beat. "How much money?"

"Nearly two hundred dollars." She angled away from Bane, her arm sticking out to the side and behind her. She was as far away from him as her arm would reach but still couldn't bring herself to break their connection. "He could probably put me in jail."

"Myrt, that's not even enough for small claims court. Plus, any lawyer worth his salt would argue it was the smallest of payments for years of work. If he comes back, I'll give him the money out of my wallet. I'll give it and never miss it; that's how small an amount it is." He put pressure on her hand, trying to get her to turn and face him, but she stubbornly refused. "Myrtle, look at me, darlin'."

It was the affectionate name that did it for her. Myrt slowly swiveled to face him, rocking her head to the side so she could see him out of one eye.

"Man like him, wanting to own a woman, he's no man at all. I'm gonna take care of you, Myrtle, and make damn sure he'll never hurt you again."

She could tell from Bane's expression he utterly believed what he'd said.

If only she could be so certain.

Chapter Six

Bane

He stood at the edge of the ditch, staring down at the remains of Vanna's mailbox.

"Well?"

The demanding bark in his ear was from Truck, a man frustrated he was a couple hundred miles away and unable to return home while this was going on.

"Looks like a baseball bat." He scanned for snakes and other varmints, then stepped down into the ditch to retrieve the warped metal. "The wood post is snapped clean off. I'll pick up another box and post today."

"Don't bother. I'm getting her a goddamned PO Box. I'll be making that call the minute we hang up. Won't even give her a say in this one. Roadside mailbox is vulnerable to more than just drive-by smashings." The sigh Truck heaved out said a lot more than the man was willing to share. Either the RWMC as a whole had other issues, or he was expecting things to be on high alert at home for some reason more than a disgruntled backwoods hillbilly using a baseball bat as a dick enhancer. "Just clean up the mess for my ole lady, brother. That's good enough. Appreciate everything you're doing."

"You got it." The call disconnected, and Bane shoved the phone into his pocket, bending to scoop up the rest of the broken post. As he shifted the flattened mailbox in his hands, something rattled inside it, and he tossed it up into the yard, climbing out of the ditch slowly while keeping a wary gaze on the metal. Nothing crawled out of it, so he gave it a nudge with his boot. "Probably nothing. If it were a snake or other nasty hitchhiker, it wouldn't have rattled."

"You're right. It would have slithered."

Bane spun on his heel to see Myrt had somehow managed to walk up behind him, the early morning sun rays framing her as they streamed through the pine trees. The angle of the illumination made her nightgown and robe translucent, giving him a view of all the slightly rounded curves she kept hidden with her on-the-baggier-side clothing selections. He stifled a groan and did his best to ignore his rapidly chubbing dick. *Another vision for the spank bank.* Seemed like every time he got close to Myrt, he found something else to like about her.

"I was just convincing myself of that." He gestured to the mailbox. "Wanna be my spotter as I open it up and see what's inside? Keep me from tanglin' with a rogue rock or whatever's there?"

"What happened to it?" She peered around him at the edge of the drive where the mailbox had stood. A broken post was the only evidence left behind. "Something broke it? What broke it off like that?"

"A someone, not a something. I was on the phone with Truck just now letting him know." He shrugged and then crouched, extending his arm far to grab the bent-over handle on the twisted mailbox door. It took several tugs, but using one boot to hold the box itself still, he eventually got the door to open with a muted shriek.

"What's in it? Who would do something like this?" Bane glanced up to find Myrt crowded in behind him, her legs braced close to his hip and thigh as she leaned in to see what he was doing. The sun behind her still kept many things in shadow, but the upper swell of her breasts was on full display, the top of her robe gaping open.

"I don't know." He smiled when she transferred her gaze from the mailbox to him, the apples of her cheeks rising in a returned grin. "Let's find out, shall we?" At her eager nod, he turned back and upended the mailbox, giving it a shake. A piece of metal fell out, and as he reached out to scoop it up, Myrt gasped, sounding shocked.

Still crouched, Bane swiveled to face Myrt, not surprised to see she'd gone pale. Whatever this was, it meant something to her, which put the asshole from yesterday in prime position to be the motherfucker who'd destroyed the mailbox.

Bouncing the twisted metal in one hand, he looked between it and her, then back again, still coming up blank with what it could be. Finally he decided to give way to his curiosity, offering the scrap up balanced on one palm. Surprisingly, Myrt didn't reach for it. Arms folded across her body, she gave every impression of being terrified.

"What is this?" He plucked it from his palm and held it up, rotating it to see every side. From this close, he could see lines and angles in the metal, which hinted at what it might have been before being mangled. On one side, it looked as if it had melted, the faint details running together to make the puddled base. He looked at her again, studying her features for any clue of what was driving her reactions. "Have you seen this before?"

"One of my little brothers likes soldiers." Her trembling words didn't make sense.

He'd opened his mouth to ask what she meant when he saw it. Like a picture that tricked senses into seeing something that wasn't there before revealing the true image, things fell into place for him, and he noticed the little things that made her words terrifyingly prescient.

"It's a metal soldier." He wasn't asking a question, but she nodded all the same. "Sturdy enough. I think it's lead." He pressed his thumbnail against the metal, not leaving a dent. "Maybe aluminum. My uncle had a set. I remember playing with them when I was little." He folded it into his fist, hiding it from view. "You think this belonged to your brother?"

"It has to. Why else would he put it here and make certain we'd find it?"

Bane stood, staring down at her bowed head, shoulders drawn forward in an effort to fold herself into nothing. He took a chance and stepped nearer, and when she didn't retreat, came another stride closer, within arm's reach, and he took another chance, reaching out to bring her tight against his chest. With flexed arms around her shoulders and back, he held her firmly, ignoring her rigid frame, rewarded when finally—*fucking finally*—she relaxed. Her muscles loosened in a quick sequence, setting off an emotional avalanche he gave her time to navigate. Hand on the back of her head, he cradled her as she wept, words bubbling out of her mixed in with sobs, but repeated often enough he didn't have to fight long to understand them.

"He's not quite right in the head. Luke. He's the third youngest, seven years younger than me." Her voice wavered, and Bane could feel the fight in her to keep talking. "God touched him only lightly, and he's a good boy. Likes making people happy. That's what makes him happiest, makin' others smile. If Sallabrook went to Daddy and complained about me takin' off, I just don't know. I swear I didn't think about him doin' that when I left. I didn't think he might do such. If I had, I would still have expected Sallabrook'd believe he'd gotten his money's worth outta me. If he did, though? If he went to Daddy and said I'd shorted him, I know my daddy'd be compelled to make it right." A tremor raced through her, and Bane found himself swaying slightly, offering what comfort he could. "What if makin' it right was replacin' me with someone else?"

She pulled back, palms flat against his chest as she created space between them. Looking up, her pale face streaked with tears, she was still the most beautiful woman Bane had ever seen. Thin, but with round, ripe breasts, and enough curve to her ass to make a handful. Full, plush lips that were gorgeous temptation and begged to be kissed, doe eyes that—when the lids dipped halfway—promised anything a man could want.

"You don't know he went to your father or asked for shit." It was faint reassurance, and he lost his view of her face when her forehead plunked heavily against his chest. "Does your father have a phone? Can we call and ask?" Her head rocked back and forth. "Sallabrook?" Another silent headshake. "You said he was a preacher. Would the church have a phone?"

"Weren't a church like that. Not like the one down in town." Her accent had grown thicker with the tears. "That one had a building, were a proper church. Sallabrook's flock met in the front yards and barns of the members. At the cemetery if they had a burial to tend to. There's nobody to call." She rocked her head sideways, resting her cheek against his chest. "What'll I ask, anyway? 'Hey, y'all know if my daddy sold my brother to that mean old man, too?' That won't go well for me. The holler takes care of their own, and I come at them asking questions, I'd be treated as if I'm from off."

"They'd close ranks against you, not caring if you had family in trouble." She nodded, validating his statement. He tightened his arms around her and gave a squeeze. "What if we went there in person? We could head to Sallabrook's place, see if your brother's there, scoop him up if he is, and bring him back here." He didn't have to wonder for even an instant if the boy would be welcome. Knowing Truck as he did, it wasn't a question if the man would open his home to the boy, especially if he were in trouble. "What about your other younger siblings? Would they be in danger, too?"

"Just Luke and my other brother, Thaddeus. When my sister married, she took the other littles with her. Her husband was older, said he didn't mind a noisy household."

"How old is Thaddeus?"

"Luke's seven under me, and Thaddie's three under that."

Bane did some quick math. Figure Myrt for twenty-five, maybe, just four years younger than him, and the years don't matter as much anyway, not when it came to measuring against experience. "So Luke's eighteen, and Thad's fifteen?" From this angle, he could see her cheek move with her smile. "What'd I get wrong?"

"I'm not as old as that." He held his breath, waiting, because in form, she appeared to be a woman, albeit young, and every other impression he'd gotten from her had been filled with maturity. "I'm twenty-one, Bane. I've belonged to Sallabrook since I was fourteen. Luke's the age I was when Daddy sent me there. That's one of the reasons I think Daddy could and would give him away."

"Okay, so we go get Luke and Thad and bring them here. You think the other little ones are okay at your sister's, then that's well and good, but we don't leave your father anyone to use as financial leverage." He thought back over their conversations and landed on something she'd said. "Your sister Marian, you said she's with your father?"

"Daddy'd never give up Marian. She's the glue what holds his household together. He's said it countless times."

"But what does Marian want? How much older is she?"

"I don't know for sure. She was from Daddy's second wife. Maybe ten years older? I don't know."

"That's okay. We'll get the boys, and then we can find and talk to her about what she wants." Jaw clenched, he tried to reassure her about a situation he didn't have any real knowledge of. "It'll take us a couple of days, max."

"Bane." Myrt leaned back again, fingers clutching his shirt, this time holding tight instead of pushing away. "You can't try to save my whole family."

"You say try like it's not a given I'll succeed." He offered her a smile, happy to see the frown creasing her brow relax, smoothing out. "Maybe Marian won't take the offer.

Doesn't mean I won't make damn sure she understands it's there and waiting if she wants it. Also doesn't come with a time limit. If she decided five years down the road she wanted something different, better, I'd be there to make sure she had opportunity."

"Vanna said you were a good man."

"Vanna exaggerates sometimes." He let the corner of his mouth curl a little to show he wasn't being serious. "You shouldn't listen to her about me." He dipped his head, bringing his face closer to Myrt's. Close enough he could feel the heat of her blush, the delicate ghosting touch of her breath across his lips. Bane adjusted, angling his hips away so she wasn't confronted by his self-serving interest in making her smile. "Listen to me about me. I won't ever lie to you."

"Promise?" It felt as if she were asking a thousand questions with the one word. Like she'd stretched an arm into the future and was plucking at the strings that were tangling, tying them together.

He gave it back to her, completely invested in his response, something he would stand by for the rest of his life.

"Promise."

Chapter Seven

Myrtle

She rounded the corner into Vanna's bedroom, drawn there by Vanna's hand holding hers, led up and away from the kitchen filled with a conversation still going on between Bane and Sharon. As their voices dimmed with distance, she rolled her shoulders, suddenly aware of how tense she'd become.

Vanna stopped next to a mirrored dresser and pulled out the tiny stool hidden in the kneehole. "Sit," she commanded. The steel in her voice shouldn't have been a surprise, given everything Myrt knew about Vanna, but it startled her into movement, her bottom meeting the fabric cover of the stool with a thump. Vanna disappeared for an instant. Through the open door, the splashing of running water preceded Vanna coming out of the bathroom with a dampened rag in hand.

Myrt startled again when Vanna reached past her to pick up a brush. "Hush, child. We need to think while we talk, and I've always thought best when I had something to do." She arranged Myrt's locks so they draped over her shoulders, stroking the length with the flat side of the brush. "I have fond memories of sitting at this very vanity while my mother talked me through some hard decisions. Different house, but the vibe is still the same." Vanna chuckled and started drawing the bristles of the brush through Myrt's hair. "To my teenaged self, the most devastating thing was being asked to the prom by the wrong boy." She rested her wrists on Myrt's shoulders, leaning down to whisper near her ear, "Your decisions are a long sight more critical, methinks."

Myrt's head drooped on her neck, chin angled down so she could see her hands twisting in her lap. "I don't know what to do." She swallowed, hating how her throat made sounds, the scarcely stifled sobs betraying her emotions. "I know what I want to do, but I don't know how it can happen."

"Tell me what you want to happen." The steady drag of the brush through her hair was soothing, a dependable pull that was easily resisted, Myrt able to hold her head steady and still. "Don't think, not yet. Just tell me."

"I want to go to the holler and make sure my brothers are safe."

Each stroke evenly spaced, the movement of the brush in Vanna's hand was hypnotizing.

Myrt found herself opening up to Vanna about all the things that had happened, good and bad. About her fears for her brother, and even her siblings hosted at her sister's husband's place. She talked until her throat croaked, and her voice broke, sipping from a bottle of water that appeared as if by magic, easing the way for her to talk even more.

At uneven intervals, Vanna drew the damp rag across the bristles, settling static electricity threatening to have Myrt's hair standing on end.

Through it all, Vanna's movements never stopped. Myrt's hair hung in shining sheets, but the brush continued to make its patient way from root to tip, again and again. Vanna reacted in other ways, soft humming when Myrt confessed her puzzlement at Sallabrook's treatment, and quiet murmurs of encouragement during more difficult stretches of the story. When Myrt was all talked out, unable to think of another detail worth mentioning, Vanna finally spoke.

"Oh my sweet, sweet girl. The trials you've been through. Look at how strong you are, though, rising above every time." The passage of the brush paused as Vanna leaned her wrists on Myrt's shoulders again, bending close to press her lips to the crown of Myrt's head.

The soft kiss broke the dam on the final secret. "I think I'm pregnant."

Vanna hummed as she returned the brush to the surface of the vanity, using both hands to arrange Myrt's hair down her back. Vanna separated out chunks and started braiding, the movement nearly as soothing as the brushing had been. "I'm not past time to take care of it. I just need the herbs to start my flow again."

"Is that what you want, sweet girl?" Vanna's gaze met hers in the mirror, just long enough for Myrt to understand this woman wouldn't think worse of her either way. "Support your choice, however it happens."

"I never wanted to bring a child into that life." Vanna tsked when Myrt tried to shake her head, using a sharp tug to get her to still again. "Sorry."

"No sorries, honey. No worries in the world." Vanna worked steadily, the brush of knuckles against Myrt's back evidence of the over-and-under movement. "You're not in *that* life now, though, are you?"

The meaning behind Vanna's question barreled over and through Myrt in an instant. Understanding flooded her eyes with tears, causing her throat to close tightly as her heart lurched in her chest. In the mirror, she experienced a look of stark terror and longing on her own face, one emotion coinciding with how she felt, the other something she'd never allowed herself to have before. She slammed her eyes closed, unable to take in the hope beginning to bloom on her face.

"Honey." Vanna cupped her shoulders, drawing her back against the strong body behind her. "Oh, honey. It's okay. You don't have to make a decision today. Nothing has to change right now." Boots rattled a quick pace up the stairs, and a moment later, the rumble of Bane's voice came from the doorway.

"Everything okay up here?" Then from closer. "What'd you say to her, Vanna? She's crying."

Bane's hands replaced Vanna's, but instead of holding her steady, he turned her on the stool until she faced him. A blink showed his earnestly concerned features staring up at her, crowded as close as he could get, his knees spread on either side of her legs. She forced her eyes closed again, unable to take the unguarded expression on his face.

"She's coming to some hard realizations, Bane." Vanna's voice was retreating, coming from farther away with each word. "Be kind to her. You're a good man, Will Crow, and don't ever forget it."

Her hand was clasped in a firm grip as a spot of heat alongside her outer thigh revealed the positioning of his other hand. "Myrtle, look at me." She shook her head, surprised for an instant at the weight of the long braid swinging back and forth. "If you don't tell me what's wrong, I can't help you fix it."

From the safety of the dark behind her eyelids, she told him the one thing she'd held back earlier.

"I'm carrying a baby."

She expected him to drop her hand, to move away, to create a distance between them. What she didn't anticipate was him doing the exact opposite. When his lower body pressed against her legs, and his arms wrapped around her shoulders, drawing her close, she gave up a tiny prayer to a God she didn't know if she still believed in, because Bane wasn't running. His reaction was to draw her tight to him, press her cheek to his hard chest, and use his soothing voice to create a sense of intimacy.

"Aww, darlin'. Shush now. It's gonna be okay. Gonna be okay, Myrt. Gonna be all right." The sobs she'd tried to hold back in front of Vanna burst free, tearing their way up her throat as they escaped into the air. Bane took the harsh sounds in stride, lifting Myrt off the stool and carrying her to the bed. He sat on the edge, arranging her on his lap as he cradled her on his thighs, hands stroking and petting her, the unending litany of soothing words falling like a drought-busting rain on her ears. "I got you, darlin'. You get it all out, sweetheart. I got you. We've got all day. You take what you need."

Myrt didn't know how long it was until she could bring herself back under control. Couldn't put a timer on how long she'd sobbed into the sodden patch her tears had created on his shirt or how long he'd patiently stroked her back and sides, playing with the end of her braid as he hummed a song she didn't recognize. The tone originating from his chest was low and rasping, vibrating through her as if a reminder of his presence.

Lifting her hands to her face, she covered her hot lids with flattened palms, pressing lightly as if to verify no tears remained to be squeezed out. She dropped one hand to rest in her lap, where Bane immediately captured it. Scrubbing across her forehead, she ran her fingers through her bangs and across the top of her head, wrapping her hand around the braid and bringing it over her shoulder. Playing with the curling end, she pulled in a final shuddering breath and released it with a whimper, leaning against Bane.

"There you go." Distracted by the way his fingers were playing with hers, stroking and wedging between by turns, she didn't jolt when his other hand touched her face, wrapping around her jaw in a strong grip. He lifted, and she went with the motion, her neck stretching and bending. "Look at me, sweetheart."

Myrt's eyelids fluttered. Every blink brought her another facet of his visage. Strong jaw. High cheekbones. Concerned eyes. Wrinkled brow. Full lips bowed down in a grimace. She blinked a final time and then let her lids rest at half-mast. Anything else was too much effort.

He was close. Near enough she could hear how his breathing deepened, see his pupils dilate. So close if she'd stretched up another inch, his mouth would have been pressed against hers. Bane's fingers tightened slightly, and she thought for one insane second he'd heard her thoughts and was acting on them, but his eyes flared underneath his furrowed brow, and he stilled.

"I will always keep you safe. I told you earlier, and you said you believed me. Do you still?" She nodded as best she could, trapped by his fingers as she was. "Gonna need more than that, sweetheart." Every time he called her the softly affectionate name, a little more of her walls crumbled. *Not that I have much left to stand against him.* If Bane indicated he wanted anything from her, she would turn and bend over, presenting for him to cover her. She'd give whatever he wanted to take if he'd only keep looking at her as he was. "Come on, sweetheart." She imagined he could feel how her heart sped at the words, his palm cradling the column of her neck. "I need to know you believe me. I'll keep you safe and do my damnedest to get your brother to safety. Both brothers. Hell, Marian, too, like I said earlier. Do you believe?"

"I believe." She realized she truly did. Rough around the edges he might be, but she knew he'd never lie to her. Would never intentionally hurt her. Would bend backwards to keep his word. "I do, Bane. I believe you." Her muscles lost their rigidity, and she sagged against him, feeling comforted and safe in a way she couldn't remember reaching before. *Maybe back before Mom got sick and passed.* Back before becoming an adult meant understanding how she was expected to put her family's needs above her own. When she found the cost of her innocence equaled the price for a used tractor. She shoved her face into the crook of Bane's neck and breathed deeply. Sweat, and a musky fragrance she'd come to associate with him. Another breath of the scent pulled deep into her lungs triggered an extra wave of relaxation, and she clutched at his shirt underneath his leather vest. "I believe," she repeated softly, the bristly touch of his short beard against her cheek an anchor.

"Sharon and I have a plan." He scooted backwards on Vanna's bed until he had wedged them against the headboard. Two thumps told her he'd toed his boots off, letting them fall to the floor. "We can leave first thing in the morning. The club has friends up in the area, and if needed, we can lean on them for anything, up to and including dealin' with that asshole Sallabrook after you and me are well out of Kentucky on our way back here. Sharon's offered us the van, and it'll work great as we're carrying the boys here. Lots of room for anything they want to bring with."

"Bring them here?" Her head swam with the rush of words he'd thrown her way. "I hadn't thought about where we'd live." A band tightened around her chest, fear causing her stomach to roll and sour. "I don't even have a *place* to live."

"Hey, now, that ain't true. Vanna and Truck have basically adopted you. Remember Mister Truck? He and Vanna Mom are amazing folks, and they'd never do or say anything they didn't want to do. Them telling you this is your house means you can bring family here if needed." Curled in his lap as she was, when he spread his legs, hers fell between them. That, and the way his arms continued to cradle her against his chest, made her feel surrounded by his calming presence. "So of course the boys will come here. Lots of room to spread out as they get acclimated to the world beyond where you grew up."

"They'll need everything." *Just like I did. Like I do.* "How can I bring them here when things feel so unsettled? Is that doin' right by them?"

"The only thing unsettled is your mind, Myrt." She crinkled her nose, much preferring the sweetheart he'd been calling her. "And I don't know how to help with that. I promise you if something happens and Truck or Vanna say you've got to find somewhere else to live, I'll be right here beside you. We'll figure it out together."

Maybe it was the aftermath of the emotional whirlwind she'd been through, but Myrt felt brave enough to question him. "But why, Bane? Why would you drop everything to help me?"

His shoulders lifted, and he made a huffing sound that echoed around her ear. His arm gave her a squeeze, which had her turning her face into the crook of his neck again, and he answered her with a question. "Why not?"

Chapter Eight

Bane

Last articles of clothing in his hands, he bumped the dresser drawer closed with one hip. He was unsurprised to turn and find Vanna standing in the doorway, offering her a brusque nod as he carried the shirts to the bag unzipped and spread wide on the bed.

Clothing arranged and bag secured, he faced her once again. Vanna met his gaze with a steady stare that somehow managed to be neither judgmental nor confrontational.

Might as well get this party started. "Ma'am." She huffed and rolled her eyes, and he gave her a tiny thing, a melding of respect and appreciation for everything she'd done. Not only for Myrt, but for Blackie, and even Sharon and Gunny back in the day. "Vanna Mom."

"Bane's a good handle for you." She folded her arms across her chest, feet wide as she took a strong stance. "No idea how it was earned, and this isn't me asking you a thing about the name. But I can imagine a dozen seasoned men muttering 'of my life' every time I hear it. Suits you well."

"You're not far off from the meaning." He grinned, letting a little honest amusement seep through. "Only the bane was everyone else. I was the perfect one. Blackie's Riders were the bastages always fuckin' things up. My own words stuck, if you can imagine such a thing."

Her laughter pealed through the house, spreading the comfort of home as it went, and Bane imagined Truck's smile to hear it. Too soon, her smile faded.

"I'd feel better if you waited for some backup to be confirmed." Vanna took a step towards him, arms uncrossing so she could hold out a hand in caution. "She's not feeling very well all the time."

"She's pregnant." Might as well get it all out in the open. From the way Vanna had danced around the topic, he knew he wasn't telling tales on Myrtle out of turn, but he needed Vanna to know the depth of his knowledge. "The stress of not knowing would be worse than any confrontation we might have with the old man."

"She may not keep it." The bland statement made his chest tighten. "Her body, her choice, and no judgment from me. I think she wants it, the baby, but she can't find her way to grant herself permission." Vanna offered him a wan smile that quickly fell away. "Yet."

"Maybe we get her into a good place with her brothers and she can see her way clear to do what's right for her. Just this once, she'll have whatever she needs. She's had a shit-filled life so far. I wanna make that right." Bane lifted a hand and covered his chest, the rapid vibrations of his heart pounding through his fingertips. "I'll make sure she gets everything, Vanna Mom. That's a promise."

"You're giving her a wide-load promise. You gonna be able to keep up your end of this when the roads narrow and get steep?"

"Yes, ma'am." He'd had to bite back his initial reaction, which was to tell Vanna to mind her own and leave him and Myrt alone. For the respect his club held for her alone, he resisted, and tried instead to explain himself a little, even though it grated on him to be called to task like this. "She's got somethin' special about her. I'm not pledging love or anything like that, but she has my hands, heart, and body. Whatever she needs, I'll get it for her." Bane lifted the bag, shrugging the strap into place over his shoulder as he gave her just a little more respect. "For whatever it's worth, you've got the same somethin' special about you, too."

Vanna unsettled him by striding directly to him and placing her hands on his shoulders as she rose on her toes. Heat from the faintest brush of her lips touched his cheek. "You're a good man, Will Crow." Her fingers tightened as she pulled back, staring into his face and giving his shoulders a shake. "And if you hurt my girl, there is nowhere on God's green earth you can hide."

He stood there struck dumb as she sashayed out the door. A moment later, her voice came up the stairs, asking Sharon what the kids would like for lunch. *I bet Truck's got his hands full with her.* He settled the strap over his shoulder again and stepped into the hallway, then over a door, where he rapped gently with a knuckle. "Myrt, honey, you ready to go?" He pushed the door ajar a few inches, until she was framed in the opening with her brilliant smile curling her lips.

He couldn't help calling her sweet, affectionate names, and from the expression on her face every time he did, Myrtle didn't mind it much, which gave him zero incentive to stop. This smile was one of hundreds he'd earned all week as he settled into the names she seemed to like the most. *Darlin'* was better than okay, *honey* a real keeper, but *sweetheart* was the big guns when it came to reactions.

"Almost, Bane." She turned away to pick something up off the floor, and he stood there, puzzled, as he watched her fold a large green tarp. She attempted to stuff it into the duffel Vanna had loaned her, struggling to tuck the edges out of sight so she could zip the bag closed. "Just—" She huffed a strand of hair out of her face. "A couple more things."

"Sweetheart." He dropped his bag in the hallway and walked to where she stood. "You don't have to take everything you own. Hell, I'm leavin' half my stuff here.

Vanna won't throw anything out, Myrt. It's safe here." Taking her hands in his, he tightened his grip until she stilled. "Let's go back through what you've packed, and we'll right-size things, yeah?"

"It seems rude to expect her to store my…things." Speaking in a tiny voice, Myrt dipped her chin until all he could see was the top of her head. Voice directed towards her feet, she uttered words so soft he had to listen closely, crowd nearer, in order to hear her. "Vanna's already doing everything for me."

"And she'd do it twice over if it meant you were safe, happy, and healthy." Bane didn't meter his response, didn't whisper, didn't try to hide their conversation. He knew Myrt understood his intent when her head tilted, and she flashed an annoyed expression at him. "All of us. Vanna, Truck, Sharon, and me—we all want you to feel secure in being here, want you to know in your gut you can trust us. We get it, at least I do—trust isn't something I can simply demand from you. I can't tell you to trust me and have it happen. I gotta earn that. I hope you've seen from what you know of me so far that I'm doin' everything in my fuckin' power to earn it from you. I would never, ever hurt you, Myrtle." He lifted her hands and placed them against his chest, the feeling of her palms relaxing and pressing flat like a victory. "I know I've got a lot of work to do, but it's good work. Worthy work. Gettin' you to believe in me." He smiled down at her, pleased to see her lips quirk to one side as she fought against returning the expression. "One thing you should know about me, Myrt. I'm a hard worker when the incentive is right."

"What's your incentive here?" The way her lips rolled together, pressed tightly against her teeth, he knew the question hadn't been asked on purpose.

Love those little slips, give me insight into what she's really thinking. He'd found just because she didn't have formal school learning didn't mean Myrtle was unintelligent. From an early age she'd read every book her mother offered her, devouring college textbooks alongside mythical stories, all of that backed up by the Bible reading her father had preferred. Her accent might have been backwoods Kentucky, but her vocabulary was anything but. Everything about her pulled him in deeper, and he'd quit pretending to fight it.

Might as well lay all my cards on the table, see what she makes of it. "My incentive—my motive, is you." He tensed, ready to hold her hands in place if she tried to escape, but she surprised him by leaning in, pressing harder as her head tilted up and then back, exposing her beautiful face for his viewing pleasure. "All the reason I need, right here."

"Half the time when you're talkin', I don't understand what you mean, Bane."

That bit of truth wasn't a slip. He could tell from her expression she genuinely wanted to understand.

Seems a little truth-tellin' didn't scare her off at all. Time to go for broke, man. "I mean what I say, always, Myrt. I like you. You're funny when you let yourself react without overthinking, and your smiles are enough to light up a room. You're sweet, appreciative of other people's efforts on your behalf, don't take anything for granted, and you're kind." He released his grip on one of her hands, grazing a bent knuckle across the apple of her cheek. Spreading his fingers, he covered the edge of her jaw, cradling her face in his hand, and she leaned into the touch. "Kids and dogs love you, which tells me deep in your heart you're good as gold. You're fiercely protective of those you love and don't shy away from hard conversations. Sure, I'm holdin' out for a miracle you might one day return some of this back to me, but regardless of if you ever come around on that front, in my soul I know you're a good person, and that's all the reason I need to help you." Bending down, he brushed his lips across her forehead and pulled back. Her eyes were closed, and her face had relaxed into the most beatific expression he'd ever seen. "So if I say something that's hard to understand, ask me, and I'll tell you. I stand by my words."

"I...I believe you."

With even a tiny hesitation in there, he wasn't buying it. "Not sure I can take your words at face value when you stumble over the statement, Myrt." Bane released her hand, dropping his hold from her face as he backed away a step. *Fuckin' stings.*

"No." She crowded closer to him, fingers tangling in his shirt, gripping tightly. "I believe you. What I was going to say, and didn't, was I didn't know if I was worth all that." She shook her head. "My thoughts are all over the place, Bane." His name was accompanied by a solid thud against his chest with her fists. "I didn't mean to hurt you."

Bane slipped his arms around her, one low at her waist, the other high across her shoulders, and he pulled her into his hold as naturally as breathing. *She just fuckin' fits me.* "Oh, sweetheart. You didn't hurt…" *I don't want to lie to her, ever.* "Okay, it hurt a little, but I'll get over it. I'm already over it, hearing the why behind the what you said. I get it, honey. My brain goes a thousand miles an hour all the time, too. It's hard for my mouth to keep up, and then there're the times when my brain-mouth filter doesn't engage and should have, so I don't doubt there will be many times in the future I'll have to ask your forgiveness for something I said." She angled her head back to better look into his face, which had the added benefit of arching her pelvis towards his body. His dick woke and took notice of the soft flesh pressed against him, fattening with a delicious tingle low in his groin. "Let's get this finished so you and me can get on the road." Her face held an expression of confusion as he backed away, fingers trailing down his arm in an effort to stay connected. "Unpack everything you won't need, and I'll get it put away." He pulled the tarp out first, went to the closet, and dropped the folded plastic on the top shelf. "Just like that."

Turning back, he found her staring at him, not having moved an inch away from where he'd left her. Instead of asking, he tilted his head to the side and arched an eyebrow, waiting.

"I don't understand you." Myrt moved towards her bag, thighs pressed against the edge of the mattress as she sorted through the contents. "But I know you're being patient with me, Bane. Thank you."

"Don't have to thank me for common courtesies." He picked up the small pile of things she'd laid on the bed beside the bag, assuming they were the discard pile for their trip. She made an aborted grab for them, but he'd already turned towards the dresser. Smiling at her dismayed expression, he told her, "I got this, Myrt." Once at the dresser, he found out what had her cheeks staining such a pretty shade of pink. Working carefully, he placed the folded underwear into a top drawer, shirts in the next one down, and the shorts and pants from the pile in the one under that. He idly noted there was plenty of room for another whole person's clothes in the unused drawers. "That it, honey?" Glancing over his shoulder, he took in her still-puzzled expression. "Anything else in the bag you won't need?"

She shook her head, and he slid the bag over in front of himself, zipped it closed, and carried it to the doorway so he could scoop up his own bag. With both straps over his shoulder, he pressed one hand against his stomach, bowing slightly as he swept his other hand wide. "Milady, your humble servant."

Fingers twisting in the hem of her shirt, she stared at him. A brisk nod seemed to end her internal conflict, and she sidestepped into the hallway, not touching or brushing up against him. The movement was so calculated, it couldn't be on accident, and he chided himself for his overt display of affection a moment ago.

When a woman's had all her choices stripped away, the last thing she's gonna want is to tumble into bed with a controlling prick of a man.

He wouldn't put himself into the same low class as—he stumbled over what to call Sallabrook. Not a husband, not a lover. *Her owner? Fuck, that's messed up.* Sallabrook was levels and levels below Bane in terms of human decency, but Bane would never deny his own sense of possession could get a little intense. *Only when it's a give-and-take situation.* The woman he was with would never wonder about how he felt, and he demanded the same in return.

Which was why he'd picked up three years ago and left everything once again, moving from Wyoming to Texas. A woman he'd been involved with hadn't been honest about how she'd felt. *Wasn't like I wanted anything out of the norm. Just to be the only one in her bed.* He'd found out later the woman had been using him for a place to live and as her own personal ready supply of money. *Never loved her. Never claimed to.* Bane had finally come to understand what he'd been looking for was stability and partnership. Behaviors he'd turned a blind eye towards during their relationship had come into crystal focus once he'd realized the extent of her betrayal.

He might not have wanted to be in his brother's club, but the life itself had called to him. So, Bane had found one that seemed to be a fit for his desires. *Another time when I have to admit how wrong I was.* After his prospect period, the truth had unfolded in front of his eyes.

Behind closed doors, the club he'd become a member of had been chaos personified. In the few years he'd been part of it, they'd gone through no less than a half a dozen presidents. The little circle of men he'd grown comfortable with had provided the truth of the kind of brotherhood he'd been seeking, but it hadn't been enough. The last straw had been finding out the woman his brothers knew as his ole lady had been fucking around, giving it up mostly to men Bane couldn't stomach, members of his own club.

No matter she'd been offering, they shouldn't have ever accepted, not in a thousand years. *We were brothers, supposed to have each other's backs.* He'd fought with the men she'd fucked, encouraged to engage in multiple fights by the club officers, never mind they should have been forbidding the line-drawing behavior. And Bane had beaten each opponent with echoes of their laughter in his ears. *She wasn't innocent, not a bit.*

It had taken a couple of weeks, but he'd finally kicked her to the curb, watched her walk away, and then laughed when none of the bastards she'd been cheating with had wanted her. The first time she'd shown up crying and lonesome on his doorstep, he'd let her know in no uncertain terms she would never be welcome in his home, or bed, again. Not long after, he'd handed his vest back to the latest president and ridden south, looking for a better life for himself.

And I found it.

The Freed Riders were the kind of club he'd longed for, filled with men who stood shoulder to shoulder with their brothers, and who'd been horrified when he'd finally explained the reason behind his tendency to hold back trust. Called out during a drunken pool game with Horse, Bane had laid the stick on the felt, ready to walk away when his brother had caught at his shoulder, pulling him back around. *"I wanna understand the man, Bane. Ain't no right or wrong here. Ain't no reason for you to dodge a question. In this building, behind these doors, we're all equals, and there's no judgment. I wanna hear your side of why you patched out, man."* So, Bane had told him, an hours-long conversation finished over glasses of very good whiskey. *He earned my respect that night.*

The former club still had his enmity and hatred, a bubbling cauldron of anger that never seemed to go away.

Betrayed twice over.

He followed Myrt down the stairs, watching her ass sway with every step.

My brothers and my ole lady.

He considered the relationships he'd had back then, comparing them to what he had now with the Freed Riders MC. *No comparison. It's like night and day.* Bane knew beyond a shadow of a doubt the FRMC had his back. Wouldn't matter what the ask was, they'd meet it and go ten steps beyond just to make sure he was good. He could pull into a clubhouse with Myrtle on his bike, leave her sitting at the bar with the other ole ladies, and trust that not a single brother would hit on her, even if she asked for it.

But she wouldn't. She's class, no matter how Sallabrook treated her.

He shook his head, rounded the corner into the kitchen, and came to a stop when he saw Truck standing in the middle of the room. "Brother." Truck's hand rose to meet his as he stepped close, grasping in a warrior's hold and pulling him chest to chest. A fist pounded his back as he returned the favor, still shocked to see the man home. "Thought you couldn't break away for a couple more weeks. Good to see you, man."

"Called in a couple of markers, set up a rotation for what I needed to cover, and hied my ass home." Truck stared at him and tipped his head towards the door. "I'd like to have a chat, if you have time."

"Make it for my friends, brother." Bane settled the bags along the base of the wall near the back door. "No time like the present." He gestured Truck ahead of him, looking back at the last moment to face Myrt. "Back in a minute, sweetie." That damn smile reappeared, accompanied by a shy chin dip. *May have found a new favorite.* "Maybe rustle up some road snacks for us?"

Myrt looked puzzled, but Vanna laughed and curled an arm around her shoulders. "I've got you covered, Bane. I've got you." Turning away, she told Myrt, "Road snacks are basically anything salty or savory, nothing messy." Their continued conversation became inaudible as they moved towards the pantry on the opposite side of the kitchen.

"Man, you got it bad." Bane twisted to see Truck grinning widely at him. "Come on, brother. I'll bring you up to speed, and you can give me the same courtesy." The man's hard elbow connected with Bane's ribs, making him wince. "And you can tell me all about your intentions for my daughter Myrtle."

"Your daughter?" He caught the edge of the screen door before it slapped shut, settling it quietly into the frame. "She's not your daughter."

"She's mine same as Sharon is, same as Kitt's my boy. If they belong to Vanna, then you better believe they belong to me, too." Truck's smile dimmed. "Woman would do well with a full house, and that's what I understand you may be bringing back our way. But that'll be the second part of our discussion. I need to give you a message."

"From who?"

"Mason."

Bane froze. Davis Mason was the international president of the Rebel Wayfarers MC, and the name he'd invoked when talking to Sallabrook. Bane had banked on the old man knowing Mason's name—and still respecting and fearing it—on account of Mason being born only a handful or miles from where Myrt was from. Terror had been the initial reaction, but the bastard coming back and smashing a mailbox didn't say it continued past the moment. Also, Mason's second had a long history with not only Blackie but Peaches, his ole lady. Slate had rolled through East Texas years ago, long before he'd earned that name, and to hear Blackie talk, the man was the founder of his family in some obscure way. Mason'd had his fingers in a lot of pies over the years, so Truck saying his name, here, in the context of an urgent message—definitely caught Bane's complete attention.

"I'm listening."

"Gratitude, brother. He knows it was Blackie's call who would answer the summons, but Mason's pleased it was you. He's only laid eyes on you a couple of times but has good associations with each interaction. Promise you, it didn't hurt that Blackie talked you up, because not only Mason but Slate have a good relationship with the man." Truck pulled in a heavy breath, palm smoothing his beard. It seemed as if he were preparing for bad news, and Bane rocked back on his heels, waiting until the man blew out a stream of air in a sigh. "Shit's happening down here in Florida. Club business, and I've been authorized to be clear and transparent with you. We've absorbed the Jailbreakers over in Adken."

"Thanks for the vote of confidence, man. Means a lot." Bane shook his head side to side. "But I gotta tell you, it's not news you guys patched over that club. We all knew it was a matter of time, given the location and proximity to all the prominent folks in Adken." Mason's sister Justine lived there, and Blackie had passed along the info a while ago that both their mothers were in a care center there, too. Bane wouldn't go so far as to lay out the fullness of his knowledge, but he expected the glancing mention would be enough to get the message across.

"Shit's been changing by the day, almost. You're working off old info." Truck let one shoulder rise and drop in an uneven shrug. "Justine's in Baton Rouge with Wildman." Bane let his head rock back, allowing his surprise to show. "Yeah, so now we're tyin' RWMC and IMC in tight knots. Something which hasn't been widely advertised is we patched over Jailbreakers because otherwise Twisted was gonna scoop 'em up. He had a man who got involved with Sparks' little sister." Sparks had been the president of the former club and was now the president of the newly minted local RWMC chapter. "Hitch was the pivot, brother. Twisted had every valid argument for their claim. Good thing Mason was in the neighborhood, and we caught wind of what was goin' on. Our tech guy assisted in their raid of an enemy's camp and raised the hazard flag. So, we picked up Adken but lost out to IMC on another front."

"Shit, man. That's a lot of change in a short time." He paused, going back over everything Truck had said. "Mason's sister is paired off with an inner-circle IMC. That's some treaty-level info. Does Blackie know?" A sideswipe of an ask for permission to share, and Truck didn't hesitate to pick up on it.

"Not yet, but he will soon as you give him a call. We know you're his go-to when it comes to shit about clubs, so I wanted to make sure you got it from the source, so to speak." Truck flashed a grin, the corners of his mouth lifting his beard. "I've got more if you wanna listen. Say the word, brother. I'm auth'ed to give you a lot."

"Gimme." He returned the smile, lifting one hand and curling his fingers into a come-here motion. "Gimme, gimme. I'll take it all, man. Take it and run with it, you give me the go signal."

"Blackie's aware of Mason's interest in Texas. They've had many a conversation about the westerly toeholds we've got in the state. What Blackie won't know yet is our strong interest in a club over in Freestone County, near Fairfield." Truck paused, but Bane had an idea where this was going and wanted to finish it sooner, so he made a rolling motion with his hand, urging the man to get on with the story. "Iron Riggers. More a riding club than an MC, but we like the feel of them. Normally it would fall to the FRMC to wrap them into a support-club relationship, but we've got decent ties with a member." Bane sucked in a breath, shocked to his core. "Means this is a courtesy call passin' along the info that we'll probably be making a move in the next couple of months."

Bane remained silent, counting his breaths as he tried to re-center after internally reeling. Fairfield wasn't far from Longview, not by road or as the crow flew, and having the RWMC gain a chapter in the area felt very much like an unsubtle threat. He needed a hot minute to tone down his initial response, which had been to deny access, something he absolutely did not have authority to do. This wasn't something for a casual backyard chat between friends but a significant treaty dealt with at an official meeting at a wide table, allowing the presiding officers elbowroom to posture and advance or back away.

Rebels in Lamesa and El Paso weren't a risk. They were far enough away from any FRMC control to be nonentities. Rebels in Little Rock were the same. Not in the close orbit of the club. Fairfield, though? *Hell, half our charity rides travel through the goddamned town.* Bane slipped his tongue across the inside of his teeth, then caught the end in a pinching hold, biting down hard enough to stop the words still threatening to boil out of him. *Shouldn't be me holdin' this info.* The final thought gave him the direction he needed to begin a response.

"I will pass along the information to the proper officers about what you claim as the RWMC intentions. Blackie and Horse and the others will guide the club, as they always do, in the direction of our best interests." Chin up, he stared at Truck, not shying away as his gaze darkened in response to

Bane's rejection of the done-deal statements the man had been trying to sell. "I'm well aware of the Iron Riggers, and we have a good relationship with them. I'm sure Skyd will be fascinated to hear this as well." Skyd was the IRMC president, and not known for keeping a lid on any kind of reaction. "I'm curious to see how things shake out—" He almost withheld the honorific, deciding at the last moment to give it to Truck. "Brother."

"Our only ask is to contact Blackie first, brother." It galled a little to hear how easily Truck gave him the word back, no hesitation or change in his tone to indicate anger or irritation at all. *Bastard,* he thought affectionately. "And then do with the info as he sees fit. No worries, man."

"Is that it for club business?" Bane wanted to keep the conversation moving, needed to put distance between his emotions and the bomb Truck had handed him. "Myrt and I have a trek ahead of us."

"Yeah, brother. That'll do for now." Truck cleared his throat and glanced back towards the house, taking a sidestep towards the back door. "Vanna said Sallabrook was a dick when he showed. Your take on the event was key for me making the decision to come home, and I thank you for your insight, Bane. It didn't sit right with me knowing shit was going on in my own home and me way the fuck over on that side of the state."

"Dick and a half. Man's a total shitheel. Thought he could come in and push Vanna around, ordered Myrt to leave with him as if she were no freer to make her own decision than a goddamned trained lapdog. Pisses me off just to remember it." He relaxed his clenched fists, shaking his hands slightly to ease the sting of tension. "Tolled his story like it was a church bell, expecting me to see the rightness of his words. Said she was his when she isn't." *She's mine.* The thought didn't make him stumble, because he knew it was right, understood in his gut where his heart was headed. "Called her all kinds of names because she dared to leave his ass. Shoulda seen his face when I told him she was under the protection of a man associated with Davis Mason."

"He recognized the name, then? Mason'd hoped you'd use his reputation if needed."

"Hell yeah, I'll use any lever I've got to wedge an asshole like that out of your front yard." Bane let his lip curl like it had been wanting to, voice a growl far back in his throat. "She ain't his, Truck. Shoulda never been put in his path to begin with, but that's in the past, and there's nothin' I can do about what's happened. What's done's done." He straightened his shoulders, consciously taking up more space. "But you can bet your sweet ass I'm not letting her cross his path again, not in that way." The memory of Myrt's voice hit him, dragging scores of pain along the inside of his chest as his heart clenched. "She wasn't but a child, Truck. We've seen this kind of thing over in Texas, mostly with coyotes dragging vulnerable migrants into shit they were marked for before they ever crossed the border, but...she's from fuckin' Kentucky, man. A child shouldn't be sold into slavery, regardless of background, but Kentucky? That's unreal."

"Seen it happen here, in Florida. In Missouri, sold out of semis at the state fair. Men, women, children—doesn't seem to matter the who, as long as the merchandise matches up with the order. Turns my stomach, I tell you that much for sure." Truck folded his arms across his chest. "So what're you gonna do about this turdball? You gonna deal with him, or you gonna *deal* with him?"

"Far as Myrt knows, we're going up to grab the younger brothers she thinks are in danger. Something Sallabrook left in the mailbox has her convinced he's got his hands on at least one of them, and maybe both." Bane glanced at the house, then back to Truck. "What she won't know won't hurt her. When I'm done with him, the man won't be able to hurt anyone else, ever again."

"Good man, Bane." Truck's hand settled on Bane's shoulder, gripping and shaking him side to side. "I knew I liked ya." He recrossed his arms and leaned backwards slightly, stretching the muscles of his back. "I'm gonna hold the fort down here. Gunny's on his way, too, so you can probably count yourself off escort duty. He'll likely be here before you get back with the two young 'uns."

Bane considered Truck for a moment, then asked, "You sure you and Vanna gonna be up for two kids? Fourteen and eleven, and the older boy is challenged, according to Myrt." He shook his head. "Of course to hear *her* talk, she's backwards just because she didn't graduate from high school. Talking to her is like a breath of fresh air over any girl in a bar anywhere. She's got ideas and considers everything anyone says." Tipping his head down, he traced the toes of their boots with his gaze, caught up in the memories of these past few days. "She's good with the kids, too. Approachable for even little Josh. He's decided she's his girlfriend, wants to hold her hand wherever they're going."

"Like I said—" Truck's drawl slowed to a halt until Bane looked up, questioningly. "You got it bad, boy."

Bane didn't even try to deny the truth this time, simply meeting Truck's smile with a smirk.

"Let's get back inside and I'll gather Myrt up, get this show on the road."

"Bane." The warning tone pulled Bane's attention from the house back to his friend, and he stilled at what he saw there, waiting. "She's got a bucketload or ten of issues."

"So?" He lifted his chin, forcing his hands not to ball into fists at the perceived insult to Myrtle. "That make her any less worthy?"

"No, man. Not what I mean at all. You didn't see her when she first showed up. Beat to hell and back, bruised, and still so sweet and damned thankful for any kindness. Tough fuckin' life for anyone, and her nothin' but a kid. Just sayin' with the past couple of years of her life the way it's been—"

"Seven years, Truck. Not a couple. Myrt's twenty-one, and she spent seven years under that bastard's fist." Bane watched as understanding dawned over the man's face. "Yeah, let the knowledge settle in. Isn't seven years considered a cycle for things? Phases of life. Relationships. Bad fuckin' luck." He shook his head. "As far as I'm concerned, she's due some sweet. She's due picking her own wants and putting her own needs ahead of anyone else, and I'm standin' here tellin' you I'm the man to help her figure it all out. Me? I'm gonna be fine. Little bit of abstinence won't kill me, and I'm going to put her first, always. She decides there's somethin' here worth diggin' into and finding the real underneath it all? I'll be all over that. She gets her feet planted and decides her fate's leading her elsewhere? I'll smooth the way for her. The woman she's shown me over the past week is worth that a thousand times over."

"It's fast for you, huh?" Truck smoothed his beard, hand moving slowly down to rest against his chest. "The need to keep her safe?"

"Took about fifteen minutes." Bane confided something to Truck he hadn't bothered to think through on his own, taking at face value what his soul promised was true. "Climbed outta the van, saw her through the window, then met her upstairs." He grinned, because the memory was too damn sweet not to. "Woman choked on her own spit, but it gave me a chance to get up close and personal while I made sure she was okay." He frowned, letting the smile fade. "The instant she realized she was leaning on me, she bolted." He shrugged. "And I was hooked. Since then, every time I get her close, I find out more about her. The things that make her tick. Make her smile or even laugh aloud. I dig 'em out and keep 'em close, holding each like the precious gem it is. Yeah, it's fast for me, Truck. Lightning bolt out of the blue, and me brought to this doorstep by chance. Fate, maybe? I don't know and don't care. I just believe. You feel me?"

"Oh, yeah, brother. I feel you." Truck stepped close, one hand landing high between Bane's shoulder blades, above where the patch for the Freed Riders rode proudly on his back. "I feel you, and I see where you're headed. It's a real good place, brother. Keep reachin' and stretchin', and you'll get there sooner than you'll expect. That belief you talk about? I got a dose o' that, too." He gave Bane a gentle shove. "Get in there and get your woman. Sooner you get on the road, sooner you can sort out what kind of bullshit is shadowing her and deal with it. Call on any RWMC assets in Lexington you need. Carte blanche, man. Gonna see who I can roust for ya, but those are Mason's orders."

"That's generous." He reached for the door handle. "And probably will be needed. Much thanks."

"Anything for a brother." Truck followed him inside and broke away, stepping to the side and directly behind Vanna where she stood at the kitchen table. "Baby, did I tell you yet how much I missed you?" His head dipped, followed by Vanna's giggles, and Myrt glanced at Bane, a smile curving her softly blushing cheeks.

"Ready to go?" Myrt nodded and hefted a plastic bag by the handles, the weight of it swinging low. "Those the snacks?" Bane grabbed the straps for their duffels and slung them over his shoulder. *One final time.* "Hand it over, Myrt. I got it." He reached for the food bag, surprised when she danced backwards, swaying the object out of his reach. "What?"

"I can carry it, Bane."

"Yeah, she can carry it, Willy." Sharon slipped into the room with Josh on her hip, grinning widely. "Let the girl have it. She's more than capable."

"Oh, Lord," Vanna muttered, to Truck's chuckled, "Here we go."

"I'm only saying Myrtle isn't helpless here." Sharon pursed her lips, looking Bane up and down. "Willy needs to listen to her."

"I do listen to her." Bane locked in place, hearing the subtext loud and clear. "I listen hardest when she doesn't say anything at all. Like right now, when she's wishing you hadn't made her the center of attention." He turned his gaze to Myrt, seeing how her cheeks were flaming scarlet instead of the quiet pink he liked so much. "I'm sorry, honey." Her tiny smile was directed at the floor, but it was there. *Still, not quite the reaction I wanted.* He decided to pull out all the stops, going with her favorite. "Sweetie, you don't want me doing anything, you tell me and I'll listen." Aiming his glare at Sharon, he finished, "Just like I was about to do with the snacks, once I understood what you meant. And my name's not Willy. It's Will or William, or just fuckin' Bane."

Sharon stuck her tongue out at him, followed by a gasp from Josh. "Mommy, that's not nice."

"Yeah, Sharon, that's not nice." Truck got in on the act, his tongue poking out in Sharon's direction until Vanna's palm landed over his mouth.

Bane decided their leave-taking had developed too large an audience already; he wasn't going to wait for the girls to show up. He backed into the screen door and swept it to the side, moving out onto the first step. "I'll text when we get there and get the lay of the land. Appreciate the information, Truck. I don't envy you, man. Got your hands full with these two." Jerking his head towards the parked vehicle, he waited for Myrt to step past him before he released the door. She opened the side door of the van for him, then got into the front, placing the heavy plastic bag between her feet.

Bane leaned into the van and dropped their bags on the floor, then pushed the button to close the side door. He paused next to Myrt's open door and asked, "You ready, sweetie?" Thank God he was close enough to hear her quick intake of breath, because her tiniest reaction was reward all in itself. Her nod gave him permission, and he dragged her seat belt down from the recessed holder, stretching across her to slot it into place. "Nope, you weren't. But now you are." He backed out of the van and closed her door with a soft thunk. A glance towards the house showed him Truck shaking his head, Vanna leaning against her ole man with a swoony look on her face, and Sharon ignoring them leaving by fussing with the dogs, holding them back by their collars.

Van running, he buckled himself in and then reversed out of the drive, lifting a hand at the last moment to wave goodbye to the crew still standing in the yard.

"And away we go." He gave the phrase a tiny bit of singsong and looked over in time to catch Myrt smiling her tiny smile. Huffing with satisfaction, Bane put the van into drive and left the country house in the dust.

Chapter Nine

Myrtle

The gentle rocking of the van ended, and Myrt lifted her head from where she'd leaned it against the metal window frame, blinking as she looked out through the glass. They were parked near a familiar church that took up half a block around the county square, and she twisted in her seat to verify her instincts were right, seeing the old pharmacy and five-and-dime still where they'd always been.

How strange. On the one hand, it felt as if she'd fled the mountains forever ago. Her tiny set of experiences had changed, curtains pulling back wide and showing her the open world beyond. Myrt felt transformed, deep inside, as she'd come to understand her family and Sallabrook didn't fit into how most of the world acted. But, on the other hand, it seemed she'd closed her eyes for a mere moment and been teleported back to her past. Heart racing, she turned to find Bane watching her closely. She flashed him a smile that felt hollow and fake, then sat straight in her seat, staring out the windshield.

"We're here." Her unnecessary words sounded as fake and flat as her smile.

"I could do with a cup of coffee and a bite to eat." From the corner of her eye, she saw Bane gesture towards the town diner ahead of them, nestled between the furniture store and the church. The mention of food soured her stomach, and she bit back a grimace. He twisted towards her, and Myrt angled herself away. "Seemed a likely place. This okay with you, Myrt?"

"It feels smaller, somehow." Held up against the sprawling hustle of Atlanta, even as seen from the windows of a car while passing through, this town—her hometown, which once had seemed the epitome of grace and sophistication—looked tiny and dingy. "Old."

"It is old." She turned to look at Bane as he spoke, catching him mid-shrug. "And it's not large. But you shouldn't discount your memories of it. They're real and true, and right for when they were made. Doesn't matter you've got a little different experiences underneath your belt now. How you saw this place is how it was, and how it is."

Myrt looked behind them, then out the front windshield again. "Everything's in the same place it's always been. Dime store next to the shoe store, right next to the Bible bookstore. But after seeing the huge store we went into last night, I know the overalls folded on the shelf at the back of the five-and-dime aren't the best quality." She shook her head and glanced at the two new duffel bags lying on the floor of the passenger cabin. At Bane's instance, they'd gone shopping for Luke and Thad, and nothing she had done seemed to derail the outing. He'd bought two of everything, sizing up one from what her guesstimates had been. His reasoning was the boys could grow into the clothes, and she'd been forced to admit he'd made a lot of sense. Her stomach growled loudly, and she glanced towards Bane, seeing him smiling widely. "The diner sounds great, Bane. I've only been in there once, but the cake I had was delicious."

"You had cake but no dinner? That's cheeky, Myrt." He reached out the same time she did, fingers tangling around her seat belt buckle. "I got it, sweetie." Her hand fell away.

That word. Every time he used it directed towards her, Myrt melted inside. It was caring and intimate, bearing the weight of affection she hoped he might have towards her. *Not that I'd know a thing about affection.* But the way he'd held her when she'd cried, when she'd told him about her fears for her brothers, when she'd confessed the challenges in her past with Sallabrook and her terror about the future—everything in his actions told her he did have affection. That he did care. About her. *About me.* She marveled again how a man who hadn't known she existed two weeks ago would seem so invested. *And for no return at all.* He not only didn't demand anything from her but had gone out of his way to ensure she knew there were no strings tied to accepting his help.

"Myrt? Where'd you go?"

She startled and blinked, finding his face much closer than it had been a moment ago. Except he was on the wrong side. Somehow, she'd daydreamed through him exiting the van and making his way to her door. "Oh my lands. I'm sorry, Bane." She angled her body out of the van, sliding across the edge of the seat until her feet hit the ground.

Bane didn't step back.

Which meant her entire front slid down his front and ended with his belt buckle pressed against her belly.

Oh my lands.

Heat bled through her clothes, and she looked down to see one of his hands resting on each hip, fingers curled possessively but not gripping hard enough to hurt. His hold on her was firm, telling her without words that she was exactly where he wanted her to stay.

"Myrt," he said, bending closer and sliding his cheek along hers so he whispered directly into her ear. "You ready, baby?"

Her stomach dipped, but not in a bad way. Her chest hitched, stealing her air, leaving her with barely a mouthful she used to whisper back. "Yes."

"Okay."

His actions belied the single word, as his fingers tightened and he leaned against her a little more, the weight of his body pinning her against the side of the seat. She felt surrounded, but in a good way, like she had back at Vanna's place when he'd held her. Her stomach settled. He may have given her some of his weight, but it was metered and measured, because he held back. Always careful. Aware of his strength, his fingers flexed and tightened, then flexed, never enough to bruise or hurt. He shifted again, and she was mindful of every inch of his body as he touched her. The trail of his lips along her jaw, the tip of his nose as he explored behind her ear.

"Bane." Light and airy, her whisper of his name brought things to a close, making Myrt wish she'd kept her mouth shut. He stepped back, and she mourned the loss of heat, of strength, the glorious feeling of possession and protection. Dipping his chin, he stared into her eyes. Bane must have seen what he wanted, because he smiled, fine crow's feet crinkling next to his eyes, which were sparkling with pleasure.

"Right. Feed my girl." His bent knuckle landed underneath her chin, tipping her face up to meet his. The kiss landed to the side of where she'd hoped for, as he pressed his lips lightly at the corner of her mouth. "Come on. Let's get our grub on."

She was glad he knew the maneuverings of diners in general, because it meant she didn't have to do anything.

They walked in and she let him step in front of her, then lead the way to a table near the front window when a woman called out "Seat yourself." He took two stiff sheets of paper from underneath the napkin holder, handing her one.

"What looks good?" He was staring at the paper, declared a menu by the words at the top. Flipping it front to back, he hummed. "Oh yeah, they do breakfast all day. I hear an omelet calling my name." Glancing up, he asked, "How about you?"

"Breakfast sounds good. Something light. Couple eggs and toast would be good." She glanced around and realized every pair of eyes in the diner was fixed on their table. *On me.* Myrt didn't recognize anyone, but she had a terrifying thought. The moment of clarity drove her to lean over the table, clasping Bane's hand. "What if he comes in here? What if someone recognizes me and calls him? Bane, I didn't think. I never thought about someone seeing me."

"Someone recognizes you and wants to chat, I'll ask them how they sleep at night knowing they allowed a fourteen-year-old girl to be sent off to a grown man." Bane lifted his gaze from the menu, eyes blazing with sudden rage. "Sallabrook waltzes in here, he won't walk out." Nostrils flaring, he tightened his jaw, grinding side to side as his lips flattened. "Won't ever walk away."

She started to pull back, and he flipped his hand over, grasping tight to her wrist, holding her in place. "Bane?"

"You aren't afraid of me, Myrt." His fingers tightened, then slightly relaxed their hold, curling around her hand. "No reason to be. I'm not in the habit of hurting women. I loathe men who do. Hell's got a special place for men who prey on those younger or smaller than themselves. They're the ones who should be afraid, but you don't ever have to be afraid of me. Not ever. I'd sooner cut off my own arm before I'd hurt you."

"I'm not afraid."

"Don't lie." His head shook side to side, ponderously, as if her words had wounded him. "Don't ever lie to me. I scared you just now. Something I said about dealing with Sallabrook struck a chord and you became afraid. It's okay to be scared of wondering if he'd come bursting in here." His fingers threaded between hers with a grip both firm and steadying. "Because he's been such a terrible thing to happen to you. The totality of your youth, stolen by his greed and arrogance, thinking he could own a person. Just don't be afraid of me." He shook her hand, conveying the certainty of his words. "I will never hurt you."

"You want coffee or water to drink?" Myrt startled when she realized the waitress stood next to their table. She stared down at them with an uninterested expression, as if her thankless customers had little dramas at this table every day. "Know what you want to eat?"

Bane rattled off his order, then glanced at Myrt. She opened her mouth and tried, but she couldn't force out a word, still caught up in the feel of his hand in hers.

With a smile, he gave Myrt's order, too, ending it with a request for a chocolate shake. The waitress took it all in stride, as if strangers came in here all the time and ordered ice cream with their breakfast foods. Then she was gone, and Bane shifted around the table, moving to the chair closest to where Myrt sat. His knee crowded hers under the table, his foot tapped the side of hers, and he brought his other hand to rest on top of their joined ones, cradling hers between his own.

"Sweetie." That now-familiar sweep of comfort and pleasure swept over her, and Myrt closed her eyes to savor it a little more. "Let's talk about our next steps, okay?" She nodded and blinked, staring at him. His face was close to hers, and she found herself reliving the almost-kiss from outside. The heat and feel of him all along her, the way he'd breathed her in, as if he couldn't go another minute without having some of her, even if it were only her scent. "Baby." His voice had roughened, dropping an octave. Myrt watched as his pupils enlarged, taking over much of the iris, dimming the color to a ring of brilliant blue circling the swimming blackness. "You gotta stop lookin' at me like that." His thumb swept across the back of her hand and her nipples tingled, her core clenching.

"Then," she whispered, bending her head closer to his, "you gotta stop touching me like that." A dose of honesty never hurt anyone, and if she was looking at him weird, it was his own fault for making her believe he could want her.

"Never wanna stop touching you." His rasped whisper fell between them, creating an intimate moment Myrt wanted to keep forever. "You're gonna have to get used to it, and figure out how not to look like you want me to pounce on you every time I talk to you, or touch you."

The edge of the table bit into her ribs painfully and Myrt pulled back, suddenly glad of the furniture between them. Without it, she would be in his lap now, begging him to *please, God, please, touch me again*. Over his shoulder, she saw the waitress headed their direction and sat back a little more, their clasped hands the only connection between them, finally broken as they made room.

Plates clattered to the table in front of them, glasses of water with a cube or two of ice set next to those, and silverware wrapped in a paper napkin dropped to the center of the table. Bane's mug was flipped over and filled to the rim with dark coffee.

Bane didn't move to pick anything up. He sat and stared at Myrt, not even looking up at the waitress who'd gone and come back with a second load.

With a flourish, the shake was placed in front of him. "I'll be back," the waitress promised, and whooshed away.

Myrt reached out for a piece of toast, nibbling on one dry edge. She picked up a packet of silverware, pausing to look at Bane, who still hadn't moved. "Everything okay?"

"Yeah." Offered after several beats of silence, the single word didn't sound certain, was questioning. "Everything okay with you, too?"

She shifted on the hard chair, immediately aware the tingling had moved south during their exchange, turning to a throbbing between her legs. "Mmhmm." Gaze fixed on her hands, she tried to ignore the feeling as she carefully unwrapped the knife and fork, spending at least half a minute smoothing out the napkin and placing it next to her plate. A glance at him showed he wasn't convinced with her response, and she tried to smile. "I'm okay."

***

Bane

Still and poised, Myrt might have fooled someone who hadn't made a study of her reactions.

In the short time he'd known her, she'd been happy and sad, fearful, and—at times—uncomfortable in his presence. But never like this. Her heartbeat fluttered in her throat, the skin there exposing how her heart pounded. The dew of moisture across her upper lip spoke to discomfort, but the high color in her cheeks—much more than her normal nervous blush—called the emotion something different. If he didn't know better, he'd think she was aroused and trying to hide it.

Chance might have it that I'm gettin' through to her. He rewound their lightly teasing conversation and became more firmly convinced his words were having an effect. His thumb made another long, slow sweep across the back of her hand, the only caress he'd allow himself in this public place. If sweet words and tender touch were all it took to rev her engine in a way she'd clearly never enjoyed before, then Sallabrook was a fool to not have realized it. *If he'd changed his methods at all, I might not be sitting here with her.* Bane hated that tiny bit of satisfaction burning inside him, knowing it came at the cost Myrt had already paid.

Never again. She'd never suffer as she had, not if he had a damn thing to do about it. If he could rouse her with gentle caresses and affectionate teasing, he'd do it again and again until she showed him she was ready to take the next step. *It's all up to her.* The vows blazed through his head, echoing like truth spoken into a well following the tumbling fall of a silver coin.

Bane gave her hands a squeeze and, when Myrt lifted her eyes to meet his, told her, "You're so much more than simply okay, sweetie." Her blush deepened even as the corners of her lips curled up. "And I know you're hungry, so let's dig in before it gets cold." He indicated the chocolate shake with a glance, gaze returning to Myrt's face to see her smile had grown. "Or before it melts. Whichever you wanna tackle first." Another squeeze, then he reached for his silverware, arranging things on the table as she had. "Now, tell me about your brothers. I wanna know what to expect when we see them."

She lifted a bite of her eggs on a suddenly shaky fork, barely managing to complete the arc to her mouth. Eyes downcast, she chewed, the tiny space between her brows furrowed deeply.

"Luke's always been a sweet boy. Innocent, you know?" She gave him a sideways glance, and he nodded, then took a bite to encourage her to do the same. It worked, and her hands were steadier with this attempt. She swallowed and licked her lips, gaze fixed on her plate as she spread jelly on her already-buttered toast. "He never got into the rough-and-tumble the other boys did, hung back and watched, but didn't like being touched like that. A gentle soul, Momma's pastor used to say about him. Thad's always played the role of his protector. Marian told me how he stood between Luke and boys at school, or between him and Daddy."

Bane nudged her shake towards her, and she picked it up with a smile. He immediately regretted it when she attempted to drink through the straw. Her cheeks hollowed obscenely with the attempt when the thick liquid defied her. Frowning prettily, she tried to stir it with the straw, but it was too weak to make any headway. He grabbed his unused spoon and plunked it into the glass, wrapping his fingers around hers to hold it steady as he stirred the thick mixture. He ignored the jolt that ripped through him when she smiled at him, pink tongue flicking out to innocently lap at a drop of ice cream on her bottom lip. *Down boy.* Shifting his ass on the seat, he tried to also ignore his half-mast dick, which thought bending her over this table was the best idea it'd heard in years.

"So Thad's a protector?" Pulling his hands back, he forced himself to not watch as she attempted the straw again. "He's the youngest of you all, right?"

"Mmhmm. Even before I left, he was stepping up for Luke."

"Before you were taken." Bane gently corrected her, knowing if he couldn't get her to see she wasn't complicit in how things had shaken out for her, she'd take on a heavy burden of guilt if things had gone badly for the boys. As expected, she tipped her head to the side quizzically, teeth crunching through one corner of a piece of toast. "You didn't leave, baby." For once, Bane didn't pause to enjoy her reaction to that word. He plowed ahead. "You were taken from your family and cast into a role you would never have accepted under your own accord. Taken, baby."

She nodded slowly, the tiny frown appearing between her brows again. Just as slowly, she repeated his words, sounding out the syllables as if they were a foreign language. "Before I was taken."

Bane tightened his jaw at how confused she looked, sending her every ounce of confidence he could towards her in a single look.

"Thad, he's always been tall for his age, broad, too." Her words came faster, the story picking up steam now they were past the newly introduced concept. "He was in second grade and Luke was in third. Luke got held back because he had trouble reading. One of Momma's gravest sorrows was his challenges, because she so loved to read. Spread her joy through the rest of us, even the older ones." She shook her head and made a grimace he couldn't decipher. "Anyway, this boy in the same grade as Luke had a thing for hurting small animals. Toads, birds, chipmunks—anything that couldn't escape him easily, he'd capture and kill. But slowly."

"Serial killer in the making." Bane forked up the last of his omelet and eyed her still half-filled plate. "Eat, baby." Her face softened, and she tucked her chin to her throat as another beautiful blush crept up her cheeks. "Keep talkin', but eat, too." He reached out and pulled her shake towards him, tipping it up as he put his lips to the edge of the glass, spoon handle and straw pushed to the side so as not to poke himself in the eye. "Mmmm. That's pretty good." He took another sip and flicked his glance towards her, bursting out in laughter at her expression of complete and utter betrayal. "Just wanted a taste, baby." That time her reaction was diffused by her annoyance, and he laughed again, pushing the glass back her direction. *My baby's got a sweet tooth.* "It's good."

"You wanna hear about the boys or not?" With her head tilted to the side, her chin was raised in a posture of conscious defiance, and he wanted to stand on his chair and cheer. Gone was the girl who'd tried to melt into a wall at his presence. The girl who'd watched him from behind the window curtains had been banished. *If I'd known stealing her sweets was all it took, I'd have found this version of Myrt sooner.*

"Yes, ma'am." Bane wrinkled his nose at her and mimed locking his lips, hiding his smile when she laughed softly.

"Yes, ma'am." She snorted a laugh as she repeated his words with gentle sarcasm. "You don't fool me, William Crow. I bet you were born full of the sass."

He pushed his empty coffee cup near the edge of the table in the universal signal for a refill and nodded. "Yeap. Sass out the ass. Mom said I was both her biggest blessing and—" He shrugged, chuckling at the memory. "—the bane of her life."

"So it's not only your club name? Is it a longtime nickname?"

"Yeah. Club side of it is my own making, mostly because I'm so accustomed to it. Whole family calls me Bane."

"Not Willy?" Her giggle was musical and fluid, showing off her sense of ease with him, even in this town that held all kinds of memories—not all of them good.

"Oh, hell no. No one except Sharon's ever called me that." He caught sight of the server headed their direction, carafe in hand, and turned to face her with a smile. "Ma'am, what kind of cake do you have today?"

"Shake not enough sweets for ya?" She gave him a half-grin, telling him she'd seen his theft of a couple of swallows. Which meant she'd been paying closer attention than normal for a waitress, and he wasn't sure if that was simply because they were unfamiliar faces or she'd recognized Myrt. He filed the idea away for future questioning if needed and focused on the rest of her answer, listing off three kinds of cake on offer. Myrt's face had brightened at the mention of cake, and her teeth had nipped at her bottom lip for a particular flavor, so he turned back to the waitress with a grin.

"Big ole piece of chocolate, please, ma'am." Looping a finger through the handle of the now-filled mug, he pulled it in front of him. As the waitress turned to walk away, he added, "With two forks." Gesturing to a still-silent Myrt, he encouraged her, "I do want to hear about the boys." Her lips thinned as her mouth firmed, and he decided to keep things stirred up a little. "Flirting with you is more fun, though." He winked.

She blinked. Her mouth opened slightly, then closed. Then opened again.

Bane lifted her shake and placed the tip of the straw against her bottom lip, stifling a groan when that lip pursed as she drew in a swallow. Mindful of their audience, he didn't allow himself the reaction he wanted, which would have been to pull Myrt into his lap and chase the taste of sweetness into her mouth with his tongue, kissing her until neither of them could remember their names. Instead, he clenched his teeth and tightened the muscles of his belly, dick throbbing, and held the glass until she finished drinking with a noisy slurp.

Woman's got me tied in knots, he thought, reaching down to adjust his dick. *And damned if I don't like it.*

"Cake." With an abrupt declaration, the waitress slid a plate to the middle of the table, carrying with it the biggest slice of chocolate cake Bane had ever seen. She reached across and gathered their other dishes, leaving a pile of napkins and two clean forks next to the plate. "Enjoy, you two lovebirds."

"Oh, we're—" Myrt closed her mouth on that little lie as the waitress walked away, chuckling.

Scooping up a big bite with a fork, he aimed the tines in Myrt's direction, not surprised when she ducked her head and angled away. "Come on, honey," he cajoled. "Lemme feed my girl." Deliberately echoing the words from outside the diner, he watched as she remembered how closely they'd been pressed together. It seemed to give her courage, and for the first time she truly embraced what he was offering her, laying her hand on his forearm as she leaned closer, mouth open. *Killin' me.* Her lips closed around the fork, and he slid it from her mouth, studying how her eyelids fluttered. *Die a happy man.* "Is it any good?"

"Mmhmm."

She fumbled for the other fork, using the edge of the metal to pinch off a bite of cake. Her aim wasn't exactly on target, probably because her gaze was glued to his eyes instead of his mouth, but he swooped lower, barely in time to avoid being speared.

"It is good." He cleared his palate with a swig of hot coffee. "Rich." Deliberately lowering his voice, he continued. "Decadently sweet. So smooth on my tongue, baby. Mmmm. Real good."

She leaned closer and blinked, that slow, languorous movement he'd seen from her only a few times before, indicating her internal dialogue was directly in line with the story his body was telling. He was set to shove back from the table when a slip of paper appeared, and the plate of cake swooshed away, replaced by a to-go box.

"Pay at the register if you want change or have a card, leave it on the table if you're in a hurry. I boxed up a piece of cake to go for ya." By the time he turned to look, the waitress was halfway across the room and headed towards another table, coffee carafe in hand.

Pulling a couple of bills from his wallet, Bane dropped the money on top of the paper and stood, hand out to Myrt.

His heart thudded double-time when she took it without question, following him readily.

Chapter Ten

Myrtle

The moments after leaving the diner were a blur. Her heart and mind were waging war, and a good dose of fear had taken up residence in the middle of her belly, making Myrt regret the overload of sweets she'd indulged in.

She found herself seated in an armchair near a window overlooking a blue expanse of shining water. Something she'd never known existed in this tiny town she'd called home. At some point in the past seven years, a hotel chain had set up business, complete with an in-ground pool. Bane had rented a set of rooms side by side in the hallway, connected by an inside door. He'd used something like a credit card to open the locks on each, instructing her to go into the one on the left and unlock the passthrough door.

He'd done what he'd called a sweep of the rooms, looking for nothing she recognized, nodding with pleasure when he didn't find whatever it was.

Then he'd parked her here, one arm swooping under her feet to lift them, coming to rest on the matching chair. A bottle of water and a pack of cheese crackers purchased from a machine near the elevator lay on the table next to her.

Bane had left to drive back downtown and purchase a few things he'd "forgotten to bring."

Myrt sighed. *I'm not dumb. I might not be the sharpest stick in the woodpile, but I'm not dumb.* They couldn't be sure if Sallabrook would be on the mountain or not. Just because no one had seen him in Florida for a few days didn't mean he'd hauled himself home, either. But if he were to be home when they drove up into the yard, she knew Bane would want to deal with him somehow. He hadn't brought anything with them, but surely he had something in mind, just as he'd already known about the existence of this hotel. He was a planner, unlike Myrt, who seemed to do things flying by the seat of her pants.

She'd seen him eyeing a few things when they'd shopped for the boys. Items that didn't say a single thing about rescue but had everything to do with an offensive move. He hadn't bought them then; she didn't know why. But she was sure he'd left to see if he could find likely replacements.

Nearly an hour later, the van turned into the parking lot off the side street, not the front entrance where she'd spent most of her time staring. The two lines of parking were narrow and long, and she watched as the vehicle pulled up next to the dumpsters at the end of the building next to the hotel and Bane exited the vehicle. He looked front and back as he walked to the back of the van, opening the doors and stepping between, moving out of her line of sight. A few minutes passed, and he backed away, one arm full of what looked like trash. He shoved it into the dumpster, closed the lid, and shut the doors. Back in the driver seat, he moved the vehicle to the space underneath her window. When he climbed out, he looked up and caught sight of her. Their gazes locked before he glanced back towards where the dumpsters were, then back up at her. His head dropped, and she imagined she heard him cussing himself as he walked towards the hotel's side entrance and out of sight.

Less than a minute later, the door buzzed lightly, and he walked through, closing it gently behind him.

"You get what you needed?" She didn't know how to tell him she'd be okay with however he handled things. "All sorted?" Maybe turning it into nothing wasn't the right way, but it was all she could think of. "It'll be dinnertime soon. Got a hankering for anything special?"

Bane swooped her legs out of the chair and deposited his rear, settling her feet in his lap. She could see the moment he decided not to take the out she'd given him, teeth setting in a fierce grin. "Thanks for that, darlin'. We'll order pizza or something later. Right now, though, we're gonna finish our talk about the boys, and then get our plans set. You've talked about the roads up there. I want to get up the mountain and back down before it gets dark." He glanced at the window, then across the room to where a clock sat on a table between the beds. "So we've got about an hour to chat before getting moving."

"Luke." She shook her head. "I don't know how he'll react. It depends on what's happened. Thad will be okay."

"Okay, time for the talk, then." His fingers wrapped around her calves and made slow, soothing circles through the fabric of her jeans. "If the boys aren't there, we go to your daddy's house and get them. The fact you believe the man's capable of doing this tells me they aren't safe there, either. We talk to Marian while we're there, get her the info she'll need if she decides she doesn't want to leave quite yet." His fingers stopped moving and gripped firmly. "If the boys are there and Sallabrook's not, we take the boys and anything belonging to them, and bring them back here. I've got a friend coming in soon. He can stay with the boys tomorrow morning while you and I go out to talk to Marian." Bane dipped his chin, gaze pinning her to the chair. "You with me so far, baby?"

"I'm with you, Bane." That phrase felt like more than a simple affirmation, and she saw the words hit him the way they'd felt coming out of her throat. Real and tangible, she'd pledged him something lasting. Just to see if it felt the same, wholly unafraid of the outcome, she repeated the words, "I'm with you." A shiver crawled up her spine, and his eyes grew dark, intense.

"Jesus, baby, the things I wanna do with you." The low mutter preceded his movements, but only by a breath. Bane removed her feet from his lap and, with a smooth transfer, pulled her wholly there instead. She leaned her shoulder against his chest as he settled back in the chair, one arm draped over her legs, one curled around her waist. She looked up and his lips were *there,* within reach. So she reached.

A soft press of flesh was the start. Heat and wet followed as his mouth opened and his tongue slid along her lips. He stroked insistently across her bottom lip while working the width of her mouth with his lips. His hand gripped her hip when she opened for him, and she whimpered as Bane's taste swirled across her tongue. He kissed her, the caress waning and rebuilding, breaths coming hotter and heavier. Myrt arched her back, pressing her aching nipples against his chest. Arms twined around his neck, she let her fingers trail through the curls he always tried hard to keep tamed, pulling and plucking them back into existence around his ears and the nape of his neck. His arm across her legs slid up, a palm solid against her thigh. His other hand curled around her side and traveled side to side along her belly, then up, finally landing over one breast. His fingers stiffened and gripped, and she arched again, enamored with the way he made her feel. It was like nothing she'd known before. This wasn't an imposing of his will on hers. *He makes me want so much.* No, Bane teased and coaxed her along with every kiss and caress. Every soft touch and low moan against her skin, he brought her along willingly to see what he'd offer next. *So much.*

Heavy hammering rattled the door in its frame, and Myrt rapidly found herself deposited on the edge of the bed, Bane standing at attention between her and the potential intruder. He was breathing heavily, and she found her breaths matching the cadence, as if a connection still tied them together. He shifted and flexed, hand moving to the small of his back as naturally as if he made the movement every day, flipping his shirt out of the way to rest his fingers on the handle of a gun.

Bane leaned close to the door, one eye to the peep hole. "Son of a bitch."

She startled and flinched at the recognition of the weapon. When Bane turned around, she was immediately glad he hadn't seen. His expression was already halfway between pleased and a grimace, and she tucked her chin, waiting to hear who it was.

"Gunny's here."

"Sharon's husband?"

"Yeah, she's his ole lady. He's here to assist if needed." The pounding resumed and he turned around, shouting at the door, "Hold your fuckin' horses, asshole." Extending his arm, he pushed the lever handle down with two fingers and retreated to stand next to Myrt.

The door opened and a man as large as Bane walked in. A wave of energy coming with him had Myrt on alert. The two men met with that curious handhold and a pair of grunts, then pulled into a one-armed hug, each seeming to compete with hardest hit as they pounded the other's back.

"You must be Myrt." Gunny aimed towards her with his hand out. She stared at the large palm and scarred and calloused fingers, then began lifting hers. Bane stepped between them and brushed Gunny's hand away. The scowl on the big man's face matched his tone when he barked out, "The fuck, man?"

"Just...don't, okay?" Bane took a step backwards, crowding closer to Myrt. The outline of the gun was clear underneath his shirt, and she wondered how she hadn't noticed it before now. "Myrt, darlin', this is Gunny." In a swift movement, he shifted and was down on a knee next to her legs, faces close. "He's safe, okay." That sounded like he was trying to convince himself as much as her, and she glanced from his features to Gunny's, noting the expression of amusement now on the man's face. "Swear, he won't hurt you." The earnestness of his voice brought her gaze back to him. "If he does, I'll kill him."

"Sharon'd kill me if you didn't, man." The humor she'd seen on his features bled through to the words, and Myrt found herself smiling. "I heard a little bit about you." His chuckle filled the room, and as it trailed off, the energy she'd felt from him before rolled through again, setting her teeth on edge. "And a lot more about the mission. Got a debrief for me, brother?"

"Yeah." Bane's gaze hadn't shifted, his eyes still looking directly at Myrt. "Yeah, but…give me a minute. Got the room next door, too. Connecting's are already open. Key's on the dresser in there. Make yourself at home."

Gunny's footfalls moved away, muffled, and then disappeared as he left the room, taking that wash of dark energy with him. Myrt shivered, then relaxed as Bane's hands found hers.

"He's a dirty cockblocker." He shook himself, rattling his leather vest as he closed his eyes and pulled in a deep breath. "But it's probably for the best. Woulda been a thousand times worse if he'd been ten minutes later." Eyes open, he stared at her again. "Before I got so beautifully sidetracked earlier, what I was going to say was about Sallabrook. I'm not going to let him hurt anyone else, Myrt. Won't leave him breathing, not if he's touched a hair on those boys' heads. Might not anyway, just as painment for what he did to you."

"Painment?"

"Yeah, pain as payment. If ever a man deserved it, he's one." Myrt felt a chill as Bane shifted, releasing her hands. He reached up and cupped her cheek with a palm, and then she felt his other hand settle at her middle, covering the tiny bump she still tried to keep hidden under her clothing. "I won't ever, not ever, let him or anyone else hurt you."

His message was clear, and she felt her certainty about the right paths changing as he spoke. "No matter what, I'll keep you safe."

She pulled back a fraction and stared into his eyes, giving him the only thing she could, her trust. "I know you will."

He leaned his forehead against hers, fingers slipping along her jaw to curl around the back of her neck in a possessive hold. "Darlin', the things you say." The hand on her belly pressed tighter as she covered it with her own, cradling that tiny spark of life together. "I would do anything for you. Will do." This close, his noisy swallow emphasized the emotions raging through him. "Anything." Then his mouth was on hers, his tongue sliding inside to twist and dance. Their breathing grew heavy, fast, and he tipped her head to better feast on her lips. This time when the kiss slowed and eased, he didn't relight the flame, finishing with a series of tiny, sweet, smacking touches that escaped the frame of her mouth, dropping on her cheeks and chin, the tip of her nose, and on each eyelid. "I'm with you, too, Myrt. Body and soul." He brushed their lips together, gliding side to side. "You got me."

She blinked against the light as he moved away a fraction of an inch, as desperate to see him as she was to stay in the cocooning darkness behind her lids. He was safety. A feeling of strength and confidence suffused her whenever he was around. In the dark he changed, turning into the flame of her arousal, something so recently discovered that she resented the need to dampen it back to a flickering shadow of what had been roaring between them.

Myrt dropped her head to his shoulder, nuzzling close to his neck to get a good scent of him. She drew in a lungful of that courage, and another, then sighed. "If Sallabrook's there, I'll get the boys and get in the van. I'll do what you tell me to. I trust you, Bane. Trust you to keep us safe." She pressed his hand against her belly, listening to the catch in his breathing as he understood her meaning. "Keep all of us safe."

"If he's not there, we won't dally." Myrt startled at the stranger's voice and pressed closer, having forgotten about Gunny in the next room. "We'll get in, do what's needed, and get out. We can always come back and take care of unfinished business, brother."

"Right." Bane leaned his head against hers and took in a long breath. "Come on, Myrt." The quiet murmur had his lips touching the skin behind her ear, and she shivered. "Time to get gone, darlin'."

On the drive up the mountain, sunshine speared through the trees, creating pockets of brilliance along the road. Myrt sat in back, leaving the men to ride up front. She listened to their conversation at first, Bane's growing comfort with Gunny loosening her muscles. She watched out the window as the turns in the road came closer together, the lanes narrowing, any attempt at a shoulder falling away. Gazing out across the crowns of thousands of trees blanketing the sides of the mountain, she remembered for a moment the rhythm and joy of the holler.

Through a break in the trees, she saw the faraway roof of the church in town, tiny from this distance, diminished in importance the way she'd hoped she would be by leaving Sallabrook as she had. Then he'd come all the way to Florida to find her.

"Hateful, spiteful man." Her whisper stuck in her throat, closed around the words until she thought she might choke. The closer they got, the harder she found it to breathe. Myrt leaned forwards between the two seats and pointed, fighting through the information Bane needed. "Next right is the road to the farm. It's narrow and easy to miss."

"Next right, got it." Bane allowed gravity to bleed off the tiny bit of speed he'd gained on the last straightaway. "You doin' okay, darlin'?"

"I'm scared." She hadn't meant the words to be so loud, but there they were, hanging in the air as both men remained silent for a beat, their nonreaction screaming with surprise. "Not of you, of course. But of what we might find."

"If he touched them—" Bane reminded her of his vow, and she nodded.

"I know." She pointed again. "There, see the tree with the broken branch? The turn's there."

"Hell," Gunny muttered, his fingers wrapped tightly around the handle above his door. "I hate cages."

"Same, brother." Bane spun the wheel, making the sharp turn to the rutted road. "Same. These roads weren't made for this century." The muscles in his forearms tensed and bulged, fingers wringing the wheel for a moment. "How far is it, Myrt?"

"Not far. 'Bout a mile or so." She shrugged, staring out the front windshield. "Give or take." Sweat trickled down her spine and dampened underneath her arms. She wiped her palms on the legs of her jeans and strained forwards a little more. "Just a couple of turns and we'll be on the barn and sheds. Do you see any recent tire tracks? Does it look like he's gonna be here?"

Gunny twisted around in the seat and gazed at her. "Myrtle." His voice was low, gravelly like Bane's could get when he was trying to be serious. "Nothing is going to happen to you."

"You don't know him." She cut her eyes towards him, seeing his full focus was her. "And, all respect—you don't know me, sir."

"True." Gunny glanced at Bane, then turned to face her more fully. "I can say nothing is going to happen to you and mean it, but because you don't know me, you don't know I can back up those words." He lifted his chin pridefully, lips pressed into a tight slash across his face. "Between me...well, and me, I've got you covered."

The van skittered sideways as they rumbled across a series of washboard ruts and Bane swore so colorfully it made her want to smile. "We're nearly there. The rough spot was the dry creek."

"I see the barn." Bane's words had Gunny turning away, but not before he gave her a dignified nod. "I'm driving right up to the house. Myrt, you stay in the van until we know if Sallabrook's here or not."

"I remember, Bane." Her voice was steadier than her nerves, and she wiped her palms across her jeans again. "Doors will be locked and I'm not to touch them until you give me the go-ahead."

The van seemed to gain momentum over those last hundred yards, barreling into the empty yard. The wheels locked with a jerk, and they slid past the space where Sallabrook always parked his truck, coming to a stop only feet away from the wooden steps leading to the porch. Bane and Gunny were out of the van in an instant, Myrt scarcely getting her hands up in time to catch the keys tossed to her. She pressed the button Bane had coached her on, hearing the solid thump of the locks clicking into place. Bane's hand went to the middle of his back as he walked away from the van, rotating in a slow circle to take in the whole of the farm as the gun came free of the holster. She glanced at Gunny to see he also had a weapon in hand, his gaze fixed outwards, towards the driveway and trees, up the mountain to where nothing lived.

The engine of the van ticked softly, hot metal cooling now there wasn't any fire to drive it forwards, and she imagined it could have been Sallabrook somehow, sputtering out without her here to brutalize. In a different life.

That changed the moment she saw her brother's head peek over the windowsill, looking out of the house and towards where she sat in the now-still vehicle.

"Thad," she breathed, the word hardly stirring the air. A bone-deep tremble set up in her body, starting from the soles of her feet and moving in a rapid wave up her spine. It came out her mouth with a yell, voice unrecognizable, screaming for Bane. He pounded on the glass next to her, and Myrt whirled to face him, pointing to the house with one shaking finger. "Thad." That time she had some oomph behind her brother's name, casting it so loud it echoed back onto her from the inside surfaces of the van.

"Unlock it." Bane gestured to her with a "come along" motion, his hand making quick circles through the air. "Let's get him. Sallabrook ain't here."

She fumbled with the key fob, unlocking and relocking the vehicle a couple of times before she got things under control. Bane was there, hand out, and she laid the keys in his palm. He grunted and shoved them into his pocket, then held his hand out again, waiting until she got the hint and slipped her hand against his, palm to palm. His fingers curled around her hand and gave her a squeeze. Then he pulled her from the van and up the stairs.

It was chilling to see everything so much the same. The muck boots hung on their nails beside the outside door, high enough dogs and varmints couldn't reach to scavenge the leather, but outside so the stink of the pig pen never entered the house. The sturdy four-legged chair waited near the door, close enough to the porch railing Sallabrook could spit into the dirt with ease. *I've been gone weeks. I'd expect more of a difference.* Maybe she'd misunderstood his visit to Vanna's, because if he were doing well without her here, why would he go so far to try and drag her back?

Bane lifted his fist to pound against the door, but Myrt ducked under his arm, turned the knob, and walked straight in.

"My lands." She stopped inside the door, trying to catalog the wreckage. Pictures with the covering glass broken hung askew from their nails, as if a mighty wind had tried to sweep them away. Dirty plates and cups were on every flat surface, some with food or drink still inside. The floor held varying levels of dirt and trash, with clothing scattered here or there. "Oh my lands."

"Not much of a clean freak when he's the one doin' the cleanin', huh?" Bane moved closer to her, his hand resting protectively against the middle of her back. "Where's Thad? You saw him, right?"

Myrt jarred herself loose from the hypnotizing filth and disarray, then took in a deep breath and immediately regretted it, the stench as bad as the mess. "Thad, where are you?"

"Myrtie?" She spun towards the kitchen in time to see Luke crawl out from underneath the table.

"Myrtle?" Thad rounded the corner near the stove, eyes round in his head.

Luke was unsteady when he climbed to his feet, but Thad was right there to put his shoulder under his brother's hand, ensuring they both remained upright.

"Oh, boys." She took no more than a step towards them before they were on her, arms around her waist and neck, pulling her into a three-way hug that seemed to go on and on. Luke was crying, and she leaned her head against his, ignoring how dirty both boys were. "Hush now, everything's gonna be all right now. We've got you. Gonna get you out of here, once and for all. Put this behind us. Gonna be okay. We're all gonna be okay."

Their words ran together, a phrase from one, a sentence from the other, and she slowly built a picture of their time on Sallabrook's farm. Their daddy had done as she'd feared, giving Luke up to take her place. Thad had proven stronger than anyone could have expected an eleven-year-old to be, refusing to allow his brother to go alone. Sallabrook had gone into a rage the instant they walked through the door, raving about Myrt doing him wrong by leaving. It was hard to hear the man's words through her brothers, to see the hatred he'd held in his heart towards her all these years. Sallabrook had tried to take Luke on, but Thad hadn't allowed the abuse, had kept watch through the nights when the man was home, blocking the door of the stall so he couldn't get in to where Luke slept.

She'd known Sallabrook could be vicious; his sessions with her had always been sex with a leavening of lust intended to make him feel human in his own eyes. Malleable human clay left to the mercies of the Maker. In his eyes, it was simply his nature, not his fault. She'd heard him ranting about it often enough. Never his fault. It was the weakness of the human form. His animal nature. She didn't ask anything, not yet, letting Luke and Thad warble their way through the worst of the story. Sallabrook had finally given up on Luke, taking Thad to the house instead. Myrt's arms tightened around her brothers as Luke took over the tale, leaving Thad to hide his face against her side. According to Luke, Sallabrook had picked Thad twice, the most recent only last night. Luke's story involved his expectations of what Sallabrook and Thad had done in the cabin while he was left in the barn—movies and ice cream topped the list.

Lord God, I know better.

It seemed forever but could only have been a handful of minutes before Bane returned to the cabin, and she felt his hand come to rest on her back. A signal, quiet and gentle, considerately not interrupting the boys—who hadn't yet acknowledged the two men with Myrt. Still, it served as a reminder that they had a plan, and a timeline, and things to do. She let Luke talk himself out, voice trailing off when he neared the end, his breaths coming slower and quieter as he calmed. "Boys, is there anything you brought with you to pack up?" She knew from experience there wouldn't have been much carried from the homeplace to here. She'd come with the clothes on her back, but the melted soldier meant their father had allowed the boys something, at least.

"Got everything in a poke sack in the barn." Thad had found his voice again, weak and wavering though it was. "We were in here lookin' for food to take with us."

"Yeah, we was gonna run away, Myrt. I'm glad you found us, though." Luke stepped back and grinned down at her, Myrt's first realization her younger brother had passed her in height. "Woulda had a hard time of it if we'd made it to the woods proper."

"I'm glad I found you, too. My friends Bane and Gunny helped, and they're gonna make sure we all get outta here, safe and sound." She rattled Thad side to side. "I'm so proud of both of you." Bending down, she stared into his face. "I understand everything, and you don't have to worry, okay? I'm going to keep you safe. You're safe now." Like a watery memory, she held on to the feeling she'd had inside when Bane told her those words. *Relief and gratitude. Belief and trust.* "I swear to you...you are safe now."

Thad held her gaze, and she watched him fight a myriad of emotions. Fear and sorrow, and so much anger. The rage inside him nearly boiled over, scalding her with the heat of it as he held it inside. He wrestled with it and bested it, and finally, the only feeling she could see was relief, that sweet respite of knowing someone else was willing to carry whatever burden it was, in this case the safety of his beloved brother, his worst fear being something bad happening to Luke.

"Let's get your bag and skedaddle on outta here." Bane slid in beside her, his arm naturally going around her waist in a movement Thad didn't miss. "I'm Bane." He stuck out his hand, holding it steady until Thad gripped and shook it up and down once. "You gotta be Thad. She's talked about you a lot." He turned his attention to her other brother, trying to become invisible in the shadows behind Thad. "Luke, it's good to meet you. She's had a ton of stories about you, too." Instead of holding out his hand, he gave Luke a wave, and Myrt knew it was because he'd read the boy's body language, currently screaming discomfort. "We've got to get back to town. There's a hotel room with your name on it, and a pool for swimming." Bane's fingers dug into her side, the action telling her this was somehow important. "Myrt's going to be there with you. We'll order pizza or something, and you can tell her what all went on here. Eat, swim, do whatever." *He's going to hunt Sallabrook.* She couldn't find any sorrow inside her at the knowledge. No matter the details of what he'd done to Thad, the fact he'd done *anything* was too much. If he'd been here right now, she would have gladly taken the gun from Bane's hand and shot him herself.

"There's nothing in the house that's yours?" Both boys shook their heads in the negative, and Myrt looked around the small two-room cabin, paying close attention to everything she could see. "Nothing of mine, either."

Seven years spent in this house, and no one would ever know. She didn't have a book or Bible, no papers stowed in a box at the back of a closet, no secreted treasures under a floorboard. Nothing to show for the hard life of pain and anguish. As Luke and Thad walked past her, heading outside, she let her hand slip low on her belly, palm pressing against her flesh there. *Only one thing,* she thought, and turned to see Bane studying her closely.

"You okay?"

Myrt nodded, not trusting her voice.

"No, really, Myrt. Are you okay? It can't be easy being back here, even knowing it's for a limited time." His palm curled around the side of her neck, fingers tangling with the braid at the back of her head. "It's okay to be sad. Or mad. It's okay to be however you feel, because this is a hard reminder of an incredibly shitty time in your life."

"It really is." She caught the sob halfway up her throat, choking on it and forcing it back down. "I never realized how bad it was here."

"Pretty fuckin' shitty, you ask me." His forehead thunked gently against hers, his face so close she could see every expression, no matter how fleeting. "But the thing is, you're a survivor. And now that you're past that survivin' phase, you're gonna be a thriver."

"Thriver isn't a word, Bane. You make words up a lot." His lips pursed invitingly, and she obliged, closing the distance between them to kiss him quickly. "I find it amusing, Mr. Crow."

"Oh you do, do ya?" His lips curled and she got a flash of that elusive chin cleft before her eyes fluttered closed as he took his turn to kiss her, longer, and with the delicious sliding and twining of tongue that always seemed to curl her toes.

Myrt was shocked to find herself heating up, the flush traveling up her chest to her throat, then inviting itself into her cheeks, blazing hot. His arms wrapped around her, one hand settling low on her hip, the other sliding high to grasp her braid. With a steady pull, he tipped her head back, exposing her neck. Myrt bit back the sounds threatening to rush out of her as his lips worked their way down the column of her throat, teeth nipping and tongue soothing.

Bane stood tall and groaned, the rough noise rattling through her as Myrt pressed her cheek to his chest, getting as close as possible while still upright and clothed. She blinked and opened her eyes, shocked to see they were still surrounded by the wreckage Sallabrook had left in his wake.

Here, in the place where her worst nightmares had lived, Bane had found a way to make her forget about everything.

***

Bane

Exiting the cabin, Bane hustled Myrt towards the barn where the boys' voices echoed. They were loud but didn't sound angry, simply excited. Gunny was nowhere in sight, so Bane knew whatever was going on likely involved the man.

Going from bright sunshine into the darkness within the barn, he took a couple of seconds for his eyes to adjust, but once they did, he burst out laughing. "Good Lord, Gunny, what the hell, man?"

Gunny was halfway up a ladder bolted to the side wall of the barn and had Thad on his shoulders. The boy had leaned far back, arms over his head as he worked at something tied to the rafter. One of Gunny's hands was on the ladder, and he had the other arm wrapped around Thad's legs, holding the boy in place. Luke stood in the middle of the barn floor, head tilted back as he watched his younger brother, anxiety clear in every line of his face, arms curled around his middle defensively.

"Put a hustle on it, kid." Gunny's arms bulged with his efforts. "And shut up, Bane. Kid's gettin' his shit."

"How the hell did it get way out there?" The rafter was narrow, about a ten-inch beam. "No, don't tell me, I'm pretty sure I know." Bane shook his head. Myrt walked past him, her fingers trailing along the back of his hand for an instant as she moved to where Luke stood. "Thanks for helpin' out, Gunny."

"Wasn't about to let the kid go beam-walking thirty feet above ground." Thad had to use his hands on the rafter to bring himself back into position above Gunny, eliciting a grunt from the big man. "Seemed the best way. Give it to me, kid." Thad extricated himself from Gunny's shoulders, climbing higher on the ladder as Gunny moved downwards as if in a choreographed movement. He passed over a large sack that clanked as Gunny got to the last few rungs and jumped off, landing heavily. "Broke a sweat. Not a fan of heights."

"You were on a ladder." Bane watched Thad scramble down until he could emulate Gunny, jumping from higher. He landed awkwardly but rolled and came up to his feet, hands already stretching for the bag in Gunny's grasp. "Wasn't like you were on a tower or anything."

"Kid scared the shit outta me. I didn't even think, just went up after him. Reminds me of Kitten. Fearless." Gunny brushed his palms together. "We ready to roll, brother?"

"Yeah." He raised his voice, not that Myrt and Luke were far away, but they seemed engrossed in a conversation. "Come on, y'all. Let's get loaded up and risk the death trails they call roads around here."

The rescue had all gone much easier than expected, and Bane was pleased for Myrt that things shook out this way so far. Still, he'd have unfinished business when they rolled out of the clearing with the cabin. If he'd heard the boys right, Sallabrook was even more evil than he'd believed, discarding the older boy for the younger. Didn't matter if he'd molested the boy or not, even threatening to do anything to either of them had earned the man that death sentence Bane was gonna be happy to pronounce.

He gestured at Gunny to wait, and they hung back in the barn while Myrt, keys in hand, walked towards the van with the boys.

"I called Blackie earlier while I was out from the hotel. Not that you give a shit, but from my quick convo with him we've got full backing from the FRMC of whatever we decide to do. Rolling in here, I noted fresh tracks headed out. Boys didn't say for sure, but I don't think he'd been gone long when we got here." Bane took a moment to appreciate the view as Myrt bent slightly, leaning into the van to get the boys settled into the back seat.

Gunny interrupted his thoughts with a dire prediction. "He'll be back. Before dark. How you wanna play this?"

"I want to take them down to the hotel and get them settled. Then I want to come back up here and wreak vengeance, brother. I want to be the smiting angel who gets to deal with the gigantic sack of shit." He watched Myrt climb into the van, turning around to give him a tiny wave. "Deal with all that shit, and then go back home to my beauty."

"Angel of death, then sleepin' with an angel." Gunny grunted. "I can see things your way." He nodded. "I can see it, meet it, and get the fuck behind it. Let's haul ass out of here so we don't run the risk of your woman seein' anything she can't unsee."

"Sounds good. But you should know she says she's behind the idea." He started walking, his footsteps echoed by Gunny's beside him.

"It's one thing to say it, but seein' it? That's a whole different ballgame."

"One I've been playin' for a long time." He split from Gunny and walked to the driver side, slamming the door behind him. Hand out, he smiled at Myrt. "Keys, darlin'." She gave him that tiny smile and dug in her jeans, coming up with the fob. "We're out of here."

A quick three-point turnaround and they were headed back down the mountain, a trip that seemed to take half again as long as the one up. He was on edge with every turn and curve, waiting to see Sallabrook's face behind the windshield of a vehicle on the way back up. If they were to meet him, Bane didn't know what he'd do for sure. The urge would be to turn around and deal with business now, putting the things threatening Myrt behind them. The saner response would be to continue on his way, hauling his woman—*ain't that a sweet, sweet thought*—and her brothers down the mountain to safety.

Fortunately or not, he didn't have to make a decision; there was zero traffic on the tiny mountain roads. Branching off on the slightly larger state highway, he drove into town and out the other side, parking below their rooms. In the mirror, he watched Myrt's interactions with the boys, their eyes growing wide at the sight of the hotel and pool.

"Let's get everyone set up." Bane turned and caught Myrt's gaze, giving her a wink that made her cheeks go pink. "Get a little cleanup done and y'all can swim until dinner."

"Really?" Luke's eyes were shining as he gave Bane a broad, guileless smile. "That'd be great."

"*Really*, really." He opened his door and swung out, seeing Gunny already headed inside. Sliding the side door of the van wide, he offered his hand to Myrt, who accepted the assistance with a duck of her head. "We've got clothes and stuff for you guys, and I'm pretty sure we threw in some swim trunks, too." Luke was behind her in exiting the vehicle, followed by Thad. "Hopefully we guessed your sizes okay."

"You've both grown so much since the last time I saw you." She ruffled Luke's hair and pulled him in for a sideways hug. "I'm glad Bane had the idea of getting...well, everything."

Thad shrugged and stepped between Bane and Luke. He didn't make a big deal about it, sliding in sideways before he gave Bane his back, and then took a step backwards, forcing more space around his brother. It was the kind of move a protector would make, done on instinct, following years of practice. A glance at Myrt said she hadn't noticed.

It told Bane a lot about the homelife these boys had lived before being forced to take Myrt's place at Sallabrook's farm. School, community, or home—one of those places had trained Thad to be aware of even potential danger to his brother, and given the way he moved, Bane thought Thad had probably backed it up pretty well for a not-yet-teen.

He did it again in the upstairs hallway leading to the rooms. Myrt and Luke were out in front, walking shoulder to shoulder, heads leaned together as they talked, and Thad trailed behind by a couple of feet, carrying the burlap bag filled with the few treasures the boys had. Bane brought up the rear of their little progression and, on a whim, decided to try to pass Thad. The boy faked a believable stumble, lurching into Bane's way and keeping him separated from Luke and Myrt. That was more deliberate than the move downstairs, and Bane stared at the back of Thad's head, considering. Then the boy turned his head to glance over his shoulder, and the expression on his face was filled with so much rage that Bane slowed his pace, allowing the three to gain a larger lead.

What the hell have these boys been through to warrant that kind of anger?

Gunny poked his head out of the second room and waved them forwards. "Boys, you're in here with me." Gunny looked past the siblings and gave Bane a chin lift. "Shifted the luggage and shit around already. I'll get them started with showers, and you and Myrt can call in some grub."

Myrt slowed, breaking free from Luke's grip on her hand as she turned to face Bane. In her eyes he saw heat; then her lids dipped as she looked down, her innate shyness taking hold. Clearly she was remembering the same thing he was—the moments before Gunny had shown, the sweet touches and hungry kisses that had moved them both.

Luke went with Gunny willingly, but Thad—predictably—paused in the hallway. Bane gestured towards the doorway. "It's okay, Thad. There's a door connecting the rooms. You can see Myrt whenever you want." Hand on the doorknob, he swiped the room's keycard through the reader and pushed the door wide. Myrt stopped beside him and leaned in, her shoulder hitting his ribs as she molded herself to his side. "Myrt's not goin' anywhere. Promise."

"It's just...we barely got her back." The boy's pain bled through his words. "I can't—I don't want to lose her again."

"You won't, Thad. You and Luke didn't only regain a sister today." Bane gestured towards Gunny, who was watching Luke explore the room while keeping one eye on their exchange in the doorway. "You've got protectors now, too. Think of us as older brothers. We'll do anything needed to keep you safe."

"Thad," Myrt said, her voice soft and low, vibrating with intensity as she leaned towards her worried brother. "It's okay, I promise. I trust Bane and Gunny beyond anything."

"It's been bad." The emotions playing across his face were a mix of hurt and fear. Thad stared at Myrt before turning his gaze on Bane. "But I believe you, Myrtie."

Bane let the boy hold his gaze for a breath, then jerked his head at the door. "Go on, get Luke settled, check out the stuff we got you. Remember, Myrt is right next door." He dropped one hand to the small of Myrt's back, not missing how his touch made her lean into him more. "Get used to holdin' on to that belief, Thad. It's going to be okay." He gazed down at Myrt, who was staring up at him with an open expression of adoration. *No lie, makes me feel ten feet tall.* "Come on, darlin'. Let's us find some grub."

Without looking back at Thad, Bane ushered Myrt into the room and closed the door firmly behind them. A quick sweep of the room showed a courteously closed connecting door and he made a note to thank Gunny later. Spinning her, he crowded close, using his body to flatten hers against the wall. "First things first." One hand on her jaw angled her face up for a kiss. He brushed side to side, nibbling on her bottom lip until she made a tiny noise at the back of her throat, hands clutching his shirt under the weight of his leather vest. "Been hungry for you for hours, woman." He murmured the words as he moved along the edge of her jaw, lips finding and latching on to her earlobe.

The move pulled another noise from her, this more impatient. "Need me a taste to carry me through."

Sliding a hand down her side to rest at her waist, he felt a shiver run through her at his words. She turned her head away and arched her neck, giving him greater access he immediately put to good use. Lips to her throat, he felt the way her heartbeat pounded through her. The curves her clothing hid pressed against him, and Bane let loose a groan that made her shiver again.

"Baby, you feel so good." She shifted and lifted to her toes as he stood upright, and he complied with her clear demand, taking her mouth in another deep, wet kiss. "Wanting is a natural state around you. Need is too. Want you any way I can get you, babe. In my arms, my mouth on you." He dusted a series of kisses across her cheek as she buried her face against his throat. Mouth to her ear, he gave her a little more truth. "Wanna make you mine, Myrt. Want that in the best way. Know I'm not the right man for you, but fuck all if I can find it in me to turn away. Want to see you spread out on my bed, kiss you from your toes to your pussy, lick you until you scream." The noises she made now sounded rough, feral, and she was twisting against him. Afraid she was pushing him away, Bane pulled back, rebounding instantly when she cried out at the distance. "You want that, too, don't you, Myrt? Want to feel me against you, inside you. I'd get you ready for me with my fingers, give your clit a tongue-lashing you won't forget. Bury my face between your legs, only come up for air when I can't go anymore."

There was a thud against the wall, and Thad's voice could be heard, the words indistinguishable. A barbershop tattoo of knuckles against the connecting door snuffed out the brilliant edge of desire Bane had built up. Myrt slid sideways, head already turned away from Bane. "I need to check on them."

Laughter sounded, high and sweet, and Myrt relaxed at the reassurance her brothers were okay.

"Gunny won't let anything happen to them. You know Sharon. You think she'd put up with his shit if he weren't a good guy?" Bane let his fingers trace up the creamy skin of her throat, twining into the hair at the nape of her neck, twirling a tiny lock that had escaped her braid. "He's gonna get them comfortable, let them be boys, and in return, they'll respect him. I've seen it a dozen times with men like him. They're good to their bones, and without question they will protect the innocence of kids with their lives."

"Luke sounds good." The smile she aimed his direction was small and tight, foreshadowing something not good was coming. "Did you hear anything Thad told me? Anything either of them said at all?"

"Yeah, some. Was tryin' to give you a chance to reconnect, darlin', but some of it I couldn't block out."

"Did you hear what Sallabrook did to him?"

Bane tensed but shook his head slowly, giving her his answer in silence. She stared at him, lines etched in her cheeks as she came to grips with what she'd learned, what she was trying to share without speaking it into reality.

The knock at the connecting door wasn't light and playful this time. It sounded as a heavy rattle, slow and ponderous. Bane backed away from where Myrt stood and reached out to open the door without looking. The body in the doorway was big, too big to be one of the boys. "Yeah, Gunny?"

"Brother."

That single word was weighted more than the knock had been, and Bane held his hand out to Myrt as he turned to face Gunny.

The man was still in his vest—not surprising; Bane was too. He had a dirty rag in his hand, stained with what looked like transmission fluid. Fabric bunched between his fingers as Gunny lifted it with a grimace. "You know what happened to the boy?"

Myrt touched Bane's arm, slipping her hand down to curl around his wrist. She gripped tightly, and he pulled her close, lifting their joined arms so he could wrap his arm around her shoulder, bringing her to his side. She was shaking. Not the erotic shivers from before, but a trembling that seemed to emanate from deep inside. Her chin bumped a half a dozen times as she nodded wildly in Gunny's direction. "It's...it's why w-w-we...had to come." Took her three breaths to get the words out, stuttering and stopping in between. "I knew what he'd—" She twisted and shoved her face against Bane's chest, hiding underneath his vest. "What he'd do." She finished on a whisper, barely audible to Bane, but when he glanced at Gunny, there was no confusion, only sorrow and understanding.

Bane reached out and took the cloth from Gunny, realizing at the last moment it was a pair of briefs. "Which boy?" He ran all of the conversations back through his head in an instant and realized he already knew. "It's Thad, isn't it? Did he say anything to you?" Gunny's head swung back and forth. Bane looked back at the stained underwear, noting the overlapping circles of red. *Jesus.* "You think he needs a doc?"

"Dunno, man. I told 'em to toss me their dirty things. It came out with the rest of his stuff." Gunny angled his head down, trying to look Myrt in the face. "Shit happens, little sister. Boy's got us at his back now, and we'll make sure he's good. He's a strong little dude, big little man, makin' sure his family's safe. Without talking to him, I still know that's what happened. Know it like I know the back of my hand. Us, me and Bane, we're gonna make it so that piece of shit can't ever do anything like this again. Hand to God, little sister."

"I should have known, but I never thought about him hurting the boys." Myrt shifted, one arm circling Bane's back as she rolled her cheek across his chest so she could look at Gunny through her tears. "Deep inside, I should have known if I left, he'd find someone else to hurt. I closed my eyes and left." She shook in the circle of Bane's arms as she began to sob. "It's all my fault." She shoved her face back under his vest, taking shelter where she could.

Over the top of her head, he shared a look with Gunny. With a sharp nod, the man took a step backwards and closed the door gently behind him. Bane steered Myrt towards the bed and guided her down into his lap, keeping the close connection between them. He breathed her in, the flowery scent of her shampoo already familiar enough to be soothing. He arranged her limbs, draping her legs across his, curling around her. With her braid of hair drawn over one shoulder, Bane glided his hands up and down her arms, across her back, around the curves of her hips, touching her everywhere he could reach.

Making her mine.

When her tears had slowed, he chucked under her chin with a knuckle, drawing her face up. *She even cries pretty.* Her cheeks rouged, lips swollen, eyes puffy but not reddened—she was gorgeous no matter what happened. "Not." Bane leaned in and kissed the tip of her nose. "Your." He spoke with emphasis. "Fault." A fresh flood of tears welled in her eyes. "Baby, don't cry." She blinked, then closed her eyes tightly, lips pressed in a thin slash. "Don't, don't, don't. Baby, don't cry anymore. It's not your fault. You had no idea he'd go back to your daddy, no idea your daddy'd do what he did. Not your fault."

"But I should have known he'd do something."

The misery writ large on her face was terrible to see. Bane stroked across the apple of her cheek with the back of one finger. "Getting yourself out of a situation like that couldn't have been easy. Shows a lot of grit and courage, Myrt. I heard about what he did to you before you left. Babe, if you'd stayed, he might not have stopped the next time. Might not have stopped until you were dead. Then what would he have done? Probably the same goddamned thing, trailed back to your daddy and whined about his life. But where would the boys be then? If you hadn't saved yourself, we wouldn't be here."

"If we weren't here." Lips quivering, she pushed her way through. "It wouldn't have ended."

"No, it wouldn't have. Not for Thad. And not for Luke, either."

Her hand lifted and rested against his chest. "It's because of you we are here."

"No, baby." Bane bent close and pecked her lips in a soft kiss. "It's because of you. It's all you. The boys are safe because of you." Eyes open, he kissed her again. "All you, baby. Own that shit."

"Me?"

"Yeah, baby." He kissed her deeper, long and wet enough he got to see her eyelids sink closed as she surrendered to the sensations. Breaking off with a grin, he gave her a minute to come back to herself. Resting his forehead against hers, he told her something he hadn't been sure she'd been ready to hear, but instincts told him the time was right now. "Gettin' those boys safe is because of you, but making sure that asshole won't do shit again? That's on me. Gunny and me are gonna go back up the mountain here in a bit, catch up with Sallabrook and explain how things are gonna be."

"You'll be careful, right?" Her brows furrowed lightly, her gaze fixed on his lips in a way that told him she was reliving the kiss right now, still in his arms.

"Yeah, babe. We'll be safe. Promise." Her hand curling around the back of his neck made him smile. "We'll be back before you know it. Now"—he swung her legs so they dangled between his, then shifted backwards on the bed—"we gotta figure out what you and the boys want for dinner."

She stood, bending at the waist so their faces were still close. "You're good to me."

"Well—" He kissed her again, hard and fast. "You're good for me." Her lips curled as she looked into his eyes. *I really like that look on her. Looks good.* "Makes us even."

***

Bane

Standing at the window next to Gunny, Bane looked down to where Myrt sat on a lounge chair within a fenced-off area. Thad was perched on the concrete apron around the pool, feet disappearing into the water. His wet hair testified he'd been in the pool at some point, probably playing with Luke, who was floating on his back, arms outspread.

"They're gonna be okay." Gunny's words didn't leave any room for argument, not that Bane wanted to disagree with the man. "Myrtle, too. That's one tough chick, man. I saw pics of what she looked like when she first showed up. Vanna documented the damage, just in case, you know?"

"I heard." He blew out a stream of air. "Didn't see. Didn't need to in order to know it was bad." His phone dinged in his pocket and showed a delivery status on the food app when he pulled it out. "Food's in the lobby." Digging cash out of his wallet, he shoved it towards Gunny. "Grab the pizza and I'll round up the crew."

"Sounds like a deal." Gunny thudded a closed fist against Bane's shoulder. "I'm fuckin' ready to roll, brother. Get that piece of shit dealt with so those boys can put all this behind 'em. Time to make good memories, startin' right here and now. Those boys gonna love Truck's place, and you're givin' 'em a good fuckin' family."

Bane remained at the window, staring down at Myrt as she laughed with her brothers, ducking back as Luke flung water her direction. She glanced up and their gazes caught and held, a smile stretching across her face. It only lasted an instant until Luke was successful in splashing her, but Bane felt the connection between them grow stronger.

Somethin' about this woman.

Not too much later the boys were dried off and seated at the table in Gunny's room. Myrt perched on the edge of a bed nearby, watching her brothers eat with a satisfied expression on her face.

"Hey, Myrt?" She looked up at Bane where he leaned against the wall. Tipping her head to the side, she scrunched up her nose, questioning silently. "Happy looks good on you, babe."

Thad's chair jolted as he turned halfway around to glare at Bane.

Gunny's chuckle was dark as he muttered, "Oho, gonna have to watch out for baby brother." He brushed past Bane on his way to the door. "Let's roll, man."

"Right behind you." He tossed the van keys to Gunny and detoured to stand next to Myrt. With his back to the boys, he loomed over her, pleased to see no fear in her face as she looked up at him. "We'll be back soon." Fingers around the hinge of her jaw, he stroked her cheek with his thumb. "Stay inside. You've got food and drinks. My card if you need to order anything else. Just sign it in a scribble, they'll think it's me anyway."

"Okay." Her bottom lip pouted out the tiniest bit, turning her from pretty into even more gorgeous. "Be careful."

"I told you, we will be." He bent and brushed his lips across hers, thrilled when she chased his mouth. "Leave the door between the rooms open; that way, you can hear the boys."

Her repeated response was soft. "Okay."

With final soft kiss at the corner of his mouth, he slid his lips to her ear. "Back real soon, baby."

The noise she made was the one that made his dick get hard, and he had to fight his instinct to take more, kiss her deeper, bend her backwards on the bed until she whimpered underneath him.

Jesus.

Bane forced himself away, turning towards the door and walking through, finding Gunny chuckling in the hallway. The door clicked shut, and he thudded his fist against Gunny's chest with a muttered, "Fuck you."

Non-club-related small talk got them halfway up the mountain, rounds of "did you know" and "where is he now" weaving the threads of common connections between them. They were easy enough together so when Bane had a thought, he voiced the question without worrying Gunny'd take it the wrong way.

"When you patched over the Jailbreakers, were you cool with takin' on a bunch of members like that?" He glanced over to where Gunny lounged in the passenger seat. "Lotta new blood all at once."

"Yeah, lotta men, but they were in our pocket anyway." Gunny stared out the window. "Good guys. We nearly lost 'em to the IMC. Was glad to keep 'em in the family." He sat up and pointed. "Hey, stop a minute. Let's pick that up. I've got an idea for what we can do when we catch up to Sallabrook."

Without a word, Bane steered the van to the edge of the road and stared at what Gunny had indicated. "You fuckin' kiddin' me?"

"Naw, brother. Trust me on this. I got an idea." Gunny's chuckle was dark and wicked sounding as it rumbled out of him. "Get it."

Bane exited the vehicle, staring up and down the empty road. He walked to the back of the van and flung the doors wide, glaring into the interior and considering his options. There was a partial roll of trash bags off to the side, left over from his and Myrt's shopping trip for the boys. Plenty remained for what was needed now.

He finished and slung the bag into the back of the van, then scrubbed his hand against the damp grass, kissed by the evening dew—the dichotomy of using something so pure to cleanse away filth flashed clear in his mind, one he didn't even try to sort out.

Turning onto the narrow driveway leading up the mountainside, he and Gunny reacted to the new set of tire prints at the same time.

"Bastard came back."

"Lookie here." Gunny slapped the roof of the van in a rapid staccato. "We're gonna deal with shit. Takin' out the trash."

Bane steered the van, following the well-worn dirt track.

"You're good, Bane. We'll be outta here before you know it."

"I know."

"Then why you stranglin' the wheel, brother?"

Bane relaxed his fingers, stretching them. "I'm good, man."

Top of the driveway, Bane slowed and let the van roll to a stop before they cleared the line of trees. The van would serve as an effective plug, keeping all traffic in and out from easy passage. Even though they'd closed the barn doors upon leaving earlier, now they hung wide, a gaping block of darkness in the shadowy evening light.

The door to the house was closed, windows dark, but from where they were Bane could see the hulking shape of a man in the chair on the porch.

"There he is."

Bane opened his door and paused, shoving his head close to the overhead light, giving Sallabrook a good, long look at him. Gunny snorted as he swung out of the van, slamming the door behind him. "Let's go, brother."

Bane climbed out, letting the door swing shut, and lengthened his stride, catching and passing Gunny within a few feet. He didn't slow until he had Sallabrook out of the chair and against the wall. His arm an iron bar across the man's throat, he shoved his face close to find all the posturing he'd done had been worthless. Sallabrook had been passed out in the chair, missed the whole show. He stank of whiskey and sweat, eyes rolling as he tried to understand what was happening.

Rage swelled in Bane, black and toxic, and a tool for him to use. "Old man, you recognize me? Got a gander at my face, dickhead? I'm the one told you there was no way you'd get your hands on Myrtle again." Bane lifted the man, suspending him with the hold on his throat, lips peeling back from his teeth with the effort. He grunted, hefted him again to slam against the wall, and his voice, low and dangerous, told Sallabrook, "If I'd known at the time what you'd done, there wouldn't have been any walkin' away for you." The man's heels rattled against the wooden wall, slowing and stilling as he slumped in Bane's grip.

"Brother."

At the steadying touch against his shoulder, Bane jerked backwards and let the man slide down, the limp body slumping against the railing at the end of the porch. "Fuck!"

"We got this," Gunny said as he pushed past Bane. "You got this, man." He wrapped an arm around Sallabrook's throat and yanked him partially upright, then dragged him across the porch, the heels of his socks catching on the rough planks. Gunny shoved the door open and moved through.

Bane followed and went directly to the kitchen, finding even this backwoods cabin had a junk drawer filled with all the things needed for the evening's activities. Strapping tape in hand, he made his way across the main room to where Gunny had Sallabrook perched in the largest chair in the house. Gunny already had the man's ankles tied to the chair legs with wide straps of leather that looked like belts.

Positioning Sallabrook's wrists on the arms of the chair, Bane took his time winding the tape around and around. His final effort was to twist the tape across the back of the chair and loop a couple of straps around the man's chest to hold him upright. Leaving the cardboard holder dangling, Bane stepped to where he could see Sallabrook's face. Red and mottled, whether from drinking deep or being choked out. It didn't matter. Bane couldn't find an ounce of sympathy in him for this asshole.

"You ready for this?" Bane asked the question, already knowing the answer as he turned to look at the other man.

"Born ready, brother." Gunny stood near the doorway and thumbed over his shoulder. "Gonna go grab a couple of things from the van. Don't have too much fun before I get back." Bane lifted his chin and shifted to face Sallabrook. "Brother?" He looked over his shoulder at Gunny, their level gazes colliding and holding. Gunny's voice was low and angry when he reminded Bane, "He hurt that boy. Hurt your woman. There's only one way this ends."

"Oh, yeah, I know." Bane's chest swelled with the belief and confidence in Gunny's gaze. "He ain't walkin' out of here. Hell, he ain't crawlin' out of here. He ain't breathin' out of here." He untwisted and faced Sallabrook. "Old man dies here. Like I said before, you and me are on the same page, brother."

Sallabrook coughed. Bane watched his body jerking with the effort, wishing for an instant he'd pressed a little harder on the man's neck.

"I'll be back in a minute, Bane."

The door opened and closed at Bane's back. He didn't take his gaze off Sallabrook, watching as the man's eyes opened, pupils wide and dark. The old man's head rocked back, and he stared at the ceiling. "You took my boys." Coughs wracked him, nearly stole the words as he rasped out a whisper. "Took my girl, too."

"She took herself out of here." He allowed himself a single step towards Sallabrook, his feet straining to move farther. "The fuck kind of shit you runnin' up here? What were you even doin' goin' back to her old man? What'd you expect to get outta the deal? Did you go there hopin' to get your money back? I know you bought her from her father, low-life piece of shit."

"Made me angry. I came home and she was gone. Hadn't made supper." Sallabrook flexed his muscles, pulling at the restraints. "I went to her daddy because I thought she'd run home. She weren't there." Sallabrook laughed, breaking off in the middle with wracking coughs. "He give me the boy. The other one hitched a ride in the back of my truck. Didn't find him until after I got up the mountain. Figured it was divine intervention."

Bane's fist connected with the side of Sallabrook's face, the club ring on his middle finger splitting open the flesh over the man's eyebrow. Blood welled immediately, looking dark, an unhealthy maroon color in the shadows. *Like the motherfucker's poisoned, inside and out.* "Divine intervention my ass, motherfucker."

"Ow, shit." Sallabrook shook his head and stared up at Bane, apparently shocked at being struck. "The hell you go and do that for?" He blinked against the steady flow of blood coming from his forehead. "Shit."

"You still pissed, old man?"

"Hell yeah, I'm still pissed. More so now." Sallabrook lifted his chin and scowled at Bane.

"Took the boys and dumped them in the barn."

Sallabrook's smile smeared blood across his teeth. "Not all I did." He turned his face to the side and spat red. "But you already know that. Why don't you just kill me. Took my property. I can't run the place by myself. Might as well finish the job."

Bane leaned close and let saliva pool in his mouth. He waited a beat, until Sallabrook's gaze settled back on him, then spat in his face. The man smiled wider as the viscous liquid slid down his cheek.

"I'm gonna finish it, old man. Rest assured you're gonna die today. Slow and long, and painful." The door opened, and he watched Sallabrook's eyes dart back and forth, unsure where to settle his gaze. "It's me you gotta worry about, motherfucker. Keep your goddamned eyes on me. Tell me what your plan was for the boys. What you intended to do."

"Didn't ask for 'em. Figured I'd use what God saw fit to put in my path. The girl left. She left all her work to me. They were supposed to take care of the animals and garden. All her chores, seemed right to have her brothers deal with what she'd abandoned."

"And you goin' after Luke? That part of your plan?" Bane slammed his boot between Sallabrook's thighs, grinding the steel toe deep into his crotch. "Heard Thad protected him like a good brother. Then you took it farther."

"Boy wasn't respectful. Boy should respect his elders." Sallabrook's head rocked back again, tendons straining in his neck. "Like you give a shit about trash like them."

A memory of Myrt swam across Bane's vision, the fear when she'd talked about how Sallabrook owned her and could order her back. Bane had spoken truth to her about the common law lack in Kentucky, but he hadn't known about the child at the time. If she birthed it, Sallabrook could take the child. *She might not want it,* he reminded himself, going over Vanna's words in his head. *Her choice, either way.* Her choice, not Sallabrook's. *Fuck him.* His fist blasted against the side of Sallabrook's head again, the ring catching along the cheekbone this time, splitting the flesh to the bone and knocking blood in a wide arc.

Rage swelled, and he ground his toe harder, pinching and crushing until Sallabrook howled in pain.

"How old was she when you stuck your dick in her?" Sallabrook didn't answer him, eyes boring holes in Bane from behind the swelling flesh. "Was she even fourteen? You like 'em young, don't you. That's why you took the boys. You like 'em young, that's for sure." He swung around and looked at Gunny, needing a break from Sallabrook, even for only an instant. "How young you think he'd go?"

Gunny shrugged, flicked the edge of the window curtains back with one finger, staring out into the dark. "Guy's an ignorant dick. He prolly can't count to save his own ass."

"We should see, shouldn't we? I think we should. You wanna go get our friend from the van, man?" He didn't know Gunny, not really, not as well as he'd like to, because right now the man seemed steady-Eddie when it came to wetwork. *Me and him, we could be friends.* "You already go grab our friend? Ready to get started, brother?"

"Why the fuck not." Gunny kicked the door open and put one boot through before leaning down as Bane turned to face Sallabrook again, steeling himself to not kill the man fast. *Needs to pay and pay.*

Bane propped the sole of his boot against the edge of the chair and shoved, pleased when the rear legs of the chair caught against a seam in the floor, tipping the chair up at an angle. Sallabrook flailed as much as he could, tied up as he was, his head flopping side to side as he tried to catch his balance.

"Ooops, ooops." Bane wiggled the chair, watching the man's eyes go wide. "Watch out now." He wiggled it again. "Wouldn't wanna fall and—" With the tiniest of shoves, he tipped the chair over backwards, watching without care as Sallabrook's head bounced against the rough plank floor with a solid thud. "Hit your head, huh? Damn shame," he finished up as he leaned over the man. Still tied to the chair, Sallabrook had no leverage to change position, blood-filled eyes staring up at Bane. "You okay down there?"

A plastic bag dropped next to Bane's feet, and Gunny grunted. "Imma open all the windows. That shit's gonna be ripe, man."

"Oh, yeah. Will be even more ripe after being bagged up like this. All sealed up so the juices stay inside. Mmhmm. Sounds so…" He glanced at Gunny and grinned, the expression changing to a grimace. "Tasty."

Gunny gestured at the man on the floor. "Carry on, my brother. You're doin' fine. I'll get you a spoon."

"Gonna spoon feed you, old man. Like you're toothless and shittin' in diapers. Enjoy it while you can. You ain't gonna live that long." He pulled a pocketknife free and flicked it open, finger and thumb pinching the blade tightly. He bent and slit the plastic, flinching backwards at the buzzing noise and rancid smell rolling out of the bag.

"Wha es tha?" Sallabrook's voice shook, the words trembling as he struggled to get them out.

"Your first test to see how young you like 'em." Gunny approached noisily, and Bane held out his hand, wrapping his fingers around the metal that thumped against his palm. "You already moved on from teen to barely into double digits. Let's see how low you'll go." He bent and spread the slit he'd cut in the bag, stifling a gag as he looked at the roadkill they'd picked up on their way up the mountain. The skin of the dead possum's belly shifted slightly as he stroked a finger along the seam of her pouch. He pressed firmly, carefully teasing the opening wide so he could see the tiny bodies inside. Half were still, dead already. The others were moving jerkily, thin bodies showing bones down the spine, ribs standing out from their sides.

"Pinkie up." Gunny lifted a baby possum by the tail, arching his little finger high. "I got manners." He walked to Sallabrook's side and crouched. "Open wide, motherfucker."

Bane shifted to the other side of the prone man, pinching his nose firmly closed. When Sallabrook opened his mouth in a gasping breath, he wedged the metal spoon edgewise between the man's gaping jaws.

Sallabrook's eyes rolled wildly, gaze first landing on Gunny, then Bane, back and forth. Gunny gripped a fistful of hair and arched the man's neck before dropping the squirming gray-skinned possum into his throat. Sallabrook gagged and choked, yelling when a tooth broke as he bore down on the edge of the spoon, fractured bits of white joining the baby's body. Bane yanked the spoon out and covered the man's mouth with his hand, keeping a tight grip on his nose. Sallabrook thrashed and convulsed as Bane kept his gaze on the man's throat, smiling grimly when he saw the muscles move with intent.

"Yeah, seems like he likes 'em young." He rocked back on one foot, keeping a knee to the floor as he released his hold. "Not enough to fuck, but he took that load like a champ. Good boy, Sallabrook."

"Another one?" Gunny bent sideways, coming back with another baby possum, this one still and quiet. "This one'll be less trouble. Except," he gave it a squeeze and Bane saw something white writhing in the baby's mouth, "it's got a few hitchhikers. You know the old man don't mind those, either. Already said that's how he got his hands on Thad. Didn't bother to let the boy's daddy know he'd ridden up the mountain. Just took it like a gift."

"Gift from Satan, maybe." Bane stared down at Sallabrook, imagining him with Myrt. Fucking her. Raping her. Over and over, her crying, tears filling her eyes, sobs breaking through her voice as she begged him to stop. Each vision burned through him, leaving only rage behind, flames that grew higher and hotter with every breath this old bastard breathed. "Gonna kill him, Gunny."

"Expected no less, brother." Gunny offered him the tiny gray body. "Let you do the honors."

Bane gripped the man's jaw and wrenched it wide, feeling the pop as ligaments and joints gave way. He put weight on the tip of Sallabrook's chin and kept his mouth open, reaching for the tiny dead body. Hovering over the man's mouth, he gave the baby possum a squeeze, gritting his own teeth as the tiny white maggots dropped, scattering in writhing clumps across the man's bloody tongue. He kept squeezing until all that escaped was a thin drool of rancid liquid before stuffing the body into Sallabrook's mouth. He held out his hand in a clear demand. "Give me another one, exactly like that."

Gunny obliged.

It took a while, but eventually Sallabrook stopped breathing around the dead possums and vomit in his mouth and throat. His chest fell and didn't rise again, all the fight fading from muscles gone lax. Bane pushed to his feet, staring down at the dead man.

"What's next?" Gunny's voice was as matter-of-fact as if they were grocery shopping and Bane held the list of kitchen necessaries.

Bane looked around the cabin, taking stock. He saw the bed wedged into the corner, the foot of it exactly waist high—exactly as he'd heard described in Myrt's shaking voice. He twisted to face the kitchen, where she'd spent hours cooking for the dead man, hoping she'd make him happy enough he'd only rape her, hot food keeping his fists at bay. Bane cracked his neck and stalked to the bed. He stared down at the discolored floorboards, stomach turning as he realized what the fresh stains meant. The old man had likely raped Thad here, too.

"He died too easy." Turning, he saw Gunny with a gas can in hand. Bane stooped, blade in hand, and cut through the tape and other bindings holding Sallabrook to the chair. He angled another glance up at Gunny. "What say we make another stop after this?"

"You wanna see the in-laws before we head back to the hotel?" Gunny shrugged. "Sounds great to me. I got nothin' but time, brother."

"Her sister is there. Myrt doesn't think their daddy will ever let her leave." The man who'd sold Myrt for a few hundred dollars.

"Won't have a say in it if he can't say a thing."

Gunny grabbed Sallabrook's arm, dragging him towards the bed. Bane caught at the man's feet, disheveled socks falling to the floor as he and Gunny lifted together, throwing the body on the bed.

"I like the way you're thinkin', brother. We can talk to Marian first." Bane took the can of gas from Gunny, opening the funnel and splashing liquid across Sallabrook's body, saturating the clothing he wore and the bedding around where he lay. "Get a read on her." He splashed gas around the cabin, kicking the bag with the dead and empty momma possum to the side. "Decide what we're gonna do after we chat."

He left a trail of wet liquid towards the door and through it. Gunny stood not far off the porch, staring at the barn.

Quiet concern in his voice, Gunny asked, "You think it'll spread to the barn?"

Bane shrugged, tossing the plastic can back inside the cabin. "Doubt it."

"But it could. Even with the rain comin' tonight, it could." Gunny sighed. "Let's turn out the animals, just in case." He turned and handed Bane a cigarette and lighter. "I'll be in the barn, come help me when you're done."

"Hell, man. I didn't know you smoked."

"I don't." Gunny flashed a grin over his shoulder at Bane. "But I knew you didn't, either."

"Smart man, always thinkin' ahead." He watched Gunny pass through the wide doors into the darkened barn, then turned back to the cabin. Filter to his lips, he tilted his head as he clicked the lighter, drawing deep until the end of the cigarette glowed cherry red. Blowing out a stream of hot smoke, he flicked the ember-tipped tube of tobacco deep into the cabin, keeping his gaze on the spot until he saw the first glow of flames. It was the work of minutes for the fire to grow, following the path laid to the bed. In a whoosh the covers went up, dense, dark smoke rising from the flames.

"Little help here." An aggrieved shout from the barn cut through the noise of the blaze.

Bane grinned at the fire and tossed the lighter into the cabin as he turned to go to the barn. "On my way, brother."

They sat in the van for an hour as the flames consumed the cabin, cows and a donkey wandering through the yard.

"You think they're gonna be okay?" Gunny flexed his muscles, legs bent nearly double as he wedged his heels against the dash.

"The cows?" Bane looked at him in time to see an expression of surprise cross Gunny's face.

With a laugh, Gunny said, "No man, the boys." Elbow to the edge of the window, he propped up his head with one hand. "Somethin' like this happens, can derail all the good there is in a life. They're gonna need something to hold on to. You gonna give them that?"

"Yeah. Me and Myrt, we'll figure it out." A wall collapsed, following the path of the roof from several minutes before. He watched the embers billow up and then settle down. "I got a half-assed plan for Myrt's old man."

"Fire's burnin' low, prolly safe to say it won't spread." Gunny shifted in his seat. "Gotta get a whole-assed plan, brother." He moved again, yanking on the handle to open the door. "Gonna piss. I'll be back."

Bane didn't respond, keeping his gaze on the fire, noting as Gunny had that it was dying down. It would continue to burn for a while, long enough to finish consuming everything. If a marshal came up the mountain to look at things, Sallabrook would appear to have died in his sleep, alone in bed. The donkey sauntered into view again, staring at the flames as it lifted its tail, unconcernedly defecating on the yard. "Yeah, man. It's all a steaming pile of shit." As if it heard him, the donkey turned and looked over its shoulder. Mouth wide, it brayed loudly. "I hear ya, brother. I hear ya."

He started the van and pulled forwards into the yard, turned around in the bald dirt where Sallabrook had conducted the same maneuver uncountable times. He aimed the vehicle to where the driveway entered the trees and rolled to a stop. A moment later, the passenger door opened, and Gunny swung in, landing with a grunt.

Without another word, he drove out and down to the highway, the glow of the fire disappearing in the rearview mirror. Following the directions Myrt had offered the previous day, he turned away from town and drove deeper into the mountains.

*****

Bane

"That it?" Gunny tossed a fourth bag on the growing pile in the back of the van.

Marian spoke from inside the vehicle, her voice softer even than Bane had ever heard from Myrt. "Yes, thank you."

Bane leaned against the van door, keeping an eye on the disgruntled old man posturing on the front porch.

It hadn't taken long to determine Marian wasn't staying at her father's house by her own choice. They'd walked up, spoken to the old man for a total of two sentences, and Bane had coldcocked him, knocking him on his ass. Five minutes later and a half-spoken, half-sobbed phone conversation with Myrt, Marian had thrown her shit into bags, and Gunny was playing pack mule while Bane babysat Floyd Threadgill, Myrt's father.

"Call the hotel." Gunny paused on his way past Bane. "Book another room for the night."

"I will, once I'm done here." Bane tipped his head at the vehicle. "Don't let her watch."

"Yeah." Gunny's fist thumped in the middle of his back, conveying an unspoken message Bane understood loud and clear. "Don't draw it out."

"Don't intend to. That half-assed plan I had? Full-assed, brother. Full-fuckin'-assed." He tossed the last words over his shoulder, picking up speed as he traveled, arriving at the porch steps full steam ahead, arm cocked back and ready to piledrive Threadgill's head through the wall behind him. The old man never moved, never flinched, his gaze not wavering as he watched Bane's fist coming closer. He dropped like a fly with the hit, landing so hard and bonelessly he didn't even bounce.

Bane glanced over his shoulder to see Gunny taking up most of the windshield. Reassured Marian wouldn't be able to see anything, he pulled the gun from the waistband of his jeans and knelt over Threadgill. Each swing of his arm felt like a blow struck for Myrt. "Fuckin' sold your kid." Blood splattered up the wall, dark in the shadows. "Sold her to a fuckin' sadist." Bone crumpled at the man's temple, leaving a black concave hollow. "Gave your boys to the same man." Threadgill's nose flattened against his cheek, blood a steady river down the side of his face. "Never gonna hurt her again. Never hurt them."

Wiping his hands on the man's shirt, Bane stared down into a face that would now be unrecognizable to even his closest kin. Blood filled Threadgill's mouth, and he gurgled, sputtering to breathe. Bane could leave him and the man would probably die. Lie here and choke to death on his own blood.

Or I can take care of shit.

He reached out, took a firm grip on the man's hair, and jerked his chin towards his chest. The gurgling deepened, becoming more drawn out, the choking gasps slowing. "You don't do that to family." He kept the pressure on, wrenching at the man's neck until the sounds ceased.

"You fuckin' don't."

He pulled his phone out and looked at it. Clearing his throat, he wiped the gun across the man's shirt as he had his hands a few minutes before, then holstered it in the small of his back. Hooking a hand in Threadgill's shirt, he dragged him a few feet to the side, putting him out of easy view of the driveway. Bane shook his head, cleared his throat again, and woke the phone, thumbing into recent calls.

He listened to the auto responder when the call connected, tapping the numbers on the phone until he got to a real person. "Hi, yeah. This is William Crow. I've got two rooms booked there for another night."

"Mr. Crow. Yes, I've got your registration in front of me. Two rooms through tomorrow night." The girl on the phone sounded younger than Myrt, probably cousin to the owner, taking the late shift to help out the business.

"Yeah, that's right. What would it take to add another room to my tab?"

"One moment. Yes, it looks like I've got a single room close to your connecting rooms." She hesitated, voice coming softer. "I can't make it connect to the other rooms, though. Is that okay?"

He nodded as he stood, stepping away from Threadgill's body. "Yeah, yeah, I know it won't connect. That's fine. I need another room close by if you can. One bed is fine."

"I'll add the room to your account, Mr. Crow. It won't take me two shakes to copy the info over. I'll have the keycard ready in ten minutes or so. Be sure to check in here at the desk."

She was sweetly helpful, and he tried to smile, knowing even a grimace would translate into a softer tone for the call. "Perfect. Thanks so much."

His return trip to the van was much slower than the approach to the house had been. Gunny still took up much of the front windshield, and Bane looked over his shoulder, then checked his hands again. *Nothing to see here, folks.* He opened the door and settled behind the wheel. Listening to Gunny with only half his attention, Bane turned the vehicle around and drove away, Myrt's childhood home smaller and smaller in the mirror.

Gunny was speaking animatedly, describing Vanna and Truck, how they'd found and rescued Myrt. The man had a thousand humorous stories about the crew in Florida and kept Marian engaged the whole drive back to the hotel, letting Bane sit in silence to reconcile what he'd have to tell Myrt.

Even though it was after three in the morning, Myrt must have been watching out the window for the van, because she was downstairs and through the door before Marian was even out of the vehicle. The joy on Myrt's face when she saw her sister was worth every ounce of effort expended tonight. The two women stood still, arms wrapped around each other, faces buried in each other's necks as they babbled and wept, tiny cries breaking through at times.

Bane steered Myrt towards the door and gave Gunny a nod. The other man stepped up and began herding them both, leaving Bane free to go to the hotel office. Key retrieved, he made his way back to the room he and Myrt had been sharing. The new room was directly across the hallway, which would make things easier. He met Gunny near the stairwell, carrying one of Marian's bags.

"How're they doing?" Bane scrubbed across his forehead, exhaustion starting to creep up on him.

"About as well as you'd expect." Gunny hefted the bag over his shoulder. "Boys are sleepin'. Women are cryin'."

"Myrt ask anything about Sallabrook?" At Gunny's headshake, he expanded his query. "Her daddy?"

"She might have had a question about that. Marian said she didn't know." Gunny turned beside Bane and paced beside him. "She stopped asking after that."

"Shit."

"Yeah."

Gunny slid a keycard through the reader and pushed the door wide with his foot. Bane followed through, shouldering the door to get inside. Myrt was in a chair at the table, feet propped on the seat, knees tight to her chest. She had one arm stretched out to where her and Marian's hands were joined. Marian's position mirrored Myrt, and it struck Bane how much they resembled each other. Marian was as slight as Myrt, same features framed by the same mane of hair.

Myrt cast a trembling smile his direction, filled with a shy hope of something he thought he knew. Bane didn't slow, didn't detour to take off his boots or his cut, didn't stop until he stood in front of Myrt. He crouched low, knee to the floor as he leaned close. He left the decision up to her, hovering near but not touching, gaze locked with hers. She met him halfway, lips parting in a tiny gasp as they connected with his. Still kissing, he smiled and asked her, "You okay, baby?"

"Mmhmm." A hand wrapped around the back of his neck as her hungry mouth opened for him, tongues sliding in a sweet, sweet caress.

"Missed you." He pulled back, breathing as hard as she was. "I got another room for Marian." He jerked his head towards the door. "It's across the hallway."

Gunny cleared his throat. "Actually, thought I could cop the new one from you. Save everyone havin' to see me in the morning before my coffee." Bane twisted to look up at him. "Prolly safer for all involved." Gunny shrugged. "You know how it is."

"I do." He looked at Marian. "You be okay bunkin' with the boys tonight? They're in one bed, so you'd have one to yourself." She nodded, and he noticed the women's hands were still gripped across the table. "Or, I can bunk with the boys, let you girls—"

"No, I'm—no." Myrt clutched at his neck, and he turned to face her. "Please, Bane."

"Yeah, yeah. Shhh, baby. I'm here. You want me, I'm here." He tipped his head towards Marian and then the connecting door. "Boys are through there." He twisted and rocked back on his heels, staying close to Myrt. "It's been a long day. I know we woke you up to talk to us, and I bet you're tired, too."

"Later." The door to the hallway opened and closed, and he realized Gunny had bailed on this encounter.

"Myrt, you know where everything is over there." Bane glanced down at his hand resting on Myrt's knee and saw red embedded around the nails. *Shit.* "I'll get cleaned up. Be waiting on you." She opened her mouth to protest, and he leaned close, touching his mouth to hers again. "Promise, I'll be here." He slipped his hand off, dangling it next to his side. He remembered the chill touch of the dew from earlier in the night, but that was followed directly by the vision of Sallabrook choking to death on half-chewed pieces of dead opossum. He pulled in a deliberate breath, biting down on the inside of his cheek until he tasted blood. "Right here, baby."

She must have let go of Marian, because both Myrt's hands cradled his face, pulling him closer as she leaned her forehead against his, mirroring the pose he'd taken with her so many times. "We're all here. We're safe with you. You saved the boys." She wrapped her arms around his neck, and cheek to cheek spoke into his ear. "Saved me. I'm right here too…" The pause was long, so long he thought she was done talking. "Baby," she finished finally, and he thought it was the sweeter for having to wait.

He stood and she rose from the chair, nestling her shoulder against his ribs, fitting underneath his arm as if she'd always been there with him. Marian watched them carefully, caution keeping her features blank. "I'm going to stay over here." He thumbed over his shoulder. "Gunny's put himself across the hallway." Bane ran his hand up and down Myrt's arm, slow and sweet. "You trusted us once, Marian. You can still trust us. You're safe."

"I know." She turned sideways and took a step until she was next to the wall. He recognized Myrt's move of trying to melt into the furniture, blend with the wall—escape.

"Help your sister." He kissed the top of Myrt's head. "Come back to me when you're ready."

A minute later, both women were through the connecting door, the one from that side closed but not locked. He tested the knob quietly, turning it so slowly the women wouldn't notice. Next he went to the hall door, ensuring it was locked, and slipped the chain into place. Pausing in front of the bathroom, he returned to the connecting door, testing the knob again, only retreating to the bathroom when he was confident he wasn't locked away from Myrt.

Stripped down to skin, he made the trip a final time, hand hovering over the knob before he settled his palm on the metal and twisted slowly. The vibration through his fingers told him what he needed to know.

The water was hot, already steaming up the small bathroom, when he stepped into the shower. Forearms against the wall, he leaned underneath the stream, letting the flow of heat sluice away the stress. He grabbed and unwrapped a bar of soap, scrubbing it across his face and chest. Working it between his hands, he flexed and rubbed until he had a fistful of suds. Dunking his head under the water, he scrubbed it through his hair, ensuring he washed away any remains of his efforts from the night's activities.

Eyes closed, he ran his hands down his chest, turning to put his back to the deluge of hot water. The feel of Myrt in his hands was a memory he never wanted to lose, the soft giving touch of her skin against his. Bane stroked along his cock, root to tip and back again, fingers curling loosely in the kind of touch he liked best. Tipping his head back, he stretched his neck and tightened his abs, feeling that damned welcome tingle low in his belly. Keeping the slow pace on his dick, he reached low, cupping and gripping his balls, stretching his sack for that second welcome burn, the pain revving up the tension.

In his imagination, Myrt was moving through the room, slow and quiet, losing clothing as she came towards him. Her hand reached out, fingers trailing down his belly to his cock.

The wet slide of flesh against flesh filled the shower, the sound of his fingers bumping over the head loud with every satisfying touch.

Myrt's hands landed on his hips, pulling him towards her mouth as she sank gracefully to her knees. She looked up at him from underneath her lashes, mouth in the damned tiny, quiet smile he loved so much.

One hand tugging his sack, the other a blur on his cock, he pushed himself to the edge.

Myrt nuzzled along his cock, burying her nose in the curls near the root, in no hurry to take him in her mouth. Her tongue flicked out, teasing across the slit, dipping in to get a taste she was sure to make a show with, curling her tongue and moaning softly. He sank his fingers into her hair, loose now, a curtain around her naked body as he thrust into her mouth.

Bane groaned and froze, muscles locking in place as he painted the wall with stripes of white.

Even in my mind, she's the best I'll ever have.

He'd tested the doorknob twice since getting out of the shower, each time finding it easy to turn, unlocked, the other room accessible. After extinguishing the lights in the room, he took a chance and pulled the door open an inch. His caution was unnecessary; all four occupants of the room were snoozing. The boys had migrated towards the center of their bed, cheeks resting on the same pillow and Thad's hand covering the back of Luke's head protectively, even in his sleep.

Myrt and Marian were on the other bed in the room, Marian under the covers, her thin wrists sticking out the shirtsleeves of a shirt he didn't recognize. Slumped to one side, Myrt was half propped against the headboard, Marian's head in her lap, fingers tangled in the woman's long hair as if she'd gone to sleep combing it.

Bane glided closer, bare feet making no sound, hovering over Myrt, his hand out in a tentative and aborted caress. Waking her now would be selfish. With the sun breaking the horizon outside, letting her sleep, allowing her to find comfort in having her family all around her, that was the gift he could give her now. He retreated to the other room and grabbed a blanket off the foot of one of the beds. Back in the room with the Threadgill siblings, he draped the fabric over Myrt, tucking it closely around her bare legs and feet.

Those were the last thoughts flashing through his mind before he fell asleep, how small and vulnerable Myrt's feet had felt in his hands. How precious she felt in his arms. How much he wanted her in his life.

Gonna keep her safe.

***

Bane

Sounds rushed over him, pulling Bane from sleep. He kept still, eyes closed, running available information through his head. Everything slipped into place within a breath. The sounds were from the connecting room, a low and pleasant chatter of the boys and Gunny, along with Marian's bright laughter.

Most important wasn't what he could hear, but what he felt.

The mattress at his hip had settled, and there was heat all along his side.

Bane lifted his head, staring down along his body. He'd fallen asleep hips still wound round with the towel, but it had come undone at some point during the night, now angled only across his groin. Myrt was curled up beside him, legs tucked close, her head resting on his ribs. She had one arm stretched across his belly, her hand resting along the edge of the towel.

He dropped his head back onto the pillow with a silent groan. But not before his dick took notice, stiffening and tenting the towel, drawing it in a slow crawl across his skin.

It took willpower, but he reached down and cradled her hand, bringing it up to rest against his chest. It was another minute before he could talk himself into giving up what she'd offered him, this moment where he could see the future he wanted with such clarity he could almost taste her pussy, nearly hear the kids they'd birth and raise.

None of which was helping with the situation underneath the towel.

"Myrt." He bent his head to look at her, stroking along one cheek. "Time to wake up, baby." She sighed deeply, turning her head into him. Her fingers clenched and then spread, flattening against his chest. "Time to get up. Boys are awake."

"Mmffph."

He curled an arm around her, dragging his fingers up and down the bare skin of her arm. "Food and coffee." One thing he'd learned about her while still at Truck's place, his Myrt did love her coffee. "Hot, delicious coffee."

"Instant coffee isn't delicious." She tipped her chin up to look at him, sleepy eyes blinking slowly. "The stuff in the lobby isn't bad, but what passes for coffee in the rooms is terrible."

He stroked his hand over her head, realizing her hair was down. It wasn't the first time he'd seen it uncontained by a tie or a braid, but something about the intimacy of having her in bed with him like this made it profound, and he found himself sliding fingers through it, over and over. She groaned and rolled her neck when he started massaging her scalp. "Feel good, baby?"

"Mmffph." Her head moved, and he felt a different heat on his belly. She'd either licked him or kissed him, or both.

"That feels good, too."

Her chin lifted again, half-hooded eyes no longer sleepy but filled with something else. "Yeah?"

"Oh, yeah." The towel started tenting again, and he remembered his state of undress. "We should probably get out of bed before something happens."

She squirmed closer. "Something good?"

He took a moment to remind himself she wasn't innocent or inexperienced when it came to the mechanics of sex. But she'd never had the kind of emotional intimacy he wanted for their first time. Threading his fingers between hers, he pressed their hands flat against his chest while he stroked her cheek with his other hand. "It would be beyond good, Myrt. But not something I want with you while the door between us and your brothers and sister is partly open. When we go there, baby." He took a gentle grip of her hair, arching her neck backwards as he crunched his way into a partial sit-up. "I want." He brushed his lips across hers. "To take." And back the other way, loving how she fought his hold to chase his mouth. "My time." Covering her mouth with his, he dove deep, tongue stroking and twisting as he kissed her slowly.

She pushed him away and covered her mouth with the hand he wasn't holding. "My breath."

"Don't care." He pushed past her fingers to kiss her again, long and wet, until she was gasping for breath and had forgotten her concerns. Ending with a series of gentle, closed-mouth kisses against the corner of her lips, he smiled. "Now, sweetheart. Coffee and food, in that order."

He swung his legs to dangle from the edge of the bed and looked back at her over his shoulder. Myrt remained still for a moment, lips in a cute pout, which made him want to climb back in beside her. He grabbed the towel as he stood, not trying to hide anything as he wound the fabric back around his hips. Gratifyingly, her attention stayed fixed south, cheeks pinking in the gorgeous way she had. Then, she licked her lips and her legs shifted as her ass wiggled. *Holy shit.*

Oh, yeah, they definitely shared a common interest.

And wasn't that glorious to see.

"We're up, brother," he called towards the barely open connecting door as he walked to the bathroom, scooping up clothing as he went. "Myrt wants some coffee, man."

"Got that covered."

Myrt stirred as Gunny responded, rolling to sit on the bed, her legs in a half circle around her. Her gaze stayed fixed on Bane—and right before he went out of sight through the door, he gave her a show. Stopping and dropping the towel to the floor, he reached back and smacked his own ass lightly. "All yours, any time you want it, Myrt."

"Yeah?" *Jesus.* Her tone was breathy and low, filled with what he hoped was arousal.

"Yeap." Door closed, he leaned back against it, head thudding silently against the surface. He'd meant to tease her a little, see how much interest she had, draw out those intimate moments they hadn't been afforded many of, take them when he could. Glancing down, he chuckled at himself. Instead, he'd been teasing himself, and his cock stood out from his body, head a dark angry red. "I hear ya, little man." Root to tip, he stroked slowly, drawing out each touch until it was a tiny bit of agony with wanting more.

"Bane?" The door behind him rattled and he startled, staring at his reflection in the mirror. "Can I come in a minute?"

A hundred scenarios ran through his head in an instant, but what he chose to focus on was the reminder she wasn't innocent, and she'd clearly seen something she liked. She enjoyed their make-out sessions a lot, and she knew he was naked in here.

Shifting to the side, he kicked the towel across the floor and opened the door, staying out of sight in case she only wanted to tell him something.

Myrt rounded the door and closed it, keeping her hands on the knob and frame before whirling around. Her gasp and wide eyes kept him still; then she reached out to grip his bicep and pull him towards her. Bane hovered over her against the door, caging her in with his arms as he kept his lower body angled away. She made a tiny frustrated noise and gripped his hips, pulling him in tight against her.

Face buried against his chest, Myrt cleared her throat softly. "I know you think I'm this damaged woman. I know a lot of what you think. But I'm not delicate. You won't hurt me. I know that down to my bones, Bane. You would never hurt me. But you are hurting me, and you don't even know it."

"How am I hurting you, baby?"

"By treating me like I can't want you." One of her hands slowly descended his body, fingertips finding and exploring his nipple, then his abs, moving to his hip, and finally arriving at the base of his cock. After several soft, grazing touches, those fingers wrapped around his girth with a firm grip. It felt so good he gritted his teeth but couldn't stay still, flexing his hips to rock into her touch. She gained confidence and glided her fingers and palm up his shaft, stroking to the tip, where she made a little noise of pleasure when she found him leaking precum. She took her time, gathering up the silky fluid and spreading it around the sensitive head, toying with the bundle of nerves underneath the rim. "This doesn't hurt me, Bane." A long stroke, tip to root, then back again slowly, teasing fingertips playing with his slit. "This is something I want."

"You want this, baby?" Her head rocked against him in a nod. "You can have me anytime you want me."

She pressed a kiss against his chest, and he cradled the back of her head, guiding her lips to where she could play with one of his nipples. He hissed when she wrapped her lips around and sucked lightly, the scrape of her teeth exactly what he liked most.

Stepping closer, Myrt pressed against him, both hands folding around and stroking his length, exploring farther, fingertips grazing his sack. He widened his stance, and she looked up at him as she moved to his other nipple. Pupils fully blown, she showed only the tiniest ring of color around the dark centers. Her lips were ruby red and shiny, pursing slightly as she latched on and sucked harder than she had before. Her lids dipped closed as she appeared to give herself over to experiencing him in this way. Myrt's hot palm cradled his balls, gently rolling and tugging as her other hand increased speed, pulling and stroking faster.

Bane kept his eyes on what he could see of her face, focused on the smoothness of her brow, the lift of her cheeks, everything that told him she was doing exactly what she wanted right now. "Damn, baby. Got all kinds of surprises for me, seems like. Lovin' this, watching you take what you want. I want your mouth, Myrt." She disengaged and sagged, and he realized she'd misunderstood him. "Not on my dick, darlin'. Although in the future, not too far from now, I'll take you up on that." He guided her back to standing and leaned down, fingers thrust into the hair at the back of her head as he tilted her neck. "Wanna kiss you, baby." The last word was whispered against her lips, and then his mouth covered hers.

Fucking into her hand, he took possession of her mouth as he started chasing his orgasm in earnest. She moaned and he ate it down, sharing breaths with her, tongues dueling in a sweet joust as hers retreated and he chased into her mouth, teeth on her bottom lip in a tender bite.

"Baby." Her use of the sweet word wasn't tentative, as confident as her hands on his body, and he reveled in her courage within this encounter.

The pleasure sat in the middle of his belly, growing with every glide of her skin against his, and he wanted to have her in bed, be over her, driving into her. That vision mixed with the reality of the kiss and her touch, and he grunted as he came over her hands in long spurts of creamy heat. She didn't stop, the fluid providing more lube until her fingers glided over the too sensitive head in a slippery grip.

Bane broke the kiss with a gasp, shoving her head into the crook of his neck as he panted and tried to slow his pounding heart. "Jesus God, woman. That was phenomenal, baby. Fucktastic all around. Nearly killed me, but I'd have died a happy man."

The belling of Myrt's laughter made him smile. Still resting against him, seemingly uncaring her hands were covered in his spunk, she kissed along his collarbone. "That's not a word."

"Should be. I'm gonna get a shirt that says 'I'm with her and she's fucktastic.' It should be a word."

"It's a good word." She laughed again, that sound tripping pleasure inside him, his gut tightening in reaction. "I wouldn't say that about me, though."

"Did you just have your hand on my dick?" Bane pulled her head back so he could see her face. While he was sweaty and exhausted, she looked only a little flushed but entirely pleased with herself. "And jerk me until I came?" Myrt's lips spread into a wide smile, teeth holding the tip of her tongue as she nodded. "Then let me be the judge of fucktasticability. Which you have in spades, darlin'."

"Another non-word." She dipped her head and pressed a gentle kiss in the center of his sternum. "But another good one." Myrt stepped backwards and he let her go with reluctance, showing it in how he kept his fingers on her, curled around her arms. Bane found himself wishing they had more time so he could explore her newfound confidence. "I need to clean up, and you were going to shower."

"I wasn't." He looked down at the smears of white on his belly and thighs, slathered over his dick. "I am now, though." Glancing up at her in the mirror over the sink, he winked and then grinned. "Wanna join me?"

"I shouldn't." She turned, towel in hand as she looked him up and down, that flush growing to a blush as he made no move to cover himself. "You were such a tease. I couldn't resist."

"I can tease more." He stepped closer, dropping his mouth to hover above hers. "Happy to do all the teasin' you want, baby."

Myrt closed the distance, and he let her lead them down a path of sweet and slow, caresses more than kisses. She ended with her forehead pressed against his, a position he'd initiated many times, and one she seemed to have grown fond of. Gazes locked, they stayed like that for a dozen breaths; then she lowered off her toes and broke the connection with a sigh.

"I'm going to see what they've left for breakfast." She stepped to the door and opened it slightly, hand on the knob keeping it from swinging wide. Looking back over her shoulder, she smirked. "If you're quick, I'll save you a plate."

"You want quick, you get quick." He reached into the shower and turned on the water, the sound of the pulsating flow filling the small room. "Later, baby, you'll get slow."

Cheeks pink, she fled the bathroom, door closing with a firm snick behind her.

Holy shit. Did that really just happen?

Bane glanced down, his dick already twitching and trying to get back into the game at the idea of a later with Myrt.

Oh yeah, that just happened.

Now he had to figure out a way to have it be an everyday occurrence with Myrt. Needed to find a way to fold her into his life, even as they'd barely taken on the responsibility for her brothers and her older sister.

"Don't matter the challenges."

Bane stepped into the shower.

"She's worth it all."

Chapter Eleven

Myrtle

Seated on the edge of the bed farthest from the connecting door, Myrt was giggling with Luke over a tale he was spinning, which included a knight in shining white cotton on a ten-speed bike, when movement caught her attention. She looked up to see Bane standing in the doorway, shoulder pressed to one side of the frame. One thumb tucked into the edge of his back pocket, he stared at her with a look she could only have described as hungry.

Myrt covered her cheeks with her palms, not surprised to find them hot. She expected embarrassment to be the overriding reaction to seeing him again after what she'd done in the bathroom, but what she was feeling was as far from that as possible. Heat coiled through her, rising past her chest and into her throat.

He winked and smirked, one corner of his mouth lifting before he turned to face Gunny.

"Save me some coffee at least, brother?"

Gunny had apparently been watching the exchange, because he stared at Bane, then Myrt, then snorted and pointed to the table in the room. "Myrt insisted on a plate, so you got cold eggs, cold sausage, and cold toast. The only thing warm is the fruit." He tugged an empty Styrofoam cup off a stack next to the coffee pot. "Coffee's hot. I took Luke with me and we sweet-talked the gal behind the counter downstairs for some real, at least." He angled his head and grinned at Luke and Myrt. "Boy's a natural."

"Like brother like sister," Bane quipped, throwing Myrt another wink. "Traits that definitely come in handy at times."

"So Marian and I were talking," Gunny started, and Myrt shot a glance at Marian, seeing her already nodding. Whatever Gunny was about to say, Myrt's sister was entirely on board with it. "We're going to take the van and head out. I'm pretty well rested, and it'll be better if we get on the road sooner than later. Wanna get back to my old lady and kids, too." He pointed at Bane. "You two—" Gesturing towards Myrt, he turned fully and faced her. "—need to take care of the local business so we don't have anyone"—he glanced at Luke, who was now engrossed in telling Thad a story—"ookinglay for the oysbay."

"How am I supposed to do that, brother?" Bane stood in front of the tiny microwave, watching his plate go round and round, not bothering to turn around for this discussion. Myrt was lost, the conversation between the two men making no sense. "Here, where I got no pull or sway?" He shrugged and took the plate out of the microwave when it beeped, turning with fork in hand, already hovering over the food. "You forget, my patch ain't your patch."

Gunny started laughing, the raucous sound rolling through the room.

"You first used his name and then bothered to gain permission. The fuck you think he'd do, play at taker-backers? Mason's word is good, and unless you hear differently from the big man himself, you've got one clear path ahead of you." He lifted his mug as Myrt's stomach flipped over. "Patch or no patch. You're no fraudy fraudy froggy frog, waitin' on the princess' kiss to start things movin'. Do your thang, brother. It's all good."

Marian blurted, "Do you mean Davis Mason? You know him?"

The boys had gone still at the name, and Myrt wondered if they felt the same paralyzing fear she did. Davis Mason's shadow fell across more mountains than just theirs. He was the powerful son of a local man. His father, Irving Mason, was remembered in cautionary tales about how not to live and what not to do. That man starred in many people's nightmares, still.

His son was known as a much better man than the father had ever hoped to be but held enormous amounts of power locally. He owned a number of businesses and was known to offer interest-free loans to help younger couples stay in the area, buying houses he sold back to them as lease-ownership deals, and brokering benefits for businesses to keep jobs from moving out of the county.

"Yeah, you know him?" Gunny tipped his head to the side and stared at Marian, then swept his gaze to Myrt and the boys. "He's a good man. Good to his core. I'd do anything for him." He shrugged. "Hell, me being here right now is because he asked. I'd planned on stayin' back with my family and letting a local crew help Bane here." Gunny's hand swept wide to indicate the man still eating, albeit more slowly. "But Mason picked up the phone and asked, and I answered."

"We—" Marian looked at Myrt, who nodded her approval, not knowing what her sister was going to say but understanding it needed to be a joint effort. "—know of him. Good things. Real good things. He's like the local guardian angel."

"His daddy was a bastid." Luke's blurted words were loud in the still room, and every eye turned towards the boy. He flushed red as a beet, hiding his face against Myrt's shoulder. "Sorry." His mumbled apology was muffled and quiet.

"His daddy was indeed a bastard and a half," Gunny agreed readily. His expression had changed, darkening as if with something remembered. "Glad as hell the old man's no longer around to dirty the same air you and I are breathin'."

"Okay." Bane set his plate down and lifted his mug, taking a long drink. "Got it. Name's got significant collateral around here and should be able to pull things into line with what we want. So if you're headed to Florida in the van, what are Myrt and I gonna ride around in?"

"On, not in." Gunny gestured towards the window. "Pulled a favor outta my ass and got a bike dropped off last night that one of the Florida boys is interested in. You'll save him the delivery fee if you ride it down. It'll be like we owe you. Kinda hilarious, if you look at it that way."

Myrt looked at Marian, who shrugged and nodded, then swung her gaze to Bane, who was studying Gunny intently. It took several beats, but he relaxed eventually, giving Gunny a sharp lift of his chin. Slowly, the movement fraught with a meaning she couldn't understand, he advanced towards Gunny with his hand extended. They collided with force, fists clasped between their chests, other arm pounding each other's backs firmly.

"Means a lot, brother." Bane pulled away as he spoke, turning to look at Myrt. "We'll visit a bike shop here in town today, get you a tie for your hair. Keep it from being a snarled mess." Lines appeared between his brows, and he shook his head. "Leathers and helmet, too. Need to keep my baby safe."

Those words landed on her like the soft drape of a protective blanket. Then her stomach gave an ill-timed lurch and she bolted for the bathroom. Closing the door was impossible, as it met something solid behind her, but she ignored that as she fell to her knees in the small room, already retching. A familiar hand, large and rough with calluses, landed on the back of her neck as water turned on in the nearby sink.

"She's okay." Bane's voice came from above her, and Myrt spared a glance for the door. Marian stood there, fingers twisting into knots in front of her belly. "Promise, little sister. She's okay. Close the door and give her some privacy, yeah?"

Myrt retched again, then spat, the soft snick of the latch telling her Marian had consented to Bane's request.

"I told her last night." She sat up and swayed sideways until her shoulder hit the wall. Scrubbing the back of her hand across her mouth, Myrt was surprised at the touch of a cool cloth on her cheek. Bane's fingers curled around her chin, and he tilted her face up, gently cleaning away the sweat brought on by her body's efforts. "The boys don't know."

"They were asleep while you and your sister had a little girl time." Understanding deepened the gentle smile he wore. "Looked like you had a lot of catching up to do."

"Her life, Bane. It's been so much worse than I knew." She pushed to her knees and wrapped her arms around his neck. "Thank you. For everything. All of it. I know you took some blackness on your soul yesterday. For me." The marvel flooded through her again, as it had every time she considered what lengths he and Gunny had gone to for her and her family. "I won't ever be able to pay back the things you've done for us."

"No need to pay back a damn thing, baby." His arms curled around her and he stood, lifting, and she instinctively wrapped her legs around his waist. "Do it again in a heartbeat. And not just for you." One of his hands slid up her back, coming to rest cradling her skull. "Do it for anyone caught in a web not of their making, where their life is miserable and hard. Where I can make a difference, I will." He laughed and leaned back, staring into her face. "Not to paint myself as a Robin Hood, because I most definitely am not one of those. I'm more of a pain-in-the-ass kind of character." He dipped closer and brushed his lips across her cheek. "Puttin' myself out there with this, hopin' you won't shoot me down." The hand on her ass squeezed, pulling her closer, and Myrt melted against him, elbows on his shoulders. "I'm countin' on the fact that I'm your kind of pain in the ass, baby. Think you'd wanna keep an old reprobate like me?"

The expression on his face was so vulnerable, filled with so much hope, that Myrt held back her smile, not wanting him to think she found his plea amusing. Instead, she rested her head against his shoulder, lips to his throat as she gave him a promise she'd never expected to say to anyone.

"I really like you, Bane. If you want to be my pain in the butt, then that makes me your pain in the butt in return. If you want to take that on, knowing everything you know about me and my—" She broke off, not sure how to frame the pregnancy.

"Your baby." Bane didn't seem to have the same problem, and she nodded at his words. "If we do this, Myrtle, then that stops being your baby." He jostled her and she sat up, staring into his face. "It's our baby. You and me, do or die. We get this right and we can deal with everything else as it comes. But puttin' it out there that I don't think I like you, baby. I know it." He kissed the tip of her nose. "I love you."

"I need to brush my teeth." Myrt clamped her lips closed and shut her eyes, willing the sudden tears away. His declaration had taken her by surprise. Even though he'd been the one starting this conversation, she hadn't known he was in as deep as she already was.

"You want a kiss, baby?" She nodded and he chuckled, bending her sideways towards the sink. "Give it a good rinse if that bothers you, and then get back up here and get your kiss on, darlin'."

Trusting he'd hold her steady, she turned on the faucet and scooped up water with both hands, filling her mouth multiple times as she swished the taste of her morning sickness away. When she straightened in his arms, Bane didn't give her a moment to think, crashing his mouth onto hers and demanding entrance with persistent swipes of his tongue.

It was only moments before she was panting for breath, heart in her throat as he sat her on the edge of the counter. Hands roaming up and down her back, he settled with a palm on each globe of her butt and gripped almost painfully as he yanked her forwards. With his hard dick grinding into the softness between her legs, she lost herself in the sensation of pressure and heat. Her head fell backwards and she arched against him as Bane dropped hard kisses along her neck, ending each with a bite that pinched and stung. She knew he was marking her and didn't care, didn't wonder why, couldn't think about anything except his body against hers.

"All good in there?" Gunny's voice was accompanied by a hard rapping against the door, and Bane groaned, breaking off from kissing her again to drop his head against hers.

"You are a serious pain in my ass." Bane's lips against hers demanded another kiss, and Myrt gladly gave it, teasing along the crease of his lips with the tip of her tongue. "And you're killin' me softly."

"We're packin' up to go, brother."

"Okay, okay. We'll be right out." Bane's eyes were dark and intense, the look he gave her filled with promises she took on faith. "Seems bathrooms aren't our thang, darlin'. Let's get them gone, and then take care of business. I'll book one room for another night, so we can leave tomorrow fresh." He kissed her hard, going from zero to a hundred miles an hour in a breath. "And tonight, tonight you're mine."

"I am." Her quiet agreement seemed to fuel him, and he pressed his mouth to hers again and again, biting her lip in that sexy way as he stared deep into her eyes. "Bane." She didn't know what she was asking for by saying his name, but he seemed to know.

"We *will* reconnect on this later." Backing up a step, he lifted her from the countertop and slid her down his body until her feet rested on the floor. "And that, my dear, is a promise from me to you."

Both boys were staring at the door as she walked out, and it was only moments before their expressions went from anxious to amused. She shook her head as Thad turned to say something to Luke, mouth hidden by one lifted hand. Marian was right there, arms out, and Myrt folded her arms around her sister, holding her close.

Last night had been a revelation, providing an unwelcome window into the rage and brutality their father had subjected Marian to over the years. She'd never been sexually abused, but the mental and physical anguish had been incessant. So much, that when two rough-looking strangers had shown out of the blue and claimed to be rescuers sent from her sister, Marian hadn't hesitated more than an instant before gathering her things and bolting. "Anything was better than there" had been the explanation, a falsity Myrt felt like contradicting, but the past was in the past, and there'd be time to teach her sister whatever life lessons were needed. Talking far into the night had drawn them closer, and Myrt couldn't wait to see how Marian would take to being free.

Free.

She lifted her gaze to find Bane looking at her. Pressing her lips together, she dipped her chin and permitted herself only the smallest of smiles. She knew beyond a shadow of a doubt that free was exactly what he was offering. Freedom to grow and learn more about herself. Freedom to trust and believe in his affections. Freedom to explore the sweeter side of life.

Free indeed.

The flurry of leave-taking activities carried her through the sudden terror at seeing her family, so recently reclaimed, drive away in the van. Myrt looked sideways at the motorcycle parked next to where she and Bane stood. The arm he had wrapped around her shoulders tightened, and he rocked her back and forth.

"I'll keep you safe, darlin'. Promise from me to you. I'll always keep you safe."

"I'm as much excited as nervous about riding with you." She followed when he turned to go inside, their joined hands a tight bond between them. "I trust you." Ducking under his arm, she went through the door he held open. "Before we go anywhere, can I ask you a couple of questions?" She took the stairs double-time so he didn't have to slow his pace.

Inside the room, he sat in a chair, drawing her to stand between his legs. "You can ask me anything, Myrtle. I'm an encyclopedia when it comes to bikes."

She settled on his thigh, steered there by his hands on her hips. Leaning against his chest, she laughed. "I don't have any questions about the bike."

"Then what, darlin'?" One large hand slipped down her arm and folded around her fingers, threading through and flexing to hold her firmly.

"Tell me about yesterday. I want to know everything." He turned to stone underneath her touch, and she pressed closer, lifting her lips to softly kiss the edge of his jaw. "They're both dead, aren't they? I just need to know for sure."

"Yeah, darlin'." His voice was soft and cautious. In between words, the only movement was the rise and fall of his breathing. She lifted her hand and placed it flat on his chest, realizing his heart was thundering. "They're both dead." He repeated her words back to her, flat and implacable. "What else do you want to know?"

"Did they die easy?" She moved her hand to curl around his neck, snuggling closer.

"No, Myrt. They didn't. They died hard." His tone was stiff. "Where you goin' with this?"

"They can't hurt anyone, ever again?"

Bane relaxed the tiniest amount as he took in a deeper breath. "No, baby. Never again."

"Daddy beat Marian. Badly and often. So much she said it was a rare Sunday she attended church, and she'd always been one to seek peace in worship." Myrt chewed on the inside of her cheek. *Could I have helped?* "I didn't know, Bane. I promise I didn't know what her life was like. Every time I saw her, I worried, but I never asked. Why didn't I ask?" That had been the thought circling her brain when talking to Marian.

"Baby, it wasn't like you were in a position to have done anything about it. Not trapped like you were with Sallabrook." Bane stroked slowly down her back, his hand coming to rest against her hip. "In over your head, both of you were drowning in different pools of shit. That's a precarious balance on a good day. Adding a layer of misery belonging to someone else could have been enough to send either of you under. Don't beat yourself up over the fact you were worn out simply trying to exist. That's not on you, but on the bastard who thought he owned you."

Tightening her hold on him, she asked again, needing reaffirmation, "He's really dead?"

"Yeah, darlin'. Yes, and yes. Sallabrook will never lay a hand on another person." She felt pressure against the top of her head and knew he'd laid a kiss there. "Not you, not the boys, and no future anybody. Never again."

"So what's next?" She rolled her head and touched her lips to the base of his neck, happily returning the affection.

"Need a decision from you." He'd gone still again, telegraphing the importance of his question. "Do you want the baby to inherit from their sperm donor? The place on the mountain, and any assets the bastard held, should go to his next of kin."

"No." She didn't have to consider or think; the response was visceral. "He's got—had—older kids. They should get his things. I—" Myrt hated the tiny bit of hesitation inside her, fear of cutting ties like this, even if it was what she wanted. Saying what she intended to say set her adrift, ending her association with a man who'd owned her for a third of her life. He might not have cared for her, but she'd had food and shelter, and by denying his relationship with the baby growing in her belly, she was condemning the child to a life without a father. *The only way forward is through the flames.* "I don't want anyone here to know the baby is his."

"Baby is ours." Growled out, the words reverberated through her, and Myrt pressed another kiss against the notch at the base of his throat. "I'm not destitute, Myrt. You want to set aside any claim to Sallabrook's estate, that's your prerogative. But I will not let you go without. Feels like I keep sayin' that I promise or askin' you to trust me, but I'm all in, baby. Gonna take care of you. Of us. And that includes the bump."

His hand slipped around to cover her low belly, and she laughed, the sound so loud in the quiet of the room that she cut if off, silencing herself. "I'm amazed by you, Bane."

"You got any other questions, darlin'?" He created space between their bodies, holding her far enough away he could look down into her face. "If not, then I need to get business taken care of so we can come back and relax. Revisit those moments we've had interrupted. See where we go next in that arena."

The hungry expression on his face gave her the courage she needed to be bold. "I know where I wanna go." Bane swallowed hard, muscles in his neck working as his jaw clenched. His reaction to her words emboldened her further. "I want to take you all the way. Want to find out what it's like to play, to tease." On impulse she stretched up, relieved and pleased when he met her halfway. The kiss was tender and passionate, one trembling along the edge of her control. Bane pulled away, and she choked off a groan, which made him laugh quietly. "Seems you've got the teasing part down already."

"Baby, we've got business to tend to first." He guided her to stand, then pushed back the chair to climb to his feet, too. "This'll be the only time you hear me say business before pleasure. We gotta deal with a couple of things, and then you're all mine."

"Or…" She grinned as he lifted her hand to his mouth, kissing her knuckles. Everything he did gave her more confidence, a willingness to pull him close. "You're all mine."

***

Bane

The day had delivered a series of surprises, and every single one of them had been positive. Bane had kept waiting for the other shoe to drop, expecting to find trouble around the corner, or at least questions that were hard to answer.

He'd first made a call to Blackie, needing to bring him up to speed on everything that had happened since their earlier conversation. He went into greater detail about the events on the mountain, and laid out their planned next steps.

Fortunately Mason had already talked to Blackie, expounding on the RWMC ask where it touched on Myrt via Truck and Vanna. With shrewd questions, Blackie had steered the conversation, ending with a musing, "Need to get my ass to Florida, seems. See you in a couple of days." The man hadn't given Bane time to respond, disconnecting and leaving only dead air in his wake.

The next call had been to Mason, wanting to give him a heads-up on the name-dropping Bane planned on doing today. Not only had the man been entirely on board with the idea, he'd immediately initiated a three-way call with the local sheriff. Obviously well known to the lawman,

Mason had been judicious with the details he'd offered, without dropping anything incriminating.

"Yeah, everyone knows Sallabrook's place burned down yesterday. I'm going to call in an investigator." Sheriff Heame laughed, the sound broken by a wet and awful cough. "Man died in bed. If you ask me, too easy a death for a bastard of a man."

"What'd it take for you to drop your investigation and take face value into your reports?" Mason's question was far more direct than one Bane would have posed, but it seemed to be the right tack with the sheriff.

"That question's enough for me." Another series of coughs. "Mountain cleansing herself, way I look at it. She kept the fire from damaging anything else in that clearing. Barn, trees—hell, Sallabrook's truck wasn't even singed. Divine intervention. Man like me?" He chuckled and Bane braced for another round of coughing, relieved when it didn't present itself. "I won't question God's plan."

"Good deal." Mason was quiet for a beat, then asked something Bane hadn't expected. "You know about the trafficking happening in your county?"

"Yeah. Can't get my hands on the bastards or I'd kill 'em myself." Heame's voice firmed, growing serious. "We ain't had shit like this since your daddy's times, Davis. Not to speak ill of the dead, but he seemed to inspire some sadistic fellas, didn't he?"

"So you wouldn't be opposed to having some shit cleared up on that patch of ground?" Mason's question was light, airy, his tone not conveying the gravity of the question. Bane held his breath, waiting.

"Nope. Count it as another blessing."

"Threadgill's dead. His girls and two youngest sons are under my direct protection as of a week ago."

"Shee-it." Heame sighed heavily, the sound echoing on the phone's speaker. "How'd he pass, if you don't mind me asking?"

"Tripped and fell into a hole of his own makin'." Mason wasn't leaving anything up for interpretation, fortunately.

"Well, that'll do it for a fella. Sure enough. Anythin' you need from me and mine?"

"Yeah. I've got a man on the line. He's in town now at my direction, you feel me?" Mason paused as Heame made an agreeable noise. "He's gonna show at your office in an hour for Threadgill's daughter to sign off on anything you need signed."

"Marian? She's a good girl. Too bad her daddy's been—that he was such a waste of space."

"No, cousin." Mason revealed his connection to the sheriff, and Bane nodded to himself at the understanding. "Threadgill's younger daughter, Myrtle."

Heame's intake of air had a hoarse whistle to it, and he hummed for a few brief notes. "I got the picture now, Davis. I got it and I'm all over it. We'll take care of the girl. My daddy's still got some rentals. I'll see if one's open, put her up until we can get her on her feet."

"She's taken care of just fine." Bane spoke for the first time, uncaring if Heame had understood Mason's reference earlier about him being on the line. "I needed to know you weren't going to try and bury her with all that's landed on your doorstep this morning."

"Hell, man, Threadgill isn't even on my radar yet. I can take my time with that one, maybe a varmint'll deal with it for me. Hate to have to euthanize me a bear, but can always relocate one if needed. I got the DNR boys on speed dial." Heame didn't miss a beat at Bane's interjecting himself into the conversation. "Good to know Myrt's landed on her feet. Sallabrook was out of his mind these past weeks, scouring the hills for anyone who mighta had sight of her."

"Where do you want us, and when?" He could let the lawman dictate this small piece of the action, giving him a message that because Mason trusted him, so did Bane. Giving away control was a risky move, but it felt right in the moment.

"Brother, sounds like you've got this. I'm gonna click off. I got places to be." Mason paused, then added, "See you in two days, yeah? Take your time, but not too much. We've plans to tend to."

Mason was referring to the same business Blackie had referenced earlier, and Bane had a brief instant of trepidation. Then Myrt strolled into view, bag in hand. He'd asked her to go through the room Marian had shared with the boys and pack up anything inadvertently left behind. Relaxed and calm, the lines of her shoulders sloped down, tendons in her neck not straining and visible for the first time in a while. She was comfortable here with just him, no more buffering presence of other people. It reminded him of how easy she'd been in the van when it had been just them.

"I hear you, brother." Myrt looked up at his words and gave him a broad smile, lifting the bag slightly as she shrugged one shoulder. "Oh, yeah, I hear you. Heame." He turned away from Myrt after shooting her a wink that had her cheeks pinking. "Did you say when?"

"Right now and the diner sound good, if you can make it that soon. No need to come to the office for this. I'll send my boy. He'll be up to speed."

"I'll buy the pie," Bane offered, and Mason's laughter cut off as he disconnected. "We'll see him in a couple minutes. We're right at the edge of town."

Seated at the table with Myrt's hand in his, he watched as a tall man in a tan shirt and dark pants strolled in. Heame Junior. had dispensed with his duty belt, wore only a simple hip holster to carry his service weapon. When his gaze landed on their table, he smiled broadly, Bane bristling at his unmistakable pleasure at seeing Myrtle.

Heame nodded at Bane, then held out his hand to Myrt, bending at the waist so she didn't have to rise from her seat. Bane stood slowly, unfolding to his full height and staring down his nose at the deputy.

"Myrtle, I'm glad to see you looking so well. You had us all worried—" Heame dashed a glance at Bane, then cut his gaze back to Myrtle. "And, well, I'm sure glad you're okay."

"I'm doing well, Thomas." The familiarity in her voice hit Bane like a brick wall. For some reason he hadn't expected her to know this man, hadn't anticipated Mason's professed cousins would have personal experience in Myrt's life that excluded Bane. He didn't like it. Myrt tugged at his hand, and he realized he'd kept his grip, holding tight. She tugged again. "Isn't that right, Will?"

Her denial to give Heame his club name was confusing until he looked at her, really looked at her. She was concerned, and he remembered she hadn't been on the call with Mason and the older Heame earlier, only having what Bane had told her to go on.

She's protecting me. He relaxed his grip, then gave her a gentle squeeze. *So fuckin' cute.*

"I didn't catch what you said, but I still agree, darlin'." He knew the hesitation Heame had showed earlier was because he'd nearly called Myrt a sweet name. "Whatever you want, babe." *Fuck this dude.* "Anything you need, honey." There, he'd covered about all of them in one fell swoop. "Sweetheart." *Nearly forgot one.*

"Silly man." Ignoring Heame, who still hadn't officially greeted Bane, she stared up at him. "I could ask you for anything and you'd cave."

"Before the request was even off your sweet lips, yes, ma'am."

"I'm gonna have sweet tea and a piece of pie, Deloris. Server's choice." Heame pulled out a chair and sat, looking over his shoulder at the waitress. "Myrt's Mr. Crow here said he's buying, so I'll take a chance on whatever looks good today."

"You got it, Thomas."

Heame tipped his head to the side and looked at Myrt for a long moment, his expression serious. "Myrt, I'm sorry to tell you I've got bad news." Myrt's muscles tensed and her fingers gripped hard. "Sallabrook's cabin burned to the ground. He was in it, unfortunately."

Her gasp was real, shocked, and Bane was glad he hadn't told her the specifics on anything that had happened. "Oh my God." She didn't glance around, staring straight at Heame. "The barn, did it burn, too?"

"No, it didn't. Funny enough the fire was completely contained to the cabin. Hardly any of the yard around got even scorched."

"Oh, thank God. Do you need to know anything about the animals or anything?"

Bane studied the side of her face, dissecting the expression he could see. She wasn't being disingenuous. This was a real question for her. Heame must have come to the same assessment, because he answered her question directly, without implying she should have any other kind of reaction.

"Nah, all taken care of." The man's lips pulled to the side in a puzzled smile. "It's all covered."

"Oh, okay." She glanced down and seemed to realize how tightly she was gripping Bane's fingers, easing up and throwing him a quick smile that didn't come close to reaching her eyes. Chin angled towards the large plate glass window across the front of the diner, she murmured, "I'm sorry for his family's loss."

"Really?" Bane cupped her chin in his palm, turning her face towards his. "You're sorry for that son of a bitch's death?"

"His kids always treated me nice. I used to tell myself they didn't know the man their daddy'd become." She gave him that tiny smile, the real one, then pressed her lips against the tip of his thumb. "I can be sorry they've lost a member of their family without mourning the death itself."

"Better person than I am, Myrt." Heame broke the moment with his interjection as Bane and Myrt both turned to look at him. "There's more news, hon—there's more news. You tell me when you're ready." The server approached with a plate of pie, a tall glass of iced tea, and the coffee carafe dangling from one finger.

By mutual unspoken agreement, they all sat quietly while food was distributed and drinks were refilled. Once the server had retreated behind the counter, Bane turned to Myrt. She was staring at Heame. "Might as well get it over with, Thomas."

Heame had just shoved a bite of pie into his mouth, and he held up a finger as he nodded. "Mmhmm." Picking up his glass, he took a series of swallows of the tea, ending with a soft "Ahhh." Fork resting on the pie plate, he looked from Bane to Myrt and back again. "No way to do this easy, and for that I'm sorry. Your father is dead." Bane noted the man didn't say was killed and didn't mention murder. He held still, waiting. Heame didn't disappoint, kicking the proverbial "other shoe" off the field entirely. "Looks like he had a heart attack drinking coffee on his front porch. No more than a couple of days ago." Myrt's breathing sped up, rasping in and out of her nose, her hold on Bane's hand rigid. "Hate to say this, but varmints got to him. It's not pretty. I talked to old man Knowles over at the funeral home and he recommends no open anything. Be easier all around to simply cremate him." He shook his head. "I know it's a lot to dump on you at once—"

"Cremate him. Tell Mr. Knowles to do with the ashes whatever is normal when the family doesn't want them." Her chin was wobbling, but she got the words out without faltering. "He's been dead to us for a long time, Thomas, and I know you know it. It's a blessing, really. Frees Marian up to live her own life."

"Where is Marian?" Heame flicked a glance at Bane, then settled his gaze back on Myrt. "She wasn't around when we did a wellness check. Looks like some of her stuff is missing."

"She's in Florida with friends." Bane leaned closer to Myrt and curled his arm around the back of her chair. "Been there for a few days." He shrugged. "Longer than Threadgill's been dead."

"Oh, I wasn't implying anything, truly." Heame shook his head. "We—I wanted to make sure she's being taken care of. Her life's been sheltered in a lot of ways, while less so in others. Would hate for someone to take advantage of her."

"My sister is being looked after, as are my brothers." Myrt stood, shoving back her chair. "I need a minute. I'll be right outside." She put her hand on Bane's shoulder when he would have risen to stand with her. "I'm good, baby." Her hesitation was almost nonexistent this time, and Bane loved seeing that swell of confidence show up again. "I just want a minute, okay?"

Hand cradling the back of her head, he brought her down to touch their lips together in a brief caress. "Okay. I'm here, baby. You need me, I'm right here. No matter what." Watching her walk away, he didn't turn back to Heame until she'd quietly closed the door behind her and gone to the curb near the bike, taking a seat. "You did that pretty well."

"Well, when Davis Mason asks for something and it's within our power, we'll do our best to make it happen." Heame's fork scraped across the empty plate, chasing the last smears of filling. "Good men do bad things with the best of intentions sometimes. Don't mean it's not the right thing, because in both of these cases those sumbitches needed to die." He shrugged, then picked up his glass and drained it. "Thanks for the pie, Mr. Crow. I appreciate your hospitality." He stuck out his hand as he stood. "I'll wait by the door. Give Myrt her couple of moments before I need to say my goodbyes. My dispatcher has all the papers she needs to sign, but Myrt don't need me around for that." He gripped tightly, and Bane stood, leaning across the little table as he bore down harder, feeling tendons pop under his fingers. "She needs you though, plain to see. Be good to her, Crow."

"Oh, I will be. She's my queen." His forearm bulged as he found another ounce or two of pressure in his grip.

Heame grimaced, his fingers flying free in surrender, and Bane let him go. He brought out his wallet and pulled two bills from the folds. Holding them between his fingers, he caught the attention of the waitress and dropped them to the table with a nod. She smiled and grabbed a tray, headed their direction.

"Thanks much, ma'am." Following Heame to the door, he waved off her question about change. "All yours,

Deloris." Outside, Myrt turned to look at them, her expression melancholy. "We've got paperwork to tend to, honey." Nodding, she stood and brushed off her ass, turning to face Heame. He didn't say anything, simply opened his arms, and she stepped near for a brief, impersonal embrace. "Thomas has somewhere else to be. You ready to ride, baby?"

"Yeah." She turned and flowed to him, her arms wrapping around him in a way they hadn't Heame, her body melding to his in a way he couldn't mistake. This was her making a statement to him, and probably to Heame. "Sooner we finish up, the sooner we can be back at the hotel." Her chin lifted and she smiled through a fake pout, something he found immediately irresistible, dropping his mouth to cover hers. "Mmmm."

The barely there hum had him ready to pounce, but they were once again in public, where the kind of activities he wanted to conduct were entirely frowned on. "Helmet." Hands on her upper arms, he set her back from him, putting needed distance between their bodies. "Or your good friend is going to have to arrest me for indecent exposure." He booped the end of her nose, glad when she smiled at the silly moment. "Paperwork, then it's you and me and a hotel bed, baby. Rest of the day."

"Y'all be safe." Bane glanced up to see Heame had turned away, walking towards his cruiser. "See you around, Myrtle."

Myrt called out a "See ya" while keeping her eyes fixed on Bane's.

"Okay, cop shop and then back to the bike dealership, see if they scrounged up the things we need." He fingered her braid as she adjusted the chinstrap on her helmet. "When we're out on the highway, the wind'll snarl all this beauty. Can't have you fighting that at the end of the day." Slinging a leg over the bike, he heeled the kickstand up and balanced the machine between his thighs. "Climb on, baby."

"What do I have to sign at the sheriff's office?" Hands on his shoulders, she stepped on the foot pegs and settled onto the seat behind him. "Just about my dad, right?"

"I suspect. But we'll know for sure when we get there." He started the bike, grinning when her fingers clamped down on his shoulders in surprise. "Ready?" Looking back, he saw and felt her let go for an instant to give him a thumbs-up before her hand returned to its position. "Here we go."

Heame hadn't lied about making things easy on Myrt. Someone somewhere had found or forged a back-dated and registered document giving her authority to make decisions about Threadgill's remains. Two signatures later, the sympathetic dispatcher was faxing the information to the funeral home.

They'd been nearly ready to leave when Bane received a text asking him to wait.

A few minutes later, a man had walked in, introduced himself as Myrt's lawyer, provided by Mason Corp., a business Bane hadn't known existed. After leading them into a private meeting room off the bullpen, he'd gone over the financial status of her father's estate, given some recommendations about escrow, and then had her sign a document giving him authority to deal with the estate disposal. The money would be split evenly between Threadgill's children from all of his wives. Then the lawyer produced an approved guardianship filing, making Myrt responsible for both Luke and Thad, so they wouldn't have to deal with the state. The dispatcher was even a notary public, and as easy as that, everything was legal, filed, documented, and final. The lawyer left without a long goodbye, reminding Myrt to let him know of any changes in the boys' status.

An hour later, Bane was following her up the stairs at the hotel, watching her hips sway underneath the waistband of the leather jacket he'd bought her. The bike shop had turned over stones to provide everything he'd been looking for. First had been a long braid-keeper to ensure her hair wouldn't become unmanageable. If she wanted to cut it, that would be her decision, but he didn't want it to be in response to something he'd initiated. Next had been a pair of boots for her, followed by the jacket. Then he'd caught Myrt fingering the fabric of a couple of soft shirts, so they'd gone into the sack, too.

Now they were here.

They were here and Bane was inordinately nervous. It was as if all the denial and interruptions were culminating in something he'd built up so much in his head that he was afraid it would be nothing at all like he hoped.

He crowded close behind her as she swiped the keycard, unlocking the door. Her half-shy smile over her shoulder at him helped dispel the unfounded fears, and then they were inside and the door closed behind them.

Bane took her hand and led her to the bed, seating himself as she moved to stand between his knees.

He cradled her hand in both of his, exploring the lines and angles of her fingers and knuckles, lifting it to his mouth as he lavished attention on each digit. Without looking up, he wanted to make sure he had her attention. "Baby?"

"Yeah, Bane?" Breathy and airy, her response exposed her arousal from something as simple as this.

"How you doin'? Was a busy day, yeah?" Her fingers trembled in his hands.

"It was a day, for sure. I'm okay, though. Better now."

"I wanna make love to you." He drew her thumb into his mouth and sucked hard, rolling his tongue around the tip. Pulling off with a pop, he told her, "Wanna kiss you all over, take my time, crawl between your legs and use all my tricks to make you feel good in all the ways I know how." Pressing his lips to her palm, he drew her hand across his face, then looked up. "If you aren't down for that, tell me now, baby."

"I'm down." She edged closer, her knees between his thighs. "Please, Bane."

"Okay, then." He rubbed his cheek against her belly, kissing and mouthing through her shirt. "Lose the jacket and boots. You do your part and I'll do the rest." She stepped back as he levered off the bed, looming over her before he swooped in for a hard, fast kiss. "Hurry, baby."

By the time she had struggled off both boots and hung up the jacket, Bane was nude and reclining on the bed. He didn't want anything coming between them if he could help it. She turned and froze, staring at his half-hard dick, her perfect mouth opening and closing.

"Come on over here, Myrt. I don't bite." When her gaze landed on his face, he winked at her. "Hard, at least." She approached the bed, and he held out a hand, beckoning her on. "That's it." Her lips stretched in a strained smile and he jackknifed, bending to meet her halfway. Hooking his hands under her arms, he pulled her onto the bed as he fell backwards, dragging her on top of him. The pressure against his dick was exquisite, verging on painful but lost in the perfection of knowing she was with him in this thing between them.

Fingers to the hem of her shirt, he lifted and she moved her arms, arching her body until he could remove it. Her bra was next, a deft flick of his fingers defeating the clasp, and he dragged the straps down each arm, flinging it to the side as he had her shirt.

He pulled in a steadying breath as he stared at her. Hooking his hands under her arms again, he dragged her higher until he could worship her breasts. Mouth and fingers, tongue and teeth, he teased and sucked until she called his name on a hoarse shout. She'd propped herself up with a hand on either side of his head, and he watched her arms shake with the effort to stay still. His hands roamed at will, skating along her sides before curling around her back to draw his nails gently along her backbone, tips of his fingers rising and falling with each vertebra. She dropped her head forwards, heavy braid falling over one shoulder, and he couldn't wait. Needed to see her with her hair down, spread out beneath him, naked and wanting.

Bane flipped them, and her cry of surprise made him bury his chuckle between her breasts. Her palms measured the width of his shoulders, curling down and around his biceps, then back up. When he nuzzled a nipple again, her fingers tangled in his hair, gripping and holding him in place, proof and testimony to how much she was liking everything he'd done so far. *Oh yeah.* He pushed up to his knees, straddling one of her legs as he worked the clasp of her belt and thumbed the buttons on her jeans. He was trying to remember why he'd found them sexy only hours ago. Hip-hugging and form-fitting looked great but were hell to remove. Bane retreated off the bed, waistband of her jeans in his hands, turning them inside out as he dragged them down her legs. Myrt was laughing, covering her face with both hands. That sound stopped when he dipped his thumbs into her panties, taking them on the same path as the jeans, but slower, teasing her with tender touches along the way.

When he spread out over her again, she was as naked as him, eyes shining as she looked up at him. *Discovery and pleasure will always go hand in hand with our love*, he vowed right then. *If I can make her laugh in bed, I'll count myself a lucky man.* She spread her legs and he notched himself between, shivering as the rightness flooded through him. Forearms against the mattress beside her head, he fumbled with the ties on the leather harness keeping her hair tamed. Her fingers joined his, and he looked down at her chest, watching how her breasts lifted and shifted with each movement. "God, baby. The things you do to me."

"Yeah?" Eyes closed, she lifted her chin, and he obliged her silent request, dropping his mouth to hers in a fierce, hot, wet, and long kiss. When he pulled back, she started working on the hair tie by feel, having stilled under his caresses. "I could do more, if you tell me what you want."

"I just want you." Bane dipped his head to lick a stripe up her neck, making his way to her earlobe. Sucking it into his mouth, he nibbled gently. "Want you every way I can have you."

"Finally." The triumph in her voice had him laughing again, and he separated from her in time to see the leather tie go flying, much as he'd done with her clothing earlier. "I want you, too." She arched her back, breasts pressing and rubbing, nipples dragging through the hair spanning his chest. Myrt put a hand on his sternum, fingers spread. "Want all of you."

He reached under the pillow, retrieving a condom stashed there earlier. Pushing back up, he knelt between her legs, staring down. Trailing a hand down her belly, he framed the curls there, then dipped his thumb lower, finding her clit and pressing gently.

Her breathy *oh* was enough to prompt his next moves, wanting to draw more surprised tones from her. It was the work of moments to roll the rubber on; then he settled on his belly. Dragging the tip of his tongue through her folds, he breathed deep, loving the scent of her. Then he went to work, determined to make this the best encounter in her life. Even knowing he didn't have much in the way of competition, Bane wanted to raise the bar so high she'd never look at anyone else but him. "Mine," he muttered, then sucked hard on her clit, tip of one finger circling her entrance. "Only mine."

He thrust inside slowly, finding her soaked and slippery. Drawing out just as deliberately, he paired his ring and middle fingers and drove them deep, fucking her with intent as he made love to her with his mouth. Lapping up her soaking sweetness, he carried some to her clit, spreading it liberally before he set to work and cleaned it all off, sucking the last bit of taste away. Bane repeated this again and again, humping the bed as the sounds she made drove him mad. Between gasps and tiny cries, her soft moans of his name, and calling on God, Myrt had the perfect reactions to everything.

When she stiffened, holding her breath, he stuffed a third finger in alongside the others, fucking her hard as she clenched down on him, her body trying to hold on to everything he had inside her. *Get yours, baby. Take what you need.* When her muscles finally relaxed, melting back into the mattress, and she took in a giant breath that broke in three places, he gently withdrew, dipping his neck deep so he could lap at the slick liquid spilling over. Hand on his dick, he wiped his fingers along his shaft, then moved over her. "Need you, baby." Poised at her entrance, he propped himself up on a hand and grabbed a corner of the sheet, wiping his mouth and beard. Then, hand to the base of his cock, he pushed inside her for the first time.

Heat. Hot and tight, even after being fingered for more than half an hour, she held him snuggly. The walls of her pussy contracted around him in time with a repeat of her surprised *oh*. Bane paused and withdrew a couple of inches, until she gave him a distressed sound.

He grinned and reversed course, gliding deeper before holding still again. Instead of pulling back, he gave her time to get used to the girth of his dick, then pushed forward, making his way inside her in inch increments. It seemed to take a lifetime before he'd bottomed out, balls snugged up against her ass. "Fuckin' hell, baby." Every muscle in his body was held in mid-spasm, not wanting to move too much too fast, afraid he was going to blow his load with the first full stroke. "Heaven, right here." Her legs lifted and he settled deeper, groaning softly as he buried his face against the side of her head. "Easy, sweetie. Easy."

It was Myrtle who demanded he carry things forwards. Bane might have been content to set up camp where he was, staying right there for the rest of his life. She rocked her hips up and down; then her fingers glided across his shoulder and down, clutching at his hip as she pulled. "Please. It's never been like this. I want, Bane."

"Whatever my baby wants." Needing to see her face and watch her body move, he propped himself up with straight arms. Wedging his knees wider, he pulled back and thudded home. Her mouth made a perfect O of pleasure, so he did it again. Her fingers dug into his ass, the other hand tangled in his hair, holding tightly. And again. Then he was moving fluidly, finding a rhythm to carry her along with him, testing angles until he found one that quickly had a constant stream of sweet words flowing from her mouth.

He pushed harder, flexing and angling and twisting, fucking her hard but keeping it sweet, wanting her to find that prize again, something he needed to see happen. Hearing her had been hot as fuck, but watching her fall apart would be better. Her hips were rolling up to meet every thrust, seeking her own pleasure in a way that was beautiful to witness. Bane fell to an elbow, lowering himself so he had a close-up view of her face and eyes, could reach her mouth and swallow down her long moans.

Shoving a hand underneath her, he cupped her ass in his palm and squeezed, lifting to guide her to a faster pace. He rocked the bed against the wall in a hard primal beat, his pleasure spiraling out of control, zaps of electricity racing through him. Fingers tingling, he curled his toes and thrust deep and held, jerking as it swept him along. He tried to get deeper, and deeper yet, and had his eyes on her face when it happened for her again. Her neck arched, chin lifting as she groaned out his name.

"Bane. Oh, God. *Bane*."

And then he got to watch her come, fall apart, soar high on the wings of desire. When she came down, he was the one she clung to. His the name she called. His chest became her pillow as he rolled them, losing the heat of her in the process. Condom removed and tied off, he dropped it to the floor, then wrapped his arms around her, holding her close as he listened to her breathe.

It struck him then. With her, he'd found something he'd never had before.

Happiness.

Chapter Twelve

Myrtle

Standing in the shower, Myrt let her fingers drift down between her legs, pressing against the tenderness she found there.

This had been different. Each encounter with Bane had changed the way her body worked and her brain thought when it came to them finally coming together. Desire bloomed instead of dread. An excited thrill with each kiss, instead of working fingers to the bone to keep attention away. She'd known it wouldn't be anything like what Sallabrook had done to her over and over, the degrading talk and forced acts.

She pressed again, fingers slipping in the slick liquid accumulating in her folds from the gentle touches she'd never attempted before.

This had been a lightbulb going on. As if she'd been walking around in the dark, thinking dim starshine was the only illumination, and suddenly the sun had risen. Bane would laugh at that, the idea the sun rose or set at his command of her body.

"It's true, though." She trapped her clit between thumb and finger and pressed, whimpering at the jolt of pleasure she'd always denied.

A rapping knuckle against the door preceded Bane's entrance by only a breath, and he swept the curtain back with one arm, gaze pinning her against the wall. She shook, unsure if it was fear—*that can't be right, because I have nothing to fear from Bane*—desire, or some wild combination of both. His gaze dropped to where her fingers lingered, and when he raised his eyes again, they were dark, pupils wide as he licked his lips.

"You're too sore to go again, baby." He reminded her of something they'd both learned this morning. "I don't want it to hurt to ride the bike."

She let her head thump against the shower, the weight of her wet hair trailing down her back. "I don't want it to hurt, either."

"Imma gonna kiss it, make it better." The husk in his voice was addictive, a tone he got when he couldn't get enough of her body. When he wanted more.

When she opened her eyes, it was to see him sliding his vest from his shoulders. After tossing it in a heap on the counter behind him, he dropped to his knees next to the edge of the tub and reached out. A hand on either hip yanked her forwards, the narrow strip of fiberglass the only reason she didn't fall. With her shoulders wedged against the wall and feet braced along the inside of the tub, her body made an arched bridge, pelvis thrust lewdly towards him.

"Bane." She tried to reach out, but removing her palm from the wall threatened to have her sliding, so she slapped her hand back into place. Myrt could do nothing in reciprocation, no touch, nothing to urge him on, couldn't find the cock she knew had to be hard and help stroke him to completion.

He used his teeth against the curve of one hip, then centered his mouth over her core and lapped at her, back to front, again and again. He held her steady with his strength and went deeper, driving his tongue into her, offering a tantalizing promise of fullness. Then Bane focused his attention on her clit and proceeded to drive her wild until all she could do was call out to him in pleasure.

When she came, it was as if a volcano had erupted inside her, muscles tensing as the erotic thrill swept up her torso until it heated her cheeks. Her legs shook and trembled and she nearly lost the strength to keep herself in the bridge position, only the grip of his hands saving her again.

He urged her upright as the water cut off; then a towel wrapped around her right before she floated into the air, drifting back through the room to the bed. He lay down beside her and Myrt snuggled close, pressing her face into the crook of his neck, where she'd get the most direct hit of his scent.

She didn't know how long she lay there, pillows soaking up the wetness from her hair, but his stomach eventually made itself known, a long rumble emitting from his middle. He chuckled and she laughed, then rolled her neck to look at him as he propped himself up on one arm.

"Hi." She didn't care if her greeting sounded as shy as she felt in this moment, unconcerned about hiding anything from him. He'd already proven he'd take her as she was, flaws and all, and being shy while covered in a towel while he was still fully clothed was simply part of her.

"Hey, baby." Bane bent and brushed his lips across hers in a gentle kiss. "Why don't you go finish getting ready. I can get us checked out of the room, and by the time you're done, we'll be ready to roll."

"Can we still go to the diner for breakfast?" She let her gaze roam his face, still shocked that this man—this gorgeous and kind, dangerous man—was hers.

"My baby wants cake, we'll get some cake." He ran a finger down her forehead and along the bridge of her nose, bumping across her lips. "How's the tummy today?"

She shrugged. The morning sickness had been hit or miss over the past week, where before it had been consistently troubling for a while. "Maybe I'm past the worst of it." She took in a breath, noting how his gaze immediately fell to where her breasts were hidden behind the terrycloth. "I'm definitely hungry this morning."

"We'll take it as it comes." He booped her nose and rolled to the edge of the bed, standing with a hand out. Helping her to her feet, he reached to loosen the knot holding her towel in place. "Ooops." He tugged the fabric free of her grip, dangling it in the air behind him. "Sorry about that."

Instead of the light shyness of only a few moments ago, she found there was a power in knowing she was in the presence of someone who loved her and liked the way she looked. Myrt sauntered towards the bathroom, putting a little extra sway in her hips as she disappeared inside, closing the door behind her. She managed to hold in her laughter until he exited the hotel room, cursing all the way.

At the diner, Deloris was their waitress again, seemingly the only one the diner employed. Myrt smiled at her and the woman gave her one right back. Once their orders were placed, Deloris leaned a hand on the table. "I know your sister, Marian." She paused and Myrt stared up at her, unsure what to say. "Tell her I said, 'Good for you,' for her getting out of this town. She'll be better off anywhere but here." Rapping her knuckles against the table, Deloris pushed upright and walked away. "Cake and coffee, with a side of cheesy scrambled eggs, coming up."

Bane showed her a little more of his playful side during the meal, teasing her with a forkful of cake, offering it, then swooping it away to place between his lips instead. Myrt found there was a different power in her expressions, as a playful pout from her turned into him dishing up another bite immediately, following through with delivering it to her tongue. He let her eat it, watched avidly as she swallowed, then closed in for a kiss, his tongue delving into her mouth in ways that had her core tingling and her breaths coming heavy.

"Mmmm. Always knew you were sweet." He rubbed his thumb across her lips. "Never knew just how sweet you could be."

Meal complete, he left money on the table for Deloris, who waved them out the door. Myrt stood on the steps near the curb and looked around at the little town square. When she'd left the first time, she'd been ducking down inside a stranger's car, hoping no one would see or recognize her. This time—she let her gaze travel over Bane, marking the broad shoulders and wide chest, faint cleft in his chin, and a sweet smile he reserved for her alone—she was leaving because the man she was with mattered more to her than anything. This time she wasn't running from anything. She was headed straight towards the future and whatever it held for her.

When he lifted a hand to her from where he sat on the bike, she didn't hesitate to lay her palm on his, balancing on the seat behind him as she adjusted her helmet. He leaned back, his weight solid against her, and turned his head for a kiss she gladly gave him. "Ready," she said without prompting.

"And away we go."

Her arms tight around his waist held her in place as he pulled away from the curb. Two turns later, they were on the highway headed out of town, and Myrt stretched to put her chin on his shoulder. She could see the courthouse roof in the mirrors, growing smaller with every moment. Myrt turned her eyes away from what was behind them and looked ahead at the road, stretching into the distance, and settled in for the ride.

***

Bane

He stifled his grin as he helped Myrt settle into a hot bath. She groaned as her ass hit the water, then groaned again when she leaned back against the tub. She'd found out today that four hundred miles on a bike was vastly different from making a trip twice the distance in a car or truck—even with stopping every hundred miles for a breather and bathroom break. When they'd ended their day at a hotel, she'd been so stiff he'd carried her to their room. Ground floor this time, thankfully.

"You good, baby?" She nodded and rolled her head to look at the back wall of the shower enclosure. *Well, that won't do at all.* "Myrt, honey, look at me." She didn't, instead arching her neck farther to keep turned away. "Baby, what's wrong?"

He crouched down next to the tub and cradled her cheek in his palm, pulling her face around so he could see her. Tears streamed from her eyes, a steady rivulet of wet rolling down to drip off her jaw.

"Oh, honey, is the water too hot?" He shuffled down to the faucets and moved her legs out of the way, preparing to temper the heat with cold.

"No, that's not it." Hiccupping between every word, Myrt kicked at him with little grace, her soreness making it hard for her to aim or connect.

"Then what is it, baby?" He knelt next to the tub, gathering her into his arms without caring about a little water. "What's wrong?"

"I'm sore." She rested her cheek against his chest, face hidden between the front panels of his vest.

"Yeah, I know you are. That's why we're doing the bath. And it's the reason I'm going to see if the gas station across the street has some over-the-counter stuff for pain. Do you know what's safe for you to take?" Myrt stared at him, not understanding. "No worries. I'll ask whoever's working what works best in the first trimester." Bane stroked her skin as he shook his head. "I didn't know it hurt that much, honey. I'm sorry. We shouldn't have covered so much ground today."

"That's not it." She was hiccupping again, tiny bursts of air between each word signaling a nearly silent sob.

"Then what is it, baby?" He let her lay back against the tub, trailing a finger across her cheek, wiping the tears away with the pad of his thumb.

"I'm too sore to...you know."

Understanding hit him in an instant, and he again had to fight a smile.

"Yeah, I know. It's okay. We've got all the time in the world."

"No, it's not okay. I wanted to...you know."

This time, he gave up fighting, grinning at her in pleasure at what she'd just given him. "My baby wanted to make love to her ole man. I get it, darlin'. Oh, I surely get it. I want that, too. But tonight, it's about making you comfortable, because tomorrow—" He winced, knowing how she'd feel in the morning. "—we're back on the bike for nearly as long before we make it home to Truck and Vanna's place." He rocked back on his heels, her hand in his, playing with her graceful fingers, trailing a touch up and down the length of each one. "You soak some of the sore out, keep the water from getting too cool, and I'll be back. I gotta run those couple of errands we talked about and grab us some grub."

"You're too good to me."

"Naw, baby. You and me, we treat each other just right. Ain't no competition here, nothin' but us doin' what feels important for us." Pushing to his feet, he stared down at her naked form lying in the water, lines of her hips and breasts obscured by the wavering ripples from her movement. Plenty enough clarity for him to like what he saw, though. "Soak. Ease that ache. I'll see if I can think of other ways to relax you when I get back."

He turned and walked out, closing the bathroom behind him to her shout of his name. "Bane!"

Laughing, he grabbed his helmet and let himself out of the room. Outside, he straddled the bike and rested the helmet on one of the rearview mirrors, kicking back with his feet up on the highway bars as he dialed Gunny's phone. They'd talked once yesterday to confirm the van had made the trip to Florida, and things had gone as expected locally with the sheriff. He'd made that call with a sleeping Myrt next to him, the conversation cut short when she'd roused, murmuring his name in the sexy, sleepy voice that got him hard instantly.

"Brother," he heard, and smiled, liking how the respect felt coming from a man he admired as much as he did Gunny. "Things're good here, man. How're you holdin' up?"

"I'm good. Real good. Few things better than a no-deadlines road trip with my woman ridin' behind me." He chuckled. "She's less good. Road ass already caught up to her."

"Sure it's the road makin' her sore?" The deep vein of humor in Gunny's voice made him smile. "Could be bein' rode makin' that happen, doncha think?"

"Maybe a touch of both," he admitted. "I'm in awe of her, man. She's taken everything life's thrown at her and then figures out how to keep goin'."

"Woman like her deserves some sweet." Laughter in the background underscored Gunny's words, and Bane wished they were there watching whatever had Gunny's girls and his boys being raucous and loud. "You the man gonna give it to her?"

"Yeah. You know it, man. She's never gotta earn anything from me. She gets everything, simply by bein' who she is." He cleared his throat. "You tell Vanna me and Myrt gonna need just the one room when we get there?"

"Nope. Peepers'll need to hear such a proclamation from you. Remember, she's gone all Vanna Mom with Myrt, so you'll have to battle that." Gunny's tone was easy and teasing, making Bane hope it wouldn't be a fight. "Let's go ahead and get said convo out of the way now." Before Bane could argue, Gunny had pulled the phone away from his face, shouting for Vanna. "Here she is now."

"Bane." That was all Vanna said, only a single word, but sweat prickled across the back of his neck at the coolness in her voice.

"Hey, Vanna, how's it goin'? Boys settling in okay? Marian?" Perhaps he could distract with a little bit of inquiry.

"They're good. Now, how's Myrt holding up with everything?" Nope, no distracting the woman when she had her sights set on something.

"She's good. She did great at the sheriff's office yesterday, asking all the right questions about her daddy's estate and shit. I think it's sinking in that the two men who caused her so much torment are never gonna be able to do that again. Yesterday evening she called her other sister, the one who scooped up the younger kids, made sure she'd heard the news. They talked for half an hour, and when she got off the phone, she was smiling through the tears." Bane clamped his lips shut, the realization he'd dumped a bunch of info on Vanna making the tips of his ears heat. "So yeah, she's good."

"I'm so glad." Vanna's voice vibrated with emotion. "So glad she's got you, that fate saw fit to cast your paths together."

"Sounds trite, but I am, too. She's burrowed deep, Vanna Mom. Under my skin and into my heart, and I do not want to *ever* lose an inch of what she's giving me." Fiddling with the helmet straps, he considered his next words, finally deciding to go with what felt right. "She's mine, you know what I mean?"

"I do know that feeling. That 'I'd do anything for this person because they're my other half' sense that bends reality so you can see into the heart and soul of your mate. Best feeling in the world, isn't it?"

"Yeah, it really is." He took a breath, wondering why this felt like facing down the parents back in his teenaged years. "We'll be sharing a room."

Vanna laughed. "Goes without saying, honey." There was the briefest of pauses, then she asked, "She decided what she's going to do with the baby yet?"

And her question was like a velvet-gloved haymaker punch to the belly, knocking all the air from his lungs, the reminder that what he'd hoped for might be mist in the wind. He straightened on the seat, boots thudding against the ground. "Not for sure. We've talked about only one outcome, though. Every conversation aims at nine months down the road, if you know what I mean?"

"Might be she's made her decision but doesn't know how to tell you, then, son." A door closed in the background, and the noise of the family came back loud, making him realize Vanna had taken the phone outside for privacy during their call. *Just another way this woman takes care of the people she likes.* He wouldn't count himself in Vanna's inner circle yet, but Myrt was, so it made sense from that angle. "Might be you should tell her what you're thinking without her prompting, so she knows it's from you, and not a reflection of her emotions and hopes."

"Might be you're a wise woman, Vanna Mom."

She laughed then, and he caught the sound of a deep bass rumble and knew Truck was nearby. "Might be I am, Will Crow. Might be I am. Travel safely, you hear me? We'll see you tomorrow."

"Yes, ma'am."

"Oh, hold on, Truck wants to speak to you."

He had to wait only a moment before the man came on the line. "Bane, road treatin' you kindly?" The noise decreased again, and he knew whatever Truck wanted to say, it would likely dip into official business.

"Yeah, it's nice havin' my ole lady wrapped around me on a long run." He chuckled. "What's with the round-robin phone call?"

"Mason wanted me to have a word."

Bane leaned back, missing the heat and solid feel of Myrt at his back, kicking one foot back up on the highway bars. "Did he now?"

"Ayeap. He and Blackie have a couple of ideas, but he wanted me to feel you out just a hair on where you saw this goin' with Myrt. I know what Gunny passed along, but I'd like to hear it from the horse's mouth myself."

Tipping his chin up, he studied the fading contrails of jets passed overhead long ago, these faint traces evidence that something, someone, had been this way. They crisscrossed in ways he knew weren't representative of the true paths of the planes. More passing glances at a distance than a true joining of forces.

Much like the posturing of the two men who waxed powerful in his world. Blackie, not wanting to lose a lieutenant after putting the time into training Bane the right way of doing things; and Mason, the acquisitive eyeing of his friends' and neighbors' patches passing into a fact of life as he angled to make his own family even more formidable.

"Do I want to patch over from the Freed Riders to the Rebels? That's the crux of it all, ain't it, Truck? Not if me and Myrt are gonna stick around, but if I'd be willing to drop my colors and pick up a different cover? Those are the questions you won't ask but need to." Huffing out a laugh, he caught himself scowling at the sky, those contrails still overlapping each other. "Let me guess. Mason wants a straight patchover. With me moving out of region, that one makes the most sense. But I bet Blackie is digging deep, because Mason done dropped the note about lookin' at the Iron Riggers, and him plannin' on catching them in one cast of the wide Rebel net. Am I close? Do I win a prize?"

"Not even in consolation prize territory." The light tone Truck adopted said whatever Bane had gotten wrong, it wasn't offensive. "Nice fiction write-up, though. You might have a career in Hollywood if this biker thing don't pan out for you." He laughed, a soft guffaw that held no heat.

"Mason's here tonight, you're here tomorrow; I should just let him lay it out for you."

"Don't do that shit to me, old man. You know my tender sensibilities. I won't be able to stand the strain of wondering and worrying."

Bane liked the easy comfort he'd found with Gunny and Truck, a different kind of relationship than he had with Blackie or even Horse. The latter were men he needed to keep impressing, keep making happy with his performance, keep on his side in the club squabbles that happened. The RWMC guys so far had been men he could see letting loose with, having a few beers without worrying about how his mouth could get him in trouble.

"Yeah, wouldn't want you distracted and shit. You're carrying precious cargo."

"That I am, so give it over. Tell me the grand master plan." He sat forwards, resettling both feet to the ground. "Give it to me straight, yeah?"

"As the crow flies." Now Truck was laughing at his play on words and Bane groaned. "Seriously, nobody wants you to patch over, least of all Blackie. He's nearly foamin' at the mouth at the idea of losin' you to another club, even one as formidable as the RWMC." Well hell, that felt good to hear, pushing Bane's chest out proudly. "Mason wants you in the area, and not only because Vanna wants to keep her hands on the girl—which my old lady does, she's following Blackie's lead with the frothing, hers at the idea of havin' a baby in the house. Sharon's kids come to visit often, but for short stretches, which means she missed out on a lot of the baby stuff." Truck cleared his throat, and Bane wished for a video call so he could watch the man try to get back on track. "Anyway, Blackie's against the idea of a patchover, Mason's in favor of it but has offered an alternative everyone's expressed interest in. Now we just need to know if you're gonna hang around here, or if Texas has a bigger draw for you."

"I'm with Myrt, wherever that leads us. We've got her brothers and sister to watch over, too, so wherever we land, we're going to need lots of support for a while." He knew it wasn't an answer, per se, so he pushed ahead. "She's fond of Vanna. Fond and then some, honestly. I think Vanna Mom's her touchstone, that person in her life who'll keep her grounded and feelin' capable. Havin' someone believe in you is a powerful thing, and your ole lady's made no bones about her feelings. I see us finding a place there near you and hanging around, for sure. So what's the idea? You're killin' me here."

"You know the Iron Riggers."

Bane's head jerked, surprise flooding through him. "I do. I've got a real good relationship with those boys."

"Blackie's against the idea of RWMC takin' IRMC under their wing, doesn't like the thought of our full shadow falling on that part of Texas, where he calls home. But he's less aggravated by the idea of putting a shoulder patch on 'em, making them a major support club."

"Back or front shoulder?" He shook his head. "Not a kidney patch, you sure?" Support patch placement mattered. A shoulder patch meant independent but supporting. If it was a front patch, it meant they were leading the way with finding other support clubs, left them open for downstream officers to approach with questions. It was a big signal for other clubs that there was a wealth of brothers at their back, ready to take up any fight on their behalf. A back shoulder meant a club was settled into their role, trusted but not lookin' for the club, meant they supported but weren't in line for consideration with anything from the dominant club. A front kidney patch meant low-ball support, typically came with high dues and was considered almost a bought-patch, frowned upon. He'd never seen an RWMC support patch positioned there, so didn't expect they'd start now. "Sorry, man, was surprised at the shift. Didn't expect Mason would back down."

"Well now, we don't see it as backin' down." *We, not he. Truck's wholly on board with whatever this is.* "Not at all. It's a considered sidestep with an eye on the eventual prize." Noise swelled in the background, and Gunny called for Truck. The man shifted the phone away from his mouth and called back, "I'm tryin' to, if you'd leave me alone for a half a fuckin' second, brother." He huffed out a laugh, then continued at a lower volume. "Asshole's downright excited about the idea. Seems you found a champion in Gunny."

"He's a good man, a good brother. I'm glad I had him at my back through all of this." Every word was true, and he hoped his depth of feeling rang through.

"That he is, and it didn't sound a hardship for him to be around you, which is high praise from Gunny. He don't trust easy." There was a pause, only a few beats, but enough to put brackets around whatever was coming next. By now Bane had an idea but didn't want to voice it in case he was wrong. "But, back to the matter at hand." Truck's voice had dropped an octave, adding an air of solemnity to his words. "Mason wants to think about startin' a new Iron Riggers chapter here. The idea would be to grow it over the course of a year or more, get a good base, get it stable, and then when he and Blackie are ready, they'll flip all the IRMC chapters at the same time. Oklahoma, Texas, and Florida."

"When Blackie's ready? What does that mean?" The phrase felt portentous, and he wanted to shine a light on what the words might mean.

"To bring his Freed Riders into the fold, too." Truck had a muttered conversation with Gunny, phone muffled in a way Bane couldn't make out any of the words. "You'll need to talk to Mason about your backstory. And then he'll have a tale to tell, but that's not for me. So give it a think while you're finishin' the trip tomorrow. Give it a think and come to a decision on what you'll want to do. I don't think Blackie would give permission for a patchover, which would mean a beatout on his end. Of course, if you're denied, it's not definite you'd get a skull and key, because RWMC has to maintain a relationship with the Riders. You're between a rock and a hard spot, that's a fact, and you'll have to find your way clear of the battleground."

"Sounds like my decision's been made for me. I gotta accept the rook to queen move Mason's playin'." The idea he'd have no say in what happened wasn't sitting well, but the alternative wasn't good, either. He couldn't ask Myrt to leave the only friend she had in the world, not when she was pregnant, newly freed from a brutal brand of slavery, just rescued her sister and brothers, and was startin' a relationship with a man like him. None of that shit was fair, it simply was, and it was up to him to make sure he smoothed her road as much as he could. "I'll see you tomorrow, Truck. We'll have a sit-down with Mason."

"And Blackie." Truck paused a beat. "He's bringin' enough men with him to deal with the beatout, if that's the route taken."

"Are you fuckin' kidding me?" He pulled in a measured breath, trying to ratchet back his anger. His single shout had a family across the way huddling closer together, shying away from even looking at him. *Shit.* "Never mind. I'll give him a call, see what's on his agenda so I know what he expects from me."

"And that right there is what makes you such a valuable member. You won't tell him what you want, not unless he asks and digs a little. But the club? That's your first priority and thought. That's why it's gonna kill him to lose you. Shifting to the support club might seem like a demotion, but it ain't. Gonna need somebody as charter president, might as well be you. I think you'll be surprised at the members you'll have flockin' to your side." Truck's voice became quick and strident, full of business. "Now, you think on what we've talked about, and we'll hear your decision tomorrow. Ride safe, brother."

Bane didn't give him a signoff, simply terminated the call. He sat there, tossing the phone lightly in his hand, flipping it back to front and back again. *Charter president, responsible for rolling up a brand-new chapter.* Not something he'd ever aspired to. The phone landed face up again, and he tapped a speed dial, listening to it ring. Voicemail picked up, and he listened to Blackie's recorded voice. "You got me in the middle of some shit or something. If this is who I think it is, then yeah, the old man has the right of it, but you gonna hafta earn it. Won't mean anythin', not a damn thing, if you don't." There was no invitation to leave a message, and the call terminated immediately after the recording cut off.

"Shit." Shoving his phone deep into his pocket, he grabbed the helmet and strapped it on. The bike roared to life underneath him, and he took a minute to appreciate the machine. It was everything he would want in a bike, plenty of power in the large engine well balanced between his legs, had ample room in the side bags for his and Myrt's shit, and the back seat was fit for his queen. Rolling the throttle as he let off the clutch, he angled out of the parking lot and towards the grocery store he'd seen a few blocks away. After the last conversation, he needed more than convenience store beef jerky and cheap beer.

Chapter Thirteen

Bane

Rolling to a stop in front of Truck's house, Bane took inventory of the bikes and other vehicles scattered throughout the drive and yard, and along the ditches in the narrow road. From the various tank paint jobs, he saw at least four separate patches represented, only one of which surprised him.

Then Luke and Thad were first through the door, with Marian and a flood of men and women and kids pouring out behind them. He killed the engine and settled the kickstand at the same time he reached a hand over his shoulder, steadying Myrt as she climbed off the bike. He fought back a grin as she hobbled towards the boys, fumbling with her helmet as her run towards her brothers looked more like someone on the chain gang than a woman scarcely in her twenties. She might be sore as hell, but he hadn't heard a single peep of discomfort from her, even as he saw the pain building with each stop along the way.

We're here now, and hopefully even with all the extra guests, we'll be able to stop movin' for a time.

Bane stepped off the bike and stretched, arms over his head before opening them wide to greet Blackie with a hard hug complete with rib-breaking pounding across their patches. The man looked good, rested and fresh—not as if he'd ridden his own ten-hour day to get here. Of course that ride had been yesterday, so the man would have had a few hours to rest up. Scanning the crowd behind Blackie, Bane spotted Peaches and grinned. He should have known the man wouldn't come visit Vanna without bringing his ole lady. Those two women were fast friends, and the stories about the shenanigans they'd gotten up to together were inspiring.

"Brother." Blackie stopped thudding his closed fist against Bane's spine and pulled back enough to stare into his face. There was fondness there, but a deep regret, as if he knew the decision was already made. "Heard about the issue management you engineered in Kentucky. Well done, my man. Well done."

"Meh, fire's a great equalizer."

"That it is, my brother. That it is." Blackie stepped to the side but kept his arm weighing heavily across Bane's shoulders. "I think you know all the players, but as you're my man in this scenario, it behooves me to ensure you're up to speed."

"Lead on, brother." Myrt paused at the top of the steps and turned to look at him. Bane gave her a grin and a chin lift, making a shooing motion with his hand. She smiled and blew him a kiss, the tips of her fingers lingering on her lips as if she were imagining something else. "Hold on, actually. Lemme give my ole lady a heads-up on my next few hours." Blackie's fingers tightened around the edge of his vest, and Bane turned to look at him, holding a finger up to keep Myrt in place. "What's that about, brother?"

"It's good to see you latched on to something, and to know your something is sweet as pie. To realize my brother's found his reason, and see the reason returned to him." Blackie pretended to wipe his eyes. "Brings a tear or two, see?"

"Oh, fuck you." Bane shoved him to the side and trotted towards the house. Myrt came back down a couple of steps to meet him near the bottom, and her arms circled him as soon as he was in reach. Bane wrapped an arm around her, lifting his other hand to cradle her cheek. "I've got some business to tend to, baby. I'll be inside soon as I can. Leave your bag, I'll bring it in when I come. Just find a place to sit and put your feet up, yeah?"

"Okay."

He captured her hand and lifted her fingers to his lips, then quirked a grin at her. "These had something that belonged to me." He kissed her fingertips again, then sucked them into his mouth. "Had to come and retrieve it, doncha know?" She leaned her cheek against his chest, and he brought their joined hands up to fold together over his heart, swaying in place. "You okay, baby?"

"Mmhmm."

"You gonna find a quiet place to rest for a bit, until I come back to you?"

"Yeah, I can do that." She sighed and leaned against him more, fingers nervously tight around his.

"I love you, you know that?" Bane stroked up her back to wrap his fingers around the tie holding her braid in place. He tugged and her neck bent backwards, chin lifting so he could capture her mouth with his, and he kissed her until some of the men in the yard catcalled. When Bane pulled back, he saw not only were her lips kiss-swollen and red as cherries but her cheeks had turned every shade of the gorgeous blush he loved so much. "Be back soon, baby. Let's get you comfy, yeah?" He scooped her up and took the steps two at a time, letting her wrestle with the door so he could carry her through. Depositing her in the kitchen, he nodded to the women standing and sitting around. "Pregnant lady here, sore from nearly a thousand miles on the bike. Got a place for her to sit a spell?"

His question was enough to trigger the reaction he'd expected, as Vanna, Peaches, Sharon, and a half a dozen more women moved around the room, vacating seats and plumping pillows for her to sit on. He passed her off into Vanna's capable hands and backed out of the room, Myrt's gaze sticking to him until he turned to head out of the house. The woman's longing look slayed him, and he knew an image of his Myrt staring at him with love in her eyes would stay with him.

The major players in what was going to go down today had all come together in a circle off to the side of the house. At a gesture from Blackie, he angled in that direction, coming to a halt a reasonable distance away, standing at his president's left shoulder.

"Bane, a steady member of the Freed Riders, and one of my most trusted." Blackie lifted a hand and indicated the place next to him, and Bane stepped into the space created as if by magic. "To your left is Retro, president of the Bama Bastards." Bane nodded, holding his tongue. He was well acquainted with the master of information, having called on him more than once in the past, both before and after joining the FRMC.

"Good to see ya, brother." Retro reached out and Bane met him halfway, clasping each other's wrists in a warrior grip. "Well met and all that jazz."

"You as well." Bane was careful with his words, not sure what the BBMC had to do at this party, but the man was in bed with a number of clubs across the region, so possibly it wasn't unexpected Retro being called in to witness whatever was going to happen.

Blackie continued the formal introductions. "Next around the ring is Twisted, president of the Incoherent. Next to him is Wrench, who holds the same position in the Caddo Hobos."

Bane cut a glance at Blackie, verifying his spiel was complete before stepping into the empty ring to meet the two men. Each had a firm handshake followed by a quick pound of his shoulder. Not a full embrace by any means, but then again, they represented the competition for many of the FRMC money-making schemes. Relations between the clubs were cordial but not effusively friendly.

He returned to his assigned position beside Blackie, looking to his president for his next cue.

Blackie gestured towards the near side of the circle, to his immediate right. "You know Mason, Rebel Wayfarers president and then some, and next to him is Gunny, someone you have a more intimate knowledge of." Noise across the circle pulled Bane's attention to Wrench and Twisted, who were fighting back smiles. "Fuck you both, not that kind of knowledge. Ain't no carnal goin' on, unless I've misread everything about Gunny."

"No offense taken or anything, but the dude's not my speed." Gunny grinned suddenly, the expression lightening his face. "And do not say a damn thing to my old lady. Sharon's got a kinky bent since Josh was born. I don't need the two of you putting any fuckin' ideas in her head."

"Not a word from me, brother." Wrench laughed softly. "But just sayin', you're missin' out, man."

"Back on track here, please." Blackie scowled at both men, then turned his glare on Bane. "And next to me is Skyd, president of the Freestone County charter of the Iron Riggers." He thumbed over his shoulder. "Seconds and more are spaced out around the place, ensuring what happens here is held close for now."

Bane nodded at Skyd as he stepped towards Mason, needing to complete the greeting process in the order Blackie had introduced the men. He didn't understand the process yet, but he knew Blackie, and there was nothing the man did that was accidental. Mason met him more than halfway, lips curled in a grin as he went for the open arm hug, pulling Bane into him, chest to chest as they slapped and pounded each other's backs. He stepped away and Gunny was there, yanking him close for a space of three breaths.

"Best motherfuckin' backup I've had in a long fuckin' time." Gunny left Bane and went to stand in front of Blackie, posturing in a way that didn't make sense. "Never met a man who thought over everything with a plan to manage alone, and then could easily take on a second pair of hands the way he did. Man to be proud of, this one is."

"I know what you're talking about. Love the man like a brother. Pull him into all major decisions, because when a deal's goin' down, a good leader always wants to bring their best to the table. So yeah, I know the man's a good'un."

Blackie closed half the distance between himself and Gunny, holding his ground with a snarled, "But I'm still not sure I fuckin' like you."

"Likewise." Gunny's shoulders lifted with a sigh. "Vanna Mom vouches for you, which puts you on the right side of the line for me."

"Why didn't we get this out of the way yesterday when I got here?" Blackie shook his head, looking around Gunny at Mason. "He always this much of a pain in the ass?"

"Sometimes worse." Mason's tone was easy, amused even, and Bane looked at the exchange between the two men with different eyes.

"Love you, old man." Gunny held out a fist, then spread his fingers wide. "Don't know what I'd do without ya."

Blackie slapped his palm on top of Gunny's, wrapping their hands in a firm grip. "Bring it in, big man. Missed the fuck outta you. Need you to come see us more often." The two men embraced, clinched tight by their clasped hands, arms spread across shoulders. Blackie muttered something into Gunny's ear that made the man laugh, and then they were stepping back, the made-up tension gone as if it had never happened.

"Well, if you're done now." Bane stepped behind Gunny to approach Skyd. They'd worked together on a number of runs and ironed out issues between the two clubs, so he wasn't surprised with the welcoming grin on the man's face. "Good to see you." A couple of pounds on his shoulder, and he broke away, returning to his place next to Blackie. Gunny had shifted Retro around and was now standing to Bane's left. The changing dynamics of the positioning spoke loud and clear about what Gunny thought, literally putting himself at Bane's back if needed.

"So...?" He looked at Blackie to see all the humor had fled, the regret back in spades, the most prominent emotion visible. "What's up, Prez?"

"What's up, he asks, like it's no big deal." Blackie cast a glance around the circle, then settled his gaze on Bane, turning so he squared up to face him. "What's up is your future. I've heard all kinds of plots and plans from every man in this group. You're a hot commodity, seems everybody wants to get a lil' bit of the Bane pie. What I want—" He thrust his thumb against his chest for emphasis. "—is to hear from your lips where you are leanin' without the interference of these bastards." Blackie nodded at Retro. "No offense to the actual Bastards."

"None taken, man." Retro stepped closer. "Witness and testify, that's my role, not to influence."

"Right." Blackie angled back towards Bane. "So, what say you? Tell us what you've found."

"What I've found? Okay." Bane shook out his hands as if for a fight, and he chuckled, because in a way this *was* a fight for him. "I found a stretch of ground that's not necessarily claimed by any regional dominant. One I think I could settle on with the patch on my back, go nomad and lose my Longview rocker. Not unlike at least one other member of an MC, who retained a city rocker, but that city is in another state, so it ain't like there's a core of members here primin' the place for a charter. I want to move to this stretch of ground, Blackie. Prez. And I'm officially asking for a nomad rocker." He glanced around the group of men, surprised to see only grins and smiles, no anger that he'd found a way around their bullshit ideas.

"Well now, that's an offer I hadn't considered." Bane bit back a laugh when Blackie stroked his beard, probably unaware Truck was making the same gesture, as was Twisted. "It's an idea, for sure, but hangs a brother out without much, if any, support. Puts you far from the parlay table when needed, would have you on the road a fuckton, because that's the nature of the nomad. You sure you wanna be away from your old lady so much?"

Shit, I didn't think about that.

His thoughts must have been visible on his face, because Blackie chuckled. "Yeah, somehow I didn't believe you'd be down for that, man."

"We'd find a happy medium, no doubt." Bane shrugged. "Devil's in the details, but we'd work it out."

"We would, but it's not optimal for anyone. You need a way to stay stuck tight to this unclaimed stretch of ground, and the easiest way would be claimin' it. I was considering what it would mean to draw my line in the sand with a new FRMC charter here." Blackie's neck twisted as he glared at

Mason. "Present a strong front to our competition, so they'll stop thinkin' they can swoop in and scoop up our territory." He pounded his chest with a fist. "My territory, bought and held with the blood of my men."

Mason's chin rose, but he held his peace. This was rightly between Bane and Blackie, and would better have been conducted without the audience.

"You're looking to spread FRMC that wide, boss?" Bane shook his head. "While I love the idea on the one hand, because it appears to solve everything in one strike, what does the distance mean for support or visiting between the charters? We want to keep the consistency of the club smooth as silk, we gotta keep the churn of rides and mixing of charters. Best way to ensure no one charter goes off on a tangent is to remind them of the overriding covenant and doctrine. It'd also be fuckin' expensive to roll up a new charter. Wouldn't be no dues comin' in, especially not if we're lookin' for men to relocate to fill the roster. They'll have money tied up in the move, wouldn't have any to spare for the club."

"You can come up with a dozen reasons not to, and I'll find a matching number of why we should." Blackie shook his head. "The previous idea was rolling up a support club here, which made sense because it'd be less threatening to the dominants who share the region." He nodded at Retro, then Twisted and Wrench, ignoring Mason, who grinned at the slight. "But we can get details worked out tonight, right here. I'm warmin' to the idea with every word. We've got the cash, and the folks who were gonna slap an IRMC patch on could as easily wear mine." Blackie straightened, feet spread, and shoved fisted hands against each hip as he stared around the group of men. "I do not see a single reason why I shouldn't plant a charter here."

"Seems a reasonable solution, brother." Mason broke from his place in the circle and came to stand in front of Blackie. "We all know where we're goin', just a few years down the road. Don't matter to me if it's FRMC or IRMC planted here, and if I'm honest, your idea makes the most sense. We both know you don't need my permission, but you've got my agreement." He thrust out a hand, and Blackie took hold slowly, each move ponderous. Understandable because this was a huge decision, made quickly, and now backed by an important dominant club president. "Congratulations, brother."

Twisted and Wrench had their heads together, both talking fast and low, the quiet buzz of their conversation all Bane could make out. They turned as one and nodded. "Sounds like a plan," Twisted said, while Wrench offered, "Best idea so far."

Blackie took in Retro's nod, then turned to Skyd, who was grinning. "Saves me the hassle of a new charter."

"Sounds like we're agreed." Blackie turned to Bane, who shoved his shoulders back, standing tall. "We'll settle the details of the new charter in a bit, but there's a couple of things to get straight now." Gunny and then Truck stepped up beside Bane, one to either side. "Mason already agreed to a patchover, but what with plans skewing slightly sideways, we might should ask him again."

"Aye." Mason called without hesitation, then laughed.

"Alrighty then." Blackie's beard split with a grin. "Meet your VP and SAA, brother."

"The fuck?" Bane spun to face the two men, feverishly studying their faces for any hint of a joke. "Are you serious?"

"As a heart attack." Gunny nodded. "My Sharon misses time with Vanna Mom, and this puts me closer to a couple of good friends down near NOLA. I'll miss my brothers in the Fort Wayne chapter, but it's time. Never thought I'd patch over, but this feels right."

Truck stepped closer and slapped a hand on top of Bane's shoulder, fingers digging deep as he held tight and rocked Bane. "What you said about me being an orphan in the region was dead on, brother. I love the Little Rock chapter, but I do not like havin' to ride hundreds of miles away from my ole lady when it comes time for church. I also miss the brotherhood, because I might have a city rocker, but it feels like I've been nomad for years at this point. You're givin' me a good reason to settle, stay in one place. We'll build something strong for the FRMC. My oath to you, as my future president. I'll work my fingers to the bone to help you create something to be proud of, brother."

"Well, shit." He looked over his shoulder at Blackie and nodded, watching as the man's beard split to show white teeth. "Looks like I'm patching up a grade, not patching over."

* * *

Myrtle

"So you've decided, then?" Vanna's quiet question stood in contrast against the controlled chaos of the kitchen. Myrt looked up to find her friend smiling down at her. Vanna nodded towards Myrt's middle, where she had a hand placed protectively over her belly. "Keeping the baby?"

"Maybe?" She hated how uncertain her voice was and cleared her throat roughly. "There's a lot to think about."

"There is." Vanna set a sweating glass of iced tea on the table near Myrt's elbow. "And a little more time before the decision's taken out of your hands. What's keeping you from settling on one side of the line or the other?"

"I don't know. I waver back and forth almost as fast as a thought. It's not like me." Myrt lifted the glass and sipped, sighing happily when she found it the perfect amount of sweet. "If I get a couple of days where I can just be, I'm sure I'll get back on an even keel." Looking around, she noted again the number of women crowded into the kitchen and dining room. "How are you doing with a houseful like this?"

"Oh this?" Vanna made a pfffft sound and flipped one hand dismissively. "Most of them are staying with friends nearby, or camping out in the field out back of the house.

It's only mealtimes we all pile in a group. Supper should have been grilled outside, but someone got a bee in their bonnet for some chicken and dumplings, so we're all wedged in here for now." Vanna lifted her chin and gave Myrt a tiny grin. "I do have a sidestep for tonight, though. I'm putting you and Bane in Truck's house down the road."

"Truck's house?" That didn't make any sense; he lived here with Vanna.

"Man bought a house sight-unseen a few years ago. Granted, it's why he and I met, and I wouldn't change our meeting for anything, but he can't be trusted when it comes to real estate deals. Him and his brothers conduct beer-time negotiations, which never end well." Tittering laughter throughout the room told Myrt that as quiet as they were being, their audience had sharp ears. "He's been fixing it up a little at a time, and it's not bad now, but Lord girl, you shoulda seen it when he first bought it. I ran down earlier today and opened the windows, freshened up the big bedroom. Put clean sheets on the bed and such. Water pressure is good, and it's got an enormous tub, perfect for soaking."

"It's like you read my mind." Myrt glanced at the door, her emotions a mix of longing and anxiety. Bane had explained how important today's decision was, and Myrt had been blown away by how much thought and consideration he'd given to how she'd feel about whichever path he chose. "How long you think they'll be out there?"

"Long as they need to." A woman who'd been introduced as Peaches settled into a chair opposite Myrt, leaning forwards with her elbows on the table. Myrt wiggled around in the chair, trying unsuccessfully to straighten herself. "Girl, leave it, you need to be comfortable. Get those feet back on the chair Bane piled up for you. We've all been there." She gestured towards the roomful of women. "Those long hauls aren't always the easiest riding bitch, but it's what we do for our men. We know you're sore, so you stay where you are. We'll take care of everything." She held out a hand for Vanna, who walked around the table to stand at Peaches' back. "I've known the man a while now, and like him. With what Vanna Mom's said about you, I kinda like you for him. You gonna be good to him?"

"Uh, yes?" Myrt was taken aback at the direct questioning from this stranger. She looked at Vanna, who was staring at her somberly, as if wondering the same things. "I mean, yes, I'm going to be good to him. If you knew the things he's done for me and my family, you'd understand. He's the best man I've ever met, and I'm blessed he's in my life."

"Oh, that's a good answer." Peaches grinned, reaching up to pat Vanna's hand on her shoulder. "She gave me a real good answer. You were right, Vanna Mom. I like this one a lot."

"Told ya. She's a keeper." Vanna turned to the front of the house, then called over her shoulder, "They're headed in; whatever kind of church this was is over."

"Church?" Myrt felt off-kilter, out of her depth suddenly as she remembered the masses of men who'd been in the front yard. There was no way Vanna's house would hold them all. Footsteps on the stairs presaged the entrance of her little brothers into the kitchen, and she realized she hadn't seen her sister since right after getting here. *I need to do a better job of being a sister.* If this were overwhelming for her, after being out in the world for several weeks, she could only imagine how it must be for her siblings. "Where's Marian?"

Peaches leaned across the table and patted Myrt's hand, clasping it gently, the movement seemingly symbolic. "Church is a members-only meeting every club has in one form or another. As for your sister, with our encouragement, Marian's been disappearing into her bedroom upstairs when things get overwhelming. Gives her a safe place to decompress without fifty sets of eyes on her." She patted Myrt's hand again, then leaned backwards, draping an elbow over the tall back of her chair. "We've all been where you two are, in one way or another, honey. None of us wants to see anyone upset or hurt, and you can trust your family with us, since you're family, too."

Bane had mentioned something similar during one of their stops along the ride yesterday. He'd been musing over how nice it was to expand his family in two ways, first taking on the boys and Marian, and then growing closer to Gunny. The bond between the two men had been palpable after they'd returned from their second trip to the mountain. *"My blood family is thin. I won't talk to my pa or brother at all, which leaves only my ma and older sis. We've all agreed to leave well enough alone, and I only call on Mother's Day. My found family, though? My brothers under the patch and their wives? We're in each other's lives every day, celebrate all the successes, no matter how small, and circle up for support whenever anything bad happens. We're there and gonna be there. Rain or shine, thick and thin, no questions asked. That's my family."*

"And if he leaves your family?" The noise around the front door swelled, and Myrt knew she only had seconds to figure out the answer that suddenly seemed so important. "What happens then?"

"He never gets to leave us, not as long as he's on this side of the sod. He's my old man's brother, and that's not only under the patch, that's standing alongside. We'll have his back, Myrt. That I can promise you." Peaches winked as she stood and turned, moving away. "And we'll have yours, darlin'."

Myrt searched the faces coming in the door, finally seeing Bane walk in, Gunny's arm around his neck pulling their heads close together. Bane looked shellshocked, as if he still couldn't believe whatever had just happened. Then he grinned and thumped his fist against Gunny's chest, pulled away, and arrowed straight into the kitchen to where he'd dropped her over an hour ago. Not even looking at her yet, but believing she'd be waiting. *I will be.* The silent vow felt small, not enough, so she added in a whisper, "Always."

"Baby." That word from his lips never failed to pull a shiver from her, and as usual, he looked thrilled with her response. Sometimes she wondered if he did it on purpose, but she didn't care. Sweet words from her...*my man.* That pulled a different shiver, one that started between her legs and rocked up through her like a tidal wave. "I understand we're bunkin' next house over. Takin' the boys and Marian with us."

"I—yeah, that's what I heard, mostly." She couldn't figure out why the idea of not having the entire house was bothersome, but brushed it off. "It's nice of Truck to let us stay in his house."

Bane's nose nuzzled in alongside her ear as he whispered, "My understanding is the primary bedroom is ours, and it's at the back of the house, well away from everything else. Gonna have my way with you again and again, my Myrt."

"I guess there's a big soaking bathtub." She wrapped her arms around his neck, holding him close when he would have pulled back. "Would you take a soak with me, my sweet William?"

"Fuck yeah." He ripped out of her arms and scooped her up with an arm under her knees and back. "We'll be back for breakfast in the morning. They'll send the boys and Marian over later." He jostled her until she shrieked and clutched his neck. "Vanna Mom, can you have 'em bring a little snack. Me and my woman gonna need sustenance, but first, gonna get her all clean." He bent his neck, bringing his mouth to her ear again. "Right before I dirty her all up again."

As he pushed through the back door and down the short set of steps to the yard, she found herself looking forward to the idea.

A lot.

***

Bane

Myrt stirred in the bed next to him, hiding her face against the mattress near his ribs, one arm and leg draped possessively over his body.

Could definitely get used to this.

The tub in the bathroom connected to their bedroom was as large as advertised, and he'd sunk into the water behind her with every expectation sexy fun times were imminent. Then, as the heat from the water drew away her soreness, Myrt had sweetly fallen asleep curled in his arms. She'd barely woken when he'd levered her from the water, standing and swaying as he dried her with a soft towel he'd found in the nearby closet. Only a few muttered words, then she'd fallen into bed clad only in panties as she'd dragged a pillow close enough to hug, quickly dropping back into sleep.

He'd gotten the boys and Marian settled when they arrived, and placed the food they brought into the refrigerator. He'd stood there a minute, staring into a well-stocked appliance, mulling thoughts through his head about what it indicated. A quick tour of the pantry and cabinets had showed the same. The house had been set up to live in, even though Truck and Vanna clearly resided in their home next door.

More questions than answers at this point. He wrapped an arm around Myrt, shifting so she was sprawled half on him. The movement, along with the early morning sunlight streaming in between the opened curtains, woke Myrt, as was his intent.

"Morin', darlin'." He skated a hand down her back, curling his fingers over one globe of her ass, and squeezed, reveling in the soft skin and giving flesh. "Mmmm. I like you all sweet and sleepy."

"I'm not sweet." Her grumbled words were broken with a soft sigh that was kissing cousins to a snore.

"So sweet, gonna make me addicted to you." Bane pressed a kiss to her forehead, holding her a little closer. "You awake, baby? I got somethin' I wanna say, but need you listenin' and not studyin' the inside of your eyelids."

"I'm awake."

The gentle slur was gone, and he felt the muscles of her body tense against him. When she tried to pull away, he held her in place, stilling her with a quiet "Shhhh. It's nothin' bad, darlin'. Promise."

"Promise?"

"Yeah, baby. Just somethin' I need you to hear, and then we'll go on about our day, however that shakes out." He waited a beat, then prompted her. "You ready?"

"Okay."

"I want to have babies with you. If our path starts with this bun in the oven we've got cookin' now, or down the road with a second chance, I want it. I want all of it with you. This ain't too fast, ain't too soon, ain't any of those put-off phrases some folks might trot out to talk about me and you. What we are is right, and good, and meant to be, baby. So I wanted to throw it out there I'd be inclined to continue this pregnancy, if you were leanin' that way. If not, then we'll find a time down the road where it's our turn." Realizing his fast-flowing words had angled off his intended target, he cleared his throat, tightened his arms around her, and tried to put a cap on it with a final thought. "You're it for me, Myrtle Threadgill. I'm sold on the idea of us, lock, stock, and barrel. I'm leavin' the decidin' up to you as should be for this decision, but I wanted to be sure you got my thoughts on how things might go."

Warmth gathered in the notch of his throat, slowly flowing down both sides of his neck, and he wrapped one arm even tighter around her, reaching up to cradle the back of her skull with his other hand.

"Oh, baby. Darlin' girl, I didn't mean to make you sad. It's all you, baby. I'm behind you, either way. Keep it, I'll love goin' through that with you. Decide the other way and I'm still right there beside you. Right there, stuck like a burr. You can't get rid of me now."

She made a strangled sound and lifted her head, pushing back against his hold until he was looking up into her face. Myrt's expression was bright and light, filled with joy. "You didn't make me sad, my sweet William." Folding an arm across his chest, she propped her chin on the back of her hand, eyes never leaving his. "I'm not sad. You—" She shook her head. "You're an amazing man."

"I thought Amazons were women?" He bucked his hips up against her soft weight, grinning broadly when her lids fluttered in response. "Amazonman? Is that even a thing?"

"That's a terrible one, you—" He bucked his hips again and her words stumbled to a halt as she gasped and sighed.

"You went to sleep last night." Hand skating around her hip, he danced fingers down the outside of her thigh as far as he could reach, sliding to take the inside track on his way back up. "So cute huggin' your pillow, I couldn't make myself wake you up. Too cute. You're a pillowsnugleoplis. All about the grrr and argh when I tried to move you." His palm encountered the curve of her ass, and he spread his fingers, slipping under the edge of her panties to cup and massage, fingers sliding in and down. "You awake now, baby?"

Ass clenching, she pressed against him with a shiver and nodded. "I sure am."

"You up for foolin' around this morning? I'm feelin' needy. Frisky and needy." Ruby lips pouted only inches from his mouth, and he arched up to capture them, his fingers threading through her hair to pull her closer. Each touch stirred a hot breath from her lips. "So fuckin' needy, baby."

Rolling so she was underneath him, he angled on one hip and slid his fingers under the front edge of her panties, kissing her deeply as he delved between her other lips to find slippery wetness. Hooking a thumb in the top edge of the fabric, he took the work of moments to whisk them away, tossed somewhere towards the corner of the room. "Need a condom, baby." Lunging across the bed to the nearest table, he prayed whoever had stocked the house had thought ahead for this eventuality, too. *Otherwise I'll have to find my pants—aha.* He pulled a whole strip of condoms out of the drawer and laughed. "Someone thinks we're gonna do the naked tango a lot. I'll have to thank them for their trust in my recovery time."

Kneeling between her thighs, he kept one hand on her, fingers traveling from one hip to the other in a teasing graze as he rolled the condom down his length. A hard squeeze of his balls set the looming orgasm back at least a few minutes, hopefully. Just seeing her like this, spread out.

She'd finger-combed her hair while he looked for the condom, so the strands were arrayed in a curtain behind her head and shoulders, perfect for him to—*Do anything. She's so fuckin' perfect for me in every way.* "Fuckin' love you, Myrtle. I fuckin' love you."

Those lips bowed into a soft smile he'd only seen directed at him, and he immediately tagged that one as his, too. Her tiny smile when she was pleased at something he'd said had been his favorite until this one. Now, he'd work every day to have her look at him as if he held her heart in his hands. She pulled in a breath and time stilled as he watched her lips move. "I love you, too." Her smile grew, chest rising and falling in a rapid rhythm as he slipped both hands up the inside of her thighs, thumbs brushing against the soft curls waiting at the center of her. "My sweet William."

"Not your Bane? You sure, darlin'?" Her proclamation quieted any tiny fears he'd still been carrying, that this was an exploration for her, and perhaps she wasn't in deep like him. Those words were worth any celebration, and he'd put that into play soon enough. Right now, though, he skated his palm across her skin. *Time enough and then some. Rest of our lives.*

"You're my Bane plenty of other times. When you're taking care of me, making sure my family is safe and healthy, visiting with our friends." Her breath caught as he pushed a finger inside her, stroking in and out slowly before pairing another with it to fill her more. "But when you look at me like you do, sweet is the only word that comes to mind."

"I'll take it." He shook his head as he leaned over her, propping himself up on his elbows. Bane tipped his head so their foreheads touched, lips a fraction of an inch from hers. "I'll take anythin' you give me, baby." His dick lined itself up with her entrance, notching into place as if it knew it was home. He rolled his hips and pushed inside slowly, not stopping until he'd seated himself deep with a single stroke. "You want your sweet William in bed with you, I can be sweet." An arched back for the withdrawal pressed his belly against hers, and he felt the tiny rounded bump that was the baby. "You want a little rough and rowdy, I can be your Bane, too. I'll be whatever you need, Myrt. Just—" He rolled his hips, faster, thrusting in and pulling back, growing the rhythm she set each time she met his movements. "—baby, you just need to need me." That felt like a vulnerable statement, maybe too vulnerable for this early, and he closed his mouth, pressing a kiss to her lips.

"I'm going to always need you. You should know by now." Each breath ghosted over his lips, and he wanted to kiss her hard, derail whatever words she was about to say. "Bane—William, you're both to me. My lover, my protector, my friend, my partner." He hadn't moved fast enough, and she'd gotten out every word, all of it, enough to shut him up for a long breath. Her head tipped back, and he attacked the side of her neck with his teeth and lips, gliding his tongue along the taut tendons as she chased her pleasure. "I won't ever not need you. Oh, please."

Pushing up on his arms, he stared down at her as she fell over the edge, body writhing, hips lifting to meet every thrust inside her. The muscles of her pussy clamped down, and he was losing the fight for control, balls drawing up tight to his body as sparks danced up and down his spine. He curled himself around her again, arm shoved under her shoulders, face buried in the pillow as he pounded harder, deeper.

"Please, Bane." Her mouth was next to his ear, words scarcely audible over the rapid slapping of flesh on flesh filling the room.

He grabbed her leg, hooking her knee over his hip, driving himself a little deeper. The need to bury himself inside her and never come out was strong, and he centered his thoughts around the give of her breasts against his chest, the tender strength in her hands as she held tight to him, the heat and silk-slick sensation of sliding in and out—the orgasm took him by storm, rolling over him so his rhythm stuttered and he held, thrust deep, and then stilled, trapped in the paroxysm of desire.

Mine.

The single powerful thought rocketed around inside his head as she lifted her other leg, wrapping her heels around his ass and pulling him tighter against her. She had him cradled to her—arms, legs, even the angle of her head had him willingly trapped, every movement showing him her love. The emotional connection would have been loud and clear even if she'd never said the words, and he knew in that moment everything he'd been feeling and thinking was right. They were destined for each other. His whole life he'd been looking, wandering place to place, trying to fill a hole with his brothers and the club—all it took was one petite woman to get him all wrapped up in knots, and slot herself inside him in a way that meant he was never gonna let her go.

"My peace, baby. You're my peace. Mine." His gusting breaths stirred the hair at the side of her head. Panting hard, trying to slow his heart, he eased them onto their sides so he didn't crush her. "Don't want to let go yet, Myrt. Hold on with me."

"You're mine, too. I'm holdin' on, my lands yes. Holdin' on." She panted and rested her head on the pillow, staring straight into his eyes as she breathed out exactly the words he'd hoped to hear. "Mine, and this baby's. You're our hope and future. I'm depending on you, Bane, but you know what?"

"What, baby?"

"I know you won't ever let us go. There's a peace in that, too. So I guess you're my shelter." She sighed softly. "My solace." Her breath hitched. "Momma woulda told me to find my answers in the Bible. I pick Job chapter sixteen, verse five."

"What's it mean, baby?"

"It's about solace, Bane." One corner of her mouth lifted. "'But my mouth would encourage you; comfort from my lips would bring you relief.' You're the embodiment of comfort for me."

Tightening his arms around her, he smiled and kissed those perfect ruby lips.

"Mine."

***

Myrtle

Footsteps pounding through the house preceded the hammering knock at the bedroom door by a few seconds. She gathered the sheet in her hands and flung it over her and Bane only a moment before the door flew open, rebounding when it hit the wall. She flinched at the idea of damage left behind.

"Luke, we're guests in this house. Take care, son." Bane's voice was gravelly and low, but not unkind, and she loved how he instinctively knew the right tactic to take with each of her brothers.

"Blackie said there's breakfast at the main house, back where we were before you came here. He said there's pan-a-cakes." Luke shuffled to the end of the bed and sat, staring at Myrt and Bane. "I want pan-a-cakes, Myrtie."

"Myrtie." Bane's voice was musing, filled with humor, and she glared at him, taking in how her expression only made his eyebrows arch more. "Rhymes with birdie. I kinda like that." He turned to look at Luke. "I also am a big fan of pancakes, so I appreciate you lettin' us know about the goodies. Right now, your sister and I need to get up and dressed, and neither of us can do so with you sittin' here. So can you skedaddle back to the kitchen and wait? We'll be there in a couple of minutes."

"Okie-dokie, Bane." Luke gave a wave and left through the open door.

"Luke." Bane's voice wasn't a roar, but it was definitely pitched to catch Luke's attention, so Myrt wasn't surprised to see the boy's head pop back into view. "Doors are like gates. You open it, you close it, yeah?"

"Oh, yeah." Luke's grin told her he wasn't upset at Bane's orders. "That actually makes a lot of sense, Bane. Got it."

"Thank you." The door closed with a snick. "You're so sweet to my brothers."

"You know, I don't think Luke's slow. I suspect his brain just works differently." Bane looked at her, expression serious. "You should have a talk with Vanna Mom. Her son has autism, and she's got a headful of knowledge about all kind of different things to do with developmental delays. I wouldn't take anything your daddy said about him as gospel. Let's find out what might really be going on, see how we can best support him."

"And that right there is one of the reasons I love you so much." She shoved the wave of emotion down, fanning her hand in front of her face. "You can't be too nice to me, Bane. I might not be pukey, but I'm weepy."

Heat covered her belly, and she knew without looking that he'd spread a hand over the baby's bump. "You're gonna have this baby." A statement, but she still nodded in confirmation. "Our baby."

Myrt felt her control dissolving, and she threw herself against him, shoving her face into the pillow. "You can't be nice." Even to her ears the words were warbling and watery, nearly indecipherable through the sudden tears.

"Oh, baby." His arms came around her, a hand flicking the sheet away as he rolled them to the edge of the bed and stood with her wrapped around him. "I'm always gonna be nice to you. You gotta get used to it."

Half an hour later, they were presentable, tramping through the woods on what looked like a well-worn path she scarcely remembered from the previous night. "Every time I went outside with the girls, we headed the other direction, across the field to the woods where the creek is. I didn't even know this house was here." Bane's fingers tightened around hers, and she looked down at their joined hands. She gave herself five seconds to remember what those hands had felt like as they roamed her body, then cut off the memory. Or tried to. It kept creeping in as she looked at his hips, his shoulders, his mouth— *Stop it. There are kids present.* She focused on the path in front of her, watching their feet trample through the dew-kissed grass.

"Baby." He sounded amused. She glanced up at him, finding a knowing look on his face. "Whacha thinkin' about?"

"Shut up." Myrt buried her head against one shoulder, heaving them both up in a great shrug she held in place. "Nothing at all to do with you."

"Methinks—" He swung around to face her, slowing their pace as the boys and Marian walked ahead talking animatedly with the man who'd come to collect them for breakfast. "My lady protests too much. You were thinking about you and me doing the nasty, weren't you?"

"I wouldn't call anything we do together nasty, Bane." Myrt lifted her chin, aiming her haughtiest expression his direction.

His laughter was easy and soft, and he stopped in the middle of the trail, pulling her against his chest. "We could step behind a tree and they'd never miss us. Boys are headed to play with Gunny's and Blackie's kids, and Marian will be swept into the woman-whirlwind happening in the kitchen right now." He trailed a finger along her cheek, booping the tip of her nose. "And you and I could do the not-nasty right here, if you wanted me. I wouldn't let anything bad happen to you, Myrt. Swear on my soul, baby."

"I believe you." She watched in surprise as his eyes closed and saw the way his Adam's apple traveled down and up his neck with a hard swallow. "Bane, baby." His continued silence made her uneasy, uncertain in a way she didn't like. "I do. I believe you."

"I know you do, baby." Rough, his voice still settled along her skin like satin, smoothing out the worrisome goose bumps that had raised her hair. "It hits deep, because it matters so much. I didn't know how much I needed that. It's a precious thing, your trust and belief." His eyes flashed open, shining with emotion. "I'll never do you wrong. Never. I'll never betray your trust, baby."

Myrt folded herself against him, loving how his arms came up naturally to wrap around her. "I believe that, too. You said earlier you were looking, didn't know what for, but you were looking. So was I. It might have taken me longer to get started, to get unstuck from where I'd been left. Still, it had to be the right time, because here you are."

"Here I am, and here you are." The weight of his cheek rested against the top of her head, and his voice rumbled reassuringly through his chest to her ears. "And here we're meant to be."

"So fuckin' sappy. I don't think I even know you anymore, brother."

Myrt groaned and Bane laughed, turning them to face their visitor. Their voices overlapped as they named him, as familiar with his voice as each other's by now. The grumbled "Brother" came from Bane, while Myrt said a laughing, "Gunny."

"Food's gettin' cold, so I was sent to retrieve the two of you." Gunny wedged his way in between them, slinging an arm across Bane's shoulders as he curved his other around Myrt's waist. He forced them into step with him, tromping through the weeds the last few yards to the defined edge of Vanna and Truck's yard. "I got you." He sounded so pleased with himself Myrt had to laugh, making Bane scowl at her around Gunny's chest.

"Woman." Whatever else he'd been about to say was interrupted by a cheer from the men and women wandering around the house in front of them.

"Patchover," Truck shouted, a fist thrust into the air. "Breakfast first, then we'll get to the patchovers."

"Brother," Bane yelled back, "you sound excited to be my second."

"Oh I am, brother. I very much am. Cannot wait to see what you're gonna do with this new chapter."

The door opened as Vanna appeared, face wreathed in a smile. "There's the happy couple." Stepping to the side, she gestured into the house. "Come on in, the boys have already finished eating, but Marian's still at the table." As Myrt and Bane passed her, she paused each for a quick kiss on the cheek Myrt was happy to return. "Hope you had a good night and a better morning." She turned away with a wink, and Myrt was glad Vanna couldn't see her cheeks heat with embarrassment.

"Everybody does it, baby. We haven't done a single thing to be ashamed of." Bane's whisper was meant for her, mouth close to her ear as he steered her to the table. "I'm not a big breakfast guy, but those pancakes seem to suit you, Miss I'll Have Cake for Breakfast." Myrt twisted her head to glare at him, but he pulled the expression right off her face when he kissed her softly. "Sit and visit. I need to take care of business."

"What's a patchover?" She turned in his arms and threaded her hands behind his neck, pulling him down for another kiss. "That's what you were talking about last night, how you'd stay in the area and work with Gunny and Truck?"

Bane smiled against her lips. "And here I thought you were fast asleep, me talkin' to myself." He brushed his mouth against hers a final time, his focus still on her. "Yeah, I get to keep my patch and my brothers, and those two'll leave the RWMC and come over to play for our team for a while. We all know it's only for a couple of years, then we'll all be under the Rebel skull and key. But it means a lot, them giving me the president patch and takin' a chance I'll be a half-decent leader."

"And your old president, he's happier with this than you leaving his club, no matter where you'd go?"

"He sure as fuck is." The booming voice from behind her startled Myrt, and she jumped forwards, plastering herself against Bane, ducking underneath the dark leather of his vest. "Shit fire, I scared your woman, Bane. Your little mouse needs to get used to me. Y'all are gonna be seein' a lot of me and my old lady."

She turned to see the man who'd fetched them from Truck's house standing next to the woman she'd met yesterday, Peaches. "You're Blackie?" Peaches' grin was wide as her husband's when he nodded, shoving a hand towards Myrt. She carefully accepted, shocked as hers was enfolded entirely by his. Tugging free, she angled her body against Bane, loving the strength at her back. "Pleased'ta meetcha." She paused a breath, then remembered he was in essence Bane's boss and added, "Sir. Blackie, sir."

Chin lifting, Blackie stroked a hand down his beard, grinning widely. "I like that. Sir Blackie." He flung an arm out, finger pointing to everyone in the room. "You heard it, she named me. I'm keepin' it. She's Bane's Little Mouse, and I'm Sir Blackie. Write alla this shit down, woman." He looked down at Peaches, who had threaded her fingers around his belt, holding herself upright while laughing. "Write. It. Down. This just fuckin' happened."

"Gonna get her situated, then I'll come outside." Bane pulled a chair out for Myrt and put his hands on her shoulders, guiding her down. "Where you wanna do this thing, Blackie?" His lips grazed her cheek, and a hand stroked down her braid to her back, heat settling where he touched her. "Who you want there?"

"Like he could keep any of us away." Myrt looked past Blackie at several men who'd crowded in behind him, all faces familiar from the brief greetings in the yard yesterday. The speaker had hair nearly as long as hers, and his face split with a grin as he flipped it over his shoulder. "Me, Mason, Twisted, Wrench—fuck, everybody is still here, man. We all want to see this shit happen. Historic. The dominants of the area not only allowing a new charter, but actively encouraging it by allowing their own men to patch over. Hell, even one of my Bastards has expressed interest, and there's another guy I'd been eyeing who's on his way down now to talk to you. This news has already spread far and wide, and has been well received."

Longer hair seemed to be the norm for some of these men, and another spoke up from his position leaning against the wall near the entrance to the dining room. "I heard tell a couple of my boys are interested too, Bane. Gonna fill your fuckin' roster before you even have to go out recruitin'. That's some shit right there." He glanced at the other man. "Retro, who you got comin' down?" Their conversation faded as Myrt turned her attention back to Bane, who seemed to be holding a staring contest with a man standing beside Blackie.

"Mason, you standing witness today, too?" Bane's fingers tightened on her shoulder, and Myrt twisted to look up at him. His expression was cautious, and she looked back at the man to whom he'd spoken, seeing lines of strain there.

Mason nodded. "You've learned of our struggles along the Gulf Coast; hell, you've lived some of them. You're the man for the job, and I want everyone in our worlds to know you've my full support. Hundred percent, brother. Rebels stand with Freed Riders, no matter the charter. My hand to God." He lifted a palm, then reached out and laid it on Blackie's shoulder, much as Bane's rested on hers. "My brother here is a lucky man to have such members as you and Horse, and the rest of them. Honored to call you my friend, too."

"Fuck, Mason." Bane stepped away, his fingers trailing along her arm until he was out of reach, then he'd pushed his hand out towards Mason. Fists clenched between their hearts, Bane and Mason came together with a collision that promised bruises, followed by heavy pounding claps against shoulders and backs. "Blackie." Bane pulled back and greeted Blackie the same way, the two men murmuring before they released. "Let's do this thing. Front porch? Give the spectators an elevated view?" He pushed past Blackie and the other men, headed to the front of the house.

"You won't want to miss this." Vanna's whisper pulled Myrt's attention around, and she saw the women filing out the back door. "They do very few things not behind closed doors, so don't get used to it, but this is open for all to see." Vanna's clasp on Myrt's hand drew her from the chair, and she followed Vanna out the door and around the house, coming to a halt in front of the group of women off to the side. Bane stood along the rail of the front porch, facing the growing group of men.

"Brothers." He propped his palms on the rail, leaning out over the edge, sweeping the small crowd with his gaze. It landed on her, and he smiled and tipped his head at her, then went back to the men in front of him.

That single gesture had nearly every man's head turning on a swivel to stare at her. Instead of being taken aback, Myrt squared her shoulders and stood tall, hearing Vanna's muffled, "Good girl," from beside her. The expression on the men's faces ran the gamut from coolly interested, to a deep study, and on to smiles and welcoming waves before they returned their focus to Bane and the men next to him.

"You know me. FRMC took me in and taught me the way a club's supposed to be. Introduced me to the reality of the brotherhood under the patch and in the life. I'm Freed Riders to the core, but beyond that, I'm all about livin' the way I always have. Free." He huffed out a laugh. "Blackie knows this next bit, as does Horse, but I need to make sure my history isn't kept a secret, not with what's being proposed. So a little bit of backstory comin' your way." He shuffled his feet. "My blood isn't something I'm proud of." He sounded like whatever was coming next would be painful.

Myrt kept her gaze on him, leaning forwards in her eagerness to help him any way she could.

***

Bane

He'd gone over this with Blackie and Mason last night. Myrt asleep in bed beside him, he'd made two calls, starting with his president. His family history needed to be laid out for Mason, because no way was he hiding anything that had the potential to come back and bite him in the ass.

The faces turned up to look at him from the front yard were open, not yet judging him, and he hoped like hell they wore the same expressions in five minutes.

"I hail from Philly. I come from an old family. Crow isn't my birth name. It's family from my momma's side, and one I took because it's about as far as possible from the one I grew up with. My father was in the family business." He laid heavy emphasis on the last two words, hoping he wouldn't have to spell out the darkness that had surrounded his childhood. "My brother didn't follow him. That motherfucker branched out, started himself an MC. MDMC is his."

"Monster Devils?" Tension filled Retro's voice as he spoke up from his position propped on the corner rail of the porch. "I know someone who had some dealings with them. One of my members used to be patched. Bad juju, brother. They are shit in my eyes, and you know I don't say things idly." He spat in the dirt. "Just the mention gives me a bad taste in my mouth."

The fact Retro still called him brother eased the binding pain around Bane's chest a little, but there was an unspoken question in there he needed to address. "He is. The only thing he seems to want is pain and death. If he's still alive, I'd be surprised. I don't keep up though. Him and my old man are dead to me. Still, I know he's fucked over a bunch of people. That's why I wanted it out there right up front how he might be blood, but he's not family, you get me?"

"Oh, I get you, man." Retro smiled slowly and turned his head, calling out, "Mudd, get a call in to Einstein. Tell him we've got some insider info comin' our way." He looked back at Bane. "You will help us out with what you might know, right?"

"Anything I have is yours, brother."

A hand slapped between his shoulder blades, right over the patch, Blackie's way of telling Bane he had his back, even in this. "Any other questions about that shit?" Shoulders hunched, Blackie glared at the crew of men, angling his chin back and forth as he darted glances to and fro. "No? You fuckin' sure? Cuz this is gonna be your one fuckin' shot at my man, so get with the program, dammit. Going once, twice." He slapped Bane's back again. "Fuckin' sold. So here's what's happening."

Bane shuffled to the side slightly, letting Blackie take center stage.

"We're expanding the FRMC. To date we've only occupied territory within the Texas national border." That quip got him a few laughs, and he beamed a grin at the men. "Yeah, you heard it here, I'm all for Texas being a nation, but that's neither here nor there, dammit. I'm expanding, takin' on the expense and strain of starting a new charter, not in a neighboring state, but way the hell over here. Why, you may ask?" Without waiting for a response, he jumped into the conversation they'd had yesterday. "Because it's fuckin' time. This area is a gray zone, used for all sorts of trafficking, and the doms of the region'd like to have some help policin' the kind of shit passin' through. Ain't gonna be no cakewalk, no sir. Bane'll have his work cut out for him. He's been doin' a hella job as an unofficial liaison between FRMC and others such as represented by the men standin' up here with me. This will kick his job up a couple of levels. We'll pass him a couple of members who're lookin' to grow. RWMC is very sweetly"—he lifted his pinched thumb and finger to his lips, as if sipping from a dainty cup, the gesture gaining him more laughter—"supporting two members' patchover without a beatout. We won't take anybody out bad, so be fuckin' sure you've got permission before you start a convo with the man." Blackie looked at Bane. "I forget anything, brother?"

"Old storefront in town was purchased yesterday. We'll fit it out as the local clubhouse." Bane nodded to Mason. "Thanks to the RWMC for the assistance." He smiled at Myrt. She still looked nervous standing next to Vanna, but he was proud of how she stood her ground. "Me and my ole lady will be lookin' for a place to stay, so if you hear of anything openin' up for a family, let us know."

"I happen to know of a place." Truck, standing at the bottom of the steps, propped one booted foot against the wooden edge. "Me and Vanna, we were talking. You and Myrt grew your family overnight, bringin' on her brothers and sister. I got a house what needs livin' in. Sounds like we can help each other out."

"Sounds like we can." He spoke slowly, remembering the way the house had been outfitted when they walked in yesterday. "I'd be happy to rent from you, brother."

"Rent? Who the fuck said anything about rent? It's our baby shower gift to you two." Truck laughed, bending double for a moment. "Oh, Jesus, you should see your face, brother. Trust me, this is more for me than for you. My woman's got a hankering to mother your old lady, and when she's happy, I get a hella lot more ass. So really, this is you doin' me a favor."

"Well, when you put it that way." He darted a glance at Myrt to see her in an embrace with Vanna, the older woman shooting him a grin over her shoulder. "How can I say no? I'm not gonna cockblock a brother."

"Who's the first to patch over?" Gunny strode up and stood next to Truck. "Where's your president patch?"

"Right here." Blackie dangled a piece of fabric from his fingers, passing it off to Bane. "Got a pin, too." A moment later, the new, stiff president label was above his nameplate, granting him an official position within the club. "Charter's here." Blackie passed over a roll of papers. Bane glanced at them, then stuck them inside his vest, making a show of buttoning the pocket to keep them safe. "Gonna have to wait on the new rockers. Rushed them, and expressed, but they couldn't be here by today. No reason to wait. We can cut off your bottom later, and then you'll have some sewing to do."

Pulling in a deep breath, Bane turned to face his friend and president, waiting.

Blackie grinned at him, an expression that came easily to the man. "My old lady musta had an idea about what'd go down. She packed not only IRMC patches, but FRMC ones, too." He shoved out a fistful of fabric towards Bane. "Here."

Bane accepted them, the weight of the patches somehow more than it should be. *Profound moment*, he thought, turning to the two men standing shoulder to shoulder on the bottom step. "You two get official permission, brothers?" Both nodded, the lines of their faces strained. Bane couldn't imagine giving up his patch, and he hadn't worn it nearly as long as these men had. "Mason, what say you to these men asking to step out from under the skull and key, taking off the colors of the Rebel Wayfarers?"

"I say aye. Pained and reluctant, but an aye from me." Mason took out a pocketknife and studied it for a moment, then gripped the blade and flung the handle away from the tang. He leaned over and handed the opened knife to Gunny, who accepted it with a scowl.

Bane felt a twist in his chest. "Brother, if you aren't—"

"Sharon and I have already put down on a house butting up against your property. We'll be neighbors, brother." Gunny shrugged out of his vest and started at the front, using the tip of the blade to pick at the threads holding on his officer patch. "Just across the creek from you and Truck seemed to be a good place to start. We're gonna be in each other's pockets from the get-go, and this"—he arrowed a glance up at Mason, then over to Bane—"is something that's been comin' a while. Had my time in the north, but this southern boy has been missin' his roots." He tipped his head to Truck. "This reprobate shacked up with my old lady's adopted mom, so it's an ask to leave the RWMC, but it's no ask at all for me to be here for him and you." His hands turned the leather over, still taking care as he removed the top and bottom rockers. "We all know the plans, anyway. Couple of years, three at the outside, I'll be sewing these damn things right back on. Gonna keep 'em for me, right, boss?" Gunny stood and passed the blade to Truck, then handed the worn and dirty patches to Mason. "Be a shame to have to break in new ones."

"I'll keep hold of them, sure." Mason folded his arms across his chest, jaw tight as he watched Truck begin the same process. "Different charters, hell, different clubs, you two are still fuckin' mine. No way around how that feels. I'll hold them for you, brother. I'll hold them."

Truck worked silently, bottom lip folded between his teeth as he snipped the threads around the edges of his patches, just as road worn as Gunny's had been. When finished, he made a show of closing the pocketknife and handing it back to Mason before turning to look at the men behind them. The crowd had grown silent and still, the only sounds from the kids off in the field playing, light laughter from a distance, while an air of solemnity lay heavily on these men. "What you see here isn't the end of an era." Truck propped a foot on a higher step, stretching to hand his patches to Mason. He nodded at Bane, then settled back on the bottom step. "It's the beginning of a new one. The king is dead—" He chuckled, and then Gunny joined in on the next line. "—long live the king."

Bane studied the distance between them and made a decision, taking his time walking down the steps to stand between the two men. He turned to Truck first, holding out the main back patch and top rocker. "Bottoms will be in soon, so I'm told." In one fist he offered the officer patch, holding it when Truck would have taken it from him. "I've known you a while, old man. Trust you with my life, and you know it. Would you step up and be my second on this ride we're takin'? Can I depend on you to be my sounding board, my conscience, my right hand?" Truck nodded and Bane released the patch, turning immediately to Gunny.

Arms wrapped around him and lifted him off his feet. He dangled there a moment, then dropped his head to Gunny's shoulder and laughed. "Put me down, you bastard."

Retro hooted, and called, "He's no Bastard, he's a Rider."

"Hell yeah, I'm a Rider, fuck yes." Gunny set him down, leaning back laughing as Bane slugged his shoulder. "Okay, okay. Let's do this."

"I'm fuckin' tryin', man." Bane cut his gaze up at Mason, who was grinning down at him. "You did this on purpose, didn't you?"

"Not sayin' anything one way or the other, man." Mason's head shook side to side slowly, his laughter still spilling out.

"Gunny," Bane snapped, and stared at the man who'd become his good friend in the space of a few days. *Forged in fire.* "You strike me as a think-everything-through kinda guy, one who'd talk first and react second, and even though I'm fuckin' lyin' through my teeth right now, we're gonna roll with it. Wanna be my enforcer and stand at my back as my SAA?"

"Hell yeah!" Gunny snatched the patches from his hands, cradling them against his chest with a crow. "Hell yeah."

A truck rolled up the road, slowing and turning in the drive as Bane and the rest of the crowd turned to look. Pulling a livestock trailer, the driver angled around the vehicles already parked to find a level space. The man who swung out was a surprise, and Bane cursed as he recognized him.

"What's Heames Junior doing here?"

"Delivering our club mascot." Gunny stalked to Sharon and wrapped an arm around her, bending her backwards with a kiss. "Hold this for me, sweetness." He shoved his vest and the loose patches into her hands, turned and walked to where the Kentucky lawman was standing staring at all the silent glares aimed his way. Gunny approached, stuck out a hand and shook, which had Mason muttering, "The fuck is he up to now."

A distinct sound split the air, and Bane turned to stare at Myrt, finding her looking just as surprised as he was. "Hey, Gunny," he called, catching the man's attention as the gate of the trailer swung out and down, creating a ramp. "What the hell you talkin' about, mascot?"

Heames disappeared from view only to reappear with the end of a lead rope in his hands. He passed the rope to Gunny and stood at the top of the ramp, apparently waiting on whatever was going to happen next.

"Club mascot, Prez." Gunny pulled steadily on the rope, backing down the ramp. Putting one dainty hoof in front of the other, a gray donkey came into view. "People always callin' me a jackass, figured we might as well have one around."

"Uh, that's a donkey, not a jackass." Bane looked up at Mason again and caught him grinning. "Swear to God, you did this on purpose."

"He's yours now." Mason threw up his hands. "Every good leader needs one immediate problem to solve."

"And Gunny's mine?"

"No, man, the donkey is."

"I'm gonna call him Randy." Gunny looped the rope around the corner post of the porch, the donkey standing placidly behind him, one hip cocked in an easy stance. "Seems fitting."

"Why, pray tell, does naming a donkey Randy seem fitting?" Bane motioned Myrt to him and wrapped an arm around her neck, then pulled her close as he dropped a kiss against the side of her head.

"Because—"

"Randy!" Gunny's words were interrupted by an excited shout from the kids, and Bane looked up to see Thad pelting across the field. The boy had the widest smile Bane had witnessed on his face, and he arrowed straight to the donkey, threw his arms around the animal's neck and held on tightly.

"Because the donkey's name *is* Randy," Myrt murmured next to him, and he looked down. "Not as in a proper name, but because he'd mount anything that stood still. So not such a great name."

Bane rolled his eyes and buried his face in Myrt's neck, laughing. "Sounds about right."

Chapter Fourteen

Bane

He stood and stretched, hands in the middle of his back as he looked over his handiwork. In the months since his charter was delivered and chapter begun, the main floor of the downtown clubhouse had come together quickly, but the second floor had taken more time. Today was the last round of painting before the community-donated furniture could be delivered from the storage lot.

Picking up the paint can and roller, he strolled to the railing edging the upstairs balcony stretching along one side of the building. They'd have four crash rooms here, for late nights that didn't warrant a ride back home. Bane laughed softly, knowing that of the men who rode under his rocker, he was the last one who'd take an empty bunk over a warm bed with his woman.

Dumping his load of stuff at the bottom of the stairs, he made his way towards the back of the building, where the bar and meeting room were. His vest swung heavily around his hips, the wide bottom rocker touting their chapter as "Baker Florida" still stiff, though it bore a beginning of the expected sheen of road dirt. Another few months and it'd look as broken in as the rest of his patches.

"Denis," he shouted, not catching sight of the prospect assigned to the main room this week. They'd shifted to weekly assignments for their three potential members, trying to spend enough time with each of them to determine if they were true brothers. There were no shortcuts to membership, and Bane was glad this was something he and his officers agreed upon.

"Yeah, boss." The man swung out of the storage closet set into the corner of the room. Bane frowned, not sure what would have drawn any interest in there. A bright feminine giggle came from that direction, and Bane's frown deepened into a scowl.

"Who's in there?" A tousled blonde head popped out, and Bane groaned when he recognized the local mayor's daughter. "Out, now." Leveling a finger at Denis, he fumed, "Prospects don't get visitation rights. Think of this as your personal purgatory from here out." After watching the girl scamper out still straightening her blouse, Bane rounded on the man. "Might want to decide today if this is gonna be somethin' you want. Because that?" He jammed a thumb over his shoulder at the door, closing in its frame. "That ain't gonna be what you get. Last thing we need is the local politicos decidin' they don't like us settin' up shop in their hometown. We've been well received so far, and I goddamned well wanna make sure it stays that way. No visitors of any kind for you, and if I find you've violated my rules, I'll take the vest off your fuckin' back."

Shoving past the man, Bane pushed the office door open, stepped inside, and kicked it closed with his heel. *This shit is harder than it looks.* Feeling like an imposter had been a frequent complaint over the first few months, and Bane was pretty sure both Blackie and Mason had gotten tired of his constant questioning their wisdom in promoting him. Then slowly, gradually, from recruiting to managing the men he and Truck selected to rousting Gunny to keep everyone in line, it seemed as if all the things with running a chapter had become easier. Blackie had told him it was like flexing a muscle, something you had to build up to until the movements came natural as breathing.

"Fuckin' hope that muscle memory kicks in sometime soon."

He walked to the table set in the center of the room and leaned on the back of one of twelve chairs set along the edge. He'd taken a leaf from Twisted's playbook and wouldn't seat himself at the end, leaving the place for whoever felt their words needed extra emphasis on any given night. No, his chair was this one, middle of the table, back to the door, and implicit was the profound trust it took to make himself vulnerable the way it did. He'd seen the respect in Truck's and Gunny's faces the first time he'd placed himself so, and a low buzz of pride had zipped through him. Not a vanity sort of pride, but one that told him he'd done a good job, had pleased his brothers, and made them think well of him.

Only half the chairs were occupied at any given meeting. Him, Truck, and Gunny had been the only bodies at the table at first.

Then he'd picked up Monday, one of Retro's boys from the Bama Bastards, as their treasurer. Monday had proven to be a steady influence on the prospects and someone Bane had trusted nearly on sight. The man had come highly recommended by Retro, and he retained connections to a club not far removed in geography, the Borderline Freaks MC.

Coolaid had been a contact from Twisted, pulling the man from where he'd been patched into the Incoherent MC Big Bend chapter. That was it for officers right now.

Their regular members were a similar mishmash of patchovers, all earning their right to drop their original colors the right way, via petitions and pledges of noninterference. On advice from Wrench, the chapter had instituted a one-year no-vote policy for all patchover members, which were all they had. At least for now. Strange but true that if they worked out, it was likely the prospects could earn votes before some of the provisional members would, something Bane would deal with if needed.

A sound from the main room made him open the door, and he looked out to see Monday sauntering in, a handful of men at his back. The former security professional had a confidence about him some of the local boys found mesmerizing. In the intake interview after Retro first put his name forwards, Monday had talked openly about why he'd wanted a change, which had nothing to do with the BBMC and everything to do with location. He'd caught his partner back in Birmingham cheating, and told Bane he'd sworn off men forever. It was the how he'd said the words that had revealed a lot to Bane, the tense posture that telegraphed Monday'd expected conflict. The sagging relief when it hadn't come had told Bane even more. This was a man looking for a home, not a quick place to hide his hurt feelings. Bane had offered his yea vote immediately, as had Truck and Gunny.

"Brother." He approached Monday, hand out, pulled into the expected one-arm clinch. "I'm headed home. Odds are my ole lady's already pulling her hair out." He scanned the room. "Don't forget, you're all comin' over for dinner." One of the men murmured, and Bane shook his head. "No discussion, no bowing out. We've got a fuckton of guests coming in tomorrow, so tonight is our family dinner. No excuses accepted."

Three hours later, the large dining room table was scattered with empty dishes, plates cleaned of food and stacked in piles to make room for glasses of whiskey and bottles of beer. Bane willingly sat in the hot seat. At this table he had no problem being the dominant, and he watched as Myrt leaned over Truck's shoulder, giggling with Vanna, who was seated on his lap. The two women cut their glances at him, and in an instant he knew they were up to something good. Now to simply let it play out.

In the months since moving into the house, Myrt had done a good job making it a home. Comfortable touches everywhere a man looked, those little things told him his woman was thinking about her family. She was healing, and he loved watching that confidence overtake the shyness that had been beaten into her for so long. Sometimes it's not time or distance that heals wounds, it's meeting the right person at the right time.

Getting the boys into school had been a revelation for all of them. Vanna said later she'd seen *some* indications, but it had been a shock to them all when they found out Luke not only wasn't cognitively delayed but was advanced. The now-fifteen-year-old was currently taking classes that carried college credits, having fit into the academic role easily. Socially was a different thing, but the school was small enough to have all classes on one campus, which meant he had Thad for the breaks and lunch periods.

Thad was turning into a sports junkie, somehow talking Bane and Myrt into both a league soccer team and Florida Pop-Warner Football. Either of them would have meant travel, but the boy playin' both meant they'd traveled a lot. He grinned as Thad came into view around Monday's shoulder, talking to the big man, who turned to focus on the boy. Good thing they'd had willing chauffeurs for the games Bane couldn't make.

"I like how you call these family dinners." Gunny spoke from Bane's immediate right, Sharon perched on her ole man's lap and their sleeping boy Josh on hers. "Means a lot, being invited into your home and lives. Shows the members and prospects it's not only the club."

"No, man. It's the whole shebang. Club, family, community—we all work together to make the most of what we've got. That's what keeps a club strong, those connections. Reminds me…" He cleared his throat. "Hey." Voice pitched to carry, he gained everyone's attention with a single word. "Tomorrow's a gathering of a lot of big players in the MC world. Best behavior and stay on our toes. We've not been quiet about who's coming, so keep an eagle eye out for anyone not invited."

"What are you expecting from tomorrow's meetings?" Monday lifted his glass, pausing before taking a drink. "Anything specific, Prez?"

"I'm expecting to be told we're golden, and how our national president is proud of what we're building here in Baker." Bane sat straighter, elbows to the table as he leaned into the message he wanted to convey. "I'm expecting to find ourselves approached by men either looking to join us or looking to steal some of us away. We've got a good thing going, and we all fit well. I'm hoping at the end of the day we'll be adding to our ranks, not detracting from." He shrugged. "I'm also expecting a stupid amount of baby stuff disguised as Christmas gifts." Laughter from all the men told him nobody'd forgotten his complaints of how the child wasn't even here yet and had taken over the house. Myrt pouted at him from over Truck's shoulder, and he beamed her a smile. "We'll also learn more about the support IMC needs to keep the cartel in check through this area. And I'm here to tell you from Blackie to me, the message is we stand with Incoherent. Not gonna see this stretch of the Gulf Coast run ragged by the Mexicans and their shit. We'll plan on a club-wide meeting next weekend to go over what I learn. We can do it around that New Year's Eve thing some of y'all plannin'."

"Sounds good, Prez." Truck tipped his chin up, hand stroking down Vanna's arm.

Bane gave him a grin. "Sure does."

***

Bane

Next morning, it wasn't the rumble of bikes that woke him, although he somehow knew the sound had been appearing off and on since right around daybreak.

No, it was the fucking donkey, braying his fucking head off.

"Remind me why we let Gunny keep Randy?" He tightened his arms around Myrt. She faced away from him, his little spoon, belly big enough to be uncomfortable in any other position. Bane ran a hand down her side to where the swelling started, curving around and down so he cradled their child.

He'd never had a second thought about claiming the little girl, sex discovered on the first sonogram and gleefully held over his head. Apparently, Gunny thought girls were far more difficult than boys to raise. Gender didn't matter to Bane; he just needed Myrt and the child healthy and whole at the end of the process. Sharon might have been considerate by not sharing her near-death experience with Myrt, but Gunny hadn't been so kind, talking at length about his ride to the hospital, finding Sharon in a fight for her life, and then after everything was all good in the end, having to go home and clean his wife's blood off the stairs. *Motherfucker.*

The donkey brayed again, sounding closer.

"I think Randy got out again." Myrt sounded groggy, and he scowled towards the window overlooking the backyard.

"Motherfucker." The last time the donkey got out, he'd tried to mount a motorcycle. It had been all Bane could do to pull Monday off Gunny that day, the big men trading blow for blow over Monday's pride and joy, his Shillelagh. "I'll go catch him and lock him up." Gunny had built a tiny barn right on the property line, barely big enough for the donkey and a few chickens. Dude had even built a stile over the fence, so the kids could come and go easily. "Motherfucker."

Running footsteps preceded a thudding fist on the door. "Bane." It was Luke. "Randy's chasing the chickens again."

"I'll be right down, son." Their transition had happened organically. After hearing the way their father had treated them, he'd vowed to do right by both boys. Calling them son had only truly stuck after the therapist they'd gotten for Thad told Bane and Myrt the younger Threadgill boy felt like he'd gotten lucky to have such great parents. It had taken Bane only an instant to catch on, Myrt a little longer, but watching the understanding bloom on her face, the look of love and devotion to her brothers replaced by a mother's fierce protection—he'd known in that moment she was going to be an amazing mother to however many kids they had, starting with their two boys.

"Okay, Dad."

Bane was smiling when he pressed a kiss to Myrt's bare shoulder. "No panties today, baby." She wasn't an exhibitionist, but both of them liked the thrill of him able to touch and caress when they wanted. "See you in a bit. Get some more shut-eye if you can."

"The big ruckus is at Vanna's. Our house is overflow for the kids. Marian's promised to be in charge of them today. I finished up all my prep yesterday, so I literally have nothing to do." She snuggled her pillow, voice muffled as she finished with, "Love you, Bane."

"Love you, too, baby." He flicked the covers over her, passing a hand over her hair, cut shorter now, but still able to be tamed into a braid for their rides.

Jeans on, he opened the curtains a sliver and looked out over the backyard and clearing in the adjoining woods. Tents populated the circle of trampled grass, bikes parked nearby. The prospects hadn't understood their task at first, cutting down perfectly healthy trees and grinding the stumps down into the ground. Using the downed trees to create rough benches and stools had brought the idea closer, and then Bane had treated the area like a golf course green, using a blowtorch on the weeds so there was no delay in liberally applying seed. This exact scene was what he'd had in mind. A place between his and Truck's homes where friends and family could come on little or no notice, a place to gather for club events—a place for his brothers to bond.

He spotted Randy a couple hundred yards from the outskirts of the clearing, fluttering wings telling him the donkey was still chasing at least one chicken. It would only be a matter of time before the damn thing saw the tents, some of which were exactly the right size to attract the donkey's attention. "Fuck." Shoving his feet into boots, he yanked on a shirt and grabbed his cut from the hook near the door. "Fuckin' Gunny. Motherfucking donkey."

Myrt's laughter chased him down the stairs.

***

Myrtle

Hand pressed against her side, she made her way down the stairs, careful to keep her skirt close to her legs with her other hand. Not that there was anyone to catch a glimpse if she happened to flash skin, but good habits were practiced even if unneeded in the moment. Or something like that.

Once on the main floor, she looked towards the living room, unsurprised to find the couch, chairs, and floor full of bodies as kids of all ages watched cartoons on their large TV. Turning to the kitchen, spanning the back of the house with the dining room, she glimpsed Marian standing at the sink. Leaning against the counter next to her sister, she looked through the window, seeing people milling around in the clearing. Their backyard was set up with various games, and it looked like several couples were making good use of the oversized Connect Four game Bane had made mild fun of when she'd offered the suggestion. He'd been in favor of the cornhole boards and croquet game, both of which were sitting unused at the moment. She yanked her phone from her pocket and snapped a picture, then texted it to him with a smiley face. It was only a moment later he responded with a devil's grin, and she shook her head as she slid the phone back into her pocket, fingers taking a moment to trace along the edges of the other item she'd stashed there.

"You want some water or juice, sister?" Marian bumped her shoulder gently, the way her sister did everything.

Myrt stifled a sigh as she shook her head. "I'll have to pee enough as it is, no reason to overwork the bladder today."

Living under their father's thumb for so long had left its mark on Marian. Before Myrt had left for Sallabrook's farm, her sister had been quick-witted, first to make a joke or join in on a game. During the years apart, the sisters had grown into women without much contact, but the woman Bane had rescued had been nearly unrecognizable. Even after these months without the constant threat of unreasonable retaliation, Marian hadn't come out of her shell much. Only around Sharon and Gunny's children and their brothers. Bane kept telling Myrt it would happen, but she found herself impatient with the slow process. The happiness she'd found made her want to help Marian with the same. *She deserves it.*

"I'm going to head over to Vanna's. You need me to do anything before I go?" Myrt leaned against Marian's shoulder. "Thanks so much for helping out with all the kids today. I'm glad we can give them a place away from the adult party, and Bane and I appreciate you so much."

"It's nothing." Marian's shoulder shifted with her shrug, and Myrt straightened. She shuffled closer so they were pressed tightly all along their sides. "You're clingy today. Everything good with the baby?"

"Yeah." Myrt stroked along the top of the beachball containing their little girl. "She's quiet, actually. Not so much imitating Thad today with her kicking."

Marian laughed softly. "That boy's found his calling."

"Yes, he has." Myrt turned and on impulse pushed to her toes to angle over her belly and plant a kiss on her sister's cheek. "Love you, Marian."

Marian's chin dipped to her neck, and she plunged her hands into the soapy water in front of her. After a moment, she nodded. "I love you, too."

Out the door and down the stairs, Myrt was careful with each step. Even though the path between the two houses was three times as wide as previous, and flattened with the feet, dirt bikes, and most recently a golf cart Truck had bought for Vanna, she didn't want to trip and wake up her daughter. Her back had been aching since she woke, and the more time the little girl slept, the less she'd spend kicking Myrt's bladder and ribs.

Halfway there, she saw a group of men approaching, no familiar faces in the midst. After knowing so many of the club members for this long, she had no fear inside her, no matter the men looked and dressed rough. They wore a mix of patches, the colors on the front of their vests telegraphing their direct alliances.

"Ma'am," one man said, tipping his head. He was in the FRMC, but not the Baker chapter.

"You're Bane's old lady?" The question by another from a different club had all the men stopping where they were, caught in mid-stride.

"I am," she responded proudly and moved to the side, intending on passing them. "Have a good day."

"We can carry you." The first speaker looked at the other men. "Wouldn't take but a couple of us, fireman's chair." General rumbles of agreement sounded, and Myrt shook her head.

"I walk this path every day, boys." It didn't matter they were all older than her, she'd found herself unable to call a group of the men anything but boys. Her boys. Bane's boys. *Bane's brothers.*

"And today, you ride in style." She studied the nameplate on his vest and realized her mistake. Horse was Bane's brother, and except for Blackie, the closest to him from the Longview chapter.

"How would that work, exactly?" Myrt palmed her skirt, lifting the hem a fraction of an inch. "I'm not dressed for lifting."

"No lifting necessary, just sitting." He clasped the other man's wrist and threaded his arm over a shoulder in a way that illustrated the fact they were creating a chair for her.

How do I turn them down without offending? She huffed out a tiny sigh. *I can't.* Stepping closer, she turned and smoothed her skirt down the backs of her thighs, ensuring they'd touch nothing they weren't expecting. *Damn Bane and his early morning orders.* "Okay." She laughed nervously. "I'm ready."

The men moved, and their arms scooped her up. Myrt squealed and threw an arm around each man's neck, being lifted higher than expected as they stood with her in their arms. The group around them chuckled, and Horse leaned his head close. "Nothing to fear, Little Mouse."

"Oh my God." She wished she felt secure enough to release her death grip on their necks, so she could cover her blazing face. "Blackie hates me."

"Far from it, little sister," the other man offered. "Way I hear it, you're the queen he always wanted for his boy Bane. I see it now. See it and understand."

She glanced ahead and found Bane standing next to Mason and Blackie, Truck at his shoulder. They'd turned to view what had become a procession, men and women filtering out from the field of tents to join them. She was struck with an idea and whispered it to Horse, who laughed as he agreed. A couple of terse exchanges with the other man—she glanced down to see his nameplate said Einstein—and the plan was set.

Gunny walked into view, Randy trailing by his lead rope. "Motherfucker tried to hump Blackie's tent again. I don't know what the man has hidden in there, but this asshole seems to like it." Myrt shook her head and tried to ignore the fact that she was being accompanied by a donkey with his dick reeled out, currently slapping his own belly in excitement. "Myrt, heard you were thinkin' about doin' somethin'. Shoulda told his brothers first, woman. We all want to be there." He dropped his head as he tapped on his phone with one thumb, the other hand still wrapped around Randy's lead. "Got 'em comin' in now. We got your back, Momma."

It was an endless couple of minutes before the men carrying her stopped only feet away from Bane. He'd turned to face them, one hand shoved into his pocket and the other propped on a hip. He was grinning widely, shaking his head. "Myrtie, doll. You got you quite an entourage."

"Wasn't intentional." She released her hold on Horse and slipped her hand into the pocket of her skirt. "But I don't mind the ride. Made me feel like a real princess. Thank you, boys." Neither man moved, and she grinned as the expression on Bane's face turned into confusion. "I've got something to ask you."

"Yeah? Ask away, baby." He took a step closer, one slow step that felt like he was stalking her. "I'm all ears."

Fingers fisted around the object, she took a breath. Vanna had appeared and was leaning against Truck's shoulder. Sharon stood nearby, frowning at Gunny. Monday, Coolio, and the rest of the local chapter stood behind Bane. *The gang's all here.* "A few months ago you reminded me how being with someone didn't mean they had a claim on me. I was glad at the time, because it gave me permission to shuck all the notions I'd had drilled into my head. Now, though, I find myself with a different feeling. See..." She shrugged, releasing her hold on Einstein to fold her hand across her belly. "Florida doesn't have a common law marriage law, either."

Bane approached several strides, rocking to a stop only feet away, gaze fixed on her face. From this position she was slightly higher than him, and she shuffled a bit. "You can put me down now," she told the men who'd been her personal carriage, and smiled as they settled her feet firmly in the grass and dirt. "Bane, my sweet William, I don't want to know there's an easy out. I want to be tied to you. So…" She held out her trembling hand and stretched out her fingers, palm up. The sunshine glinted off the gold circle. "Would you do me the honor of marrying me?"

"Oh, fuck yeah." He closed the distance and pulled her hand to his mouth, already sliding the ring into place on his hand. "Fuck yes, woman." Arms around her, he fitted her side against his front, swaying them back and forth. "Kiss me, Myrtie."

She lifted her face and closed her eyes, unsurprised when his kiss was long, hot, wet, and possessive.

Everything she'd ever wanted was tied up in this man.

So lucky.

~ ~

THANK YOU SO MUCH FOR READING
In Search of Solace!

I truly hope you enjoyed this crossover story tying things together even tighter between the Rebel Wayfarers MC and the Texas-based Freed Riders MC. Thanks for takin' this trip along with me.

~ML

ABOUT THE AUTHOR

Raised in the south, *Wall Street Journal* & *USA TODAY* bestselling author MariaLisa learned about the magic of books at an early age. Every summer, she would spend hours in the local library, devouring books of every genre. Self-described as a book-a-holic, she says "I've always loved to read, but then I discovered writing, and found I adored that, too. For reading...if nothing else is available, I've been known to read the back of the cereal box."

Want sneak peeks into what she's working on, or to chat with other readers about her books? Join the Facebook group! **bit.ly/deMora-FB-group**

deMora's got a spam-free newsletter list she'd love to have you join, too: **bit.ly/mldemora-newsletter**

~~~~~
~~~~~

My Rebel Wayfarers MC and the Neither This Nor That MC series do cross over, along with the Occupy Yourself band books, so readers have a couple of choices. The series can be read independently beginning with RWMC, OYBS, and then NTNT without too many spoilers. There's also a crossover between my RWMC world and Lila Rose's Hawks MC world. Or they can be read intertwined—in chronological order.

Here's the recommended reading order if you want to follow according to timing:

Mica, RWMC #1
A Sweet & Merry Christmas, RWMC #1.5
Slate, RWMC #2
Bear, RWMC #3
Born Into Trouble, OYBS #1
Jase, RWMC #4
Gunny, RWMC #5
Mason, RWMC #6
Hoss, RWMC #7
This Is the Route of Twisted Pain, NTNT #1
Harddrive Holidays, RWMC #7.5
Duck, RWMC #8
Biker Chick Campout, RWMC #8.5
Watcher, RWMC #9
Treading the Traitor's Path: Out Bad, NTNT #2
Living Without, Lila Rose's Hawks MC: Caroline Springs #4
Shelter My Heart, NTNT #3
A Kiss to Keep You, RWMC #9.25
Gun Totin' Annie, RWMC #9.5
Secret Santa, RWMC #9.75
Trapped by Fate on Reckless Roads, NTNT #4

Bones, RWMC #10
Gunny's Pups, RWMC #10.25
Not Even A Mouse, RWMC #10.75
Road Runner's Ride, RWMC #12.5
Never Settle, RWMC #10.5
Fury, RWMC #11
Christmas Doings, RWMC #11.25
Gypsy's Lady, RWMC #11.5
Tarnished Lies and Dead Ends, NTNT #5
Going Down Easy
No Man's Land
In Search of Solace
Cassie, RWMC #12

~~~~~
~~~~~

Also by MariaLisa deMora

Neither This Nor That MC romance series

Legends are born from moments like these. Folktales spun around a single point in time so perfect, you can almost hear the click resonating through the universe as things align. Meet Twisted, Po'Boy, Retro, and Ragman, good old boys from southern states who have many things in common. First, is a bone-deep love of the biker lifestyle. Second, would be their love of the brotherhood, and knowing that you trust the man at your back. Finally, these men have the love of a good woman. None of these come without a price, and it is our pleasure to journey along with them as they discover the blessings that can be won, and lost along the way.

This is the Route of Twisted Pain
Treading the Traitor's Path: Out Bad
Shelter My Heart
Trapped by Fate on Reckless Roads
Tarnished Lies and Dead Ends

5-Star Reviews for the stories of the NTNT MC series

This is the Route of Twisted Pain
"This is the Route of Twisted Pain is an exhilarating, gripping romance novel contrived of incredible world

building, complex yet relatable characters, and a unique, captivating plot.
Gifted storyteller MariaLisa deMora beautifully balances exciting suspense, fast action, intriguing secrets with delicious, blazing hot romance scenes. Readers will be up all night with this riveting page-turner."
~ NY Literary Magazine

I am completely tickled in my fancy for TWISTED! First off, let me state that there was one thing I didn't like about this book and that is the LAST PAGE! I hated for it to end. I dearly loved this book and its characters as well as their setting.
~Colleen M.

Gripping tale
Twisted and Penny fit together beautifully. The book covers so much more than just their love story. Great introduction to the Incoherent MC. The tale is gripping and gritty. The journey is full of twists and turns that keep you on the edge of your seat. I couldn't put it down. Cannot wait for the next one.
~Lillmil

Twisted is one of the most original and interesting characters I have read in a long time. Marialisa's character building is setting a high bar for her to follow, she will hopefully continue with Po'Boy's story. The Route of Twisted Pain was pure brilliance, and I highly recommend this read.
~Penny T.

This book obsessed me!

This may be the best book I read all year.
These people...they're not characters, they're real...
have stuck in my head from the day I met them.
MariaLisa deMora can throw words down that'll Twist
(hehe) your insides up till you can't breathe for
waiting to hear what's next!
I'm working my way through her other 'families' and
yup....she really is that good.
~DeLane

Treading the Traitor's Path: Out Bad
"Treading the Traitor's Path: Out Bad is a solidly
engrossing, well-written novel by a talented author.
MariaLisa deMora delivers a thrilling ride filled with
exciting suspense, deliciously explicit, vivid sex scenes,
and gritty, fast-paced action. Her characters are
smart, complex, and strong with sharp edges. The
settings meticulously detailed.
Fans of Motorcycle Club romance stories will not want
to miss this second installment in deMora's exciting
series."
~ NY Literary Magazine
What an amazing read! DeMora does not simply
wrote a book, she pulls you into a different world.
When you read her work, you are very much
surrounded by the characters and setting. Prepare for
a book hangover because once you finish the book,
you will still be stuck with Po Boy.
~KW

THIS WAS AMAZING. Highly recommend for a good
story line, interesting characters. I just wish there was
more more more.
~Laura

Loved This Book!
What did I just read?! Is my kindle still working? I'm pretty sure it combusted into flames while reading this story. RED HOT READ for 2017. Not what I was expecting at all! I tend to stay away from ménage a trois, because for me it's hard to say there's any kind of conflict except for jealousy, and the ending kind of leaves things unresolved and unrealistic. NOT THIS BOOK! The best one out there guaranteed.
~Linda A

...seriously this series is just WTF so freaking good. Dark, Twisted, harsh, painful and raw. Po'Boy lives for his club, his brothers and his family, there is nothing he wouldn't do for them.
~Fay

I live and breathe for books like this! Fabulously Naughty!...Wickedly Hot! This is my first book by MariaLisa deMora and it will not be my last. MariaLisa delivered a 5 STAR READ! The plot is filled with action, suspense, romance and tons of hot scenes.
~Jenny F


~~~~~
~~~~~

Alace Sweets, a dark romantic suspense 3-book series

A dark thriller, this book is not a light read. Filled with edge-of-your-seat suspense, this intense story commands the reader's attention as it drives towards the explosive ending. Alace Sweets is a vigilante serial killer, with everything that implies and is sure to trip all your triggers. Be ready.

At seventeen, Alace Sweets turned a corner in her life, taking the wrong shortcut home from school.

Resisting the harsh knowledge her attackers will never be made to pay for their actions, Alace takes a stand. Justice must be served, and if fate's scales are out of balance, she's determined to set things right as best she can.

When the laws of men fail, the rules of Alace prevail.

5-Star Reviews for Alace Sweets

"Whatever deep dark trench [deMora] pulled a character like Alace from should be revisited again and often."
~Confessions of a Serial Reader

"deMora has a superb story-line and exceptional character development. All of her characters have such depth that will intrigue the reader…"

~Turning Another Page

"Hot, sweet, dark thriller."
~Beth D

"It will keep you on the edge of your seat and give you chills."
~Escape Reality Book Blog

"Disturbing, haunting, sickly; yet hot, sexy and heart racing!"
~Amanda L

"From the first page [deMora] pulls you into the world she has created and you do not even try to escape..."
~Little Shop of Readers Blog

"A must read for all those dark, gritty romance fans out there."
~Sweet & Spicy Reads

"You will find yourself so drawn into the story that the outside world is blocked out and your locking the doors and turning on all the lights."
~Danena F

"Don't judge me for bonding with a vigilante serial killer, she's more than what she does."
~iScream Books

"Thrilling...chilling...full of suspense, nail biting edge of your seat excitement."
~Tracey H

"Every time MariaLisa deMora picks up her pen (or opens her computer), she creates characters you want to believe in."
~Gail S

"Intriguing dark storyline, beautiful love story and nail-biting conclusion, what more could a reader ask for?"
~Manda M

"This book takes you a dark and twisted ride that is gripping..."
~Renee Entress' Blog

"This book is dark and gritty and I literally had to take a day off from reading it because it's that intense."
~My Girlfriend's Couch

"This is my favourite book so far from this author ... I recommend this book if you enjoy dark romantic thrillers."
~Cheekypee Reads and Reviews

"There's not enough stars to give this book and 5 just doesn't really do it justice!"
~DeLane C

"I couldn't put this book down from page one! Tried to stop & go to bed but couldn't sleep thinking about Alace and got up & finished the book."
~Debbie M

"MariaLisa DeMora, wordsmith that she is, made this a story of the enlightenment of a woman and finding love in a life where she has had none."
~Kat W

ADDITIONAL SERIES AND BOOKS

Please note that books in a series frequently feature characters from additional books within that series. If series books are read out of order, readers will twig to spoilers for the other books, so going back to read the skipped titles won't have the same angsty reveals.

Rebel Wayfarers MC series:

Mica, #1
A Sweet & Merry Christmas, #1.5
Slate, #2
Bear, #3
Jase, #4
Gunny, #5
Mason, #6
Hoss, #7
Harddrive Holidays, #7.5
Duck, #8
Biker Chick Campout, #8.5
Watcher, #9
A Kiss to Keep You, #9.25
Gun Totin' Annie, #9.5
Secret Santa, #9.75
Bones, #10
Gunny's Pups, #10.25
Never Settle, #10.5
Not Even A Mouse, #10.75
Fury, #11
Christmas Doings, #11.25
Gypsy's Lady, #11.5
Cassie, #12
Road Runner's Ride, #12.5

Occupy Yourself band series:

Born Into Trouble, #1
Grace In Motion, #2 (TBD)
What They Say, #3 (TBD)

Neither This, Nor That MC series:

This Is the Route Of Twisted Pain, #1
Treading the Traitor's Path: Out Bad, #2
Shelter My Heart, #3
Trapped by Fate on Reckless Roads, #4
Tarnished Lies and Dead Ends, #5

Rebel Wayfarers crossover stories:

Going Down Easy
No Man's Land
In Search of Solace

Mayhan Bucklers MC series:

Most Rikki-Tik, #1
Mad Minute, #2
Pucker Factor, #3
Boocoo Dinky Dau, #4 (TBD)

Borderline Freaks MC series:

Service and Sacrifice, #1
More Than Enough, #2
Lack of Inbetween, #3
See You in Valhalla, #4

Alace Sweets series:

Alace Sweets, #1
Seeking Worthy Pursuits, #2
Embarrassment of Monsters, #3
All the Broken Rules, #4 (TBD)

With My Whole Heart series:

With My Whole Heart, #1
Bet On Us, #2

If You Could Change One Thing:
Tangled Fates Stories

There Are Limits, #1
Rules Are Rules, #2
The Gray Zone, #3

Other Books:

Hard Focus
Dirty Bitches MC: Season 3

More information available at **mldemora.com**.